LOST IN DALAT

Lost in Dalat

The Courage of a Family Torn by War

A Novel

James Luger

HIGH FLIGHT
PUBLISHING

HIGH FLIGHT
PUBLISHING

Published by High Flight Publishing LLC™
Minneapolis, Minnesota

This book is also available as an e-book, ISBN-13: 978-1-7330982-1-2

A CIP catalogue record for this title is available from the Library of
Congress.

This High Flight Publishing paperback edition published 2019

Printed in the United States of America

Interior Design by Lin White

Cover Design by Jessica Bell

For author information, comments or questions, and forthcoming book
announcements, please visit www.JamesLuger.com

To all missing-in-action military personnel and the loved ones they left behind.

Although this fictional story is very loosely based on my wartime and civilian travels and experiences in Vietnam, and my musings about the unknown fate of a long-ago brother in arms, the characters in this novel are purely fictional and the locations were chosen arbitrarily, without any reference or comparison to actual individuals or places. Any likeness to a real person, either living or deceased, is unintended and purely coincidental.

—*James Luger*

CHAPTER 1

Meggan Mondae swayed her hips to Rolling Stones riffs piping through her earbuds while tidying up the kitchen, out of sight from her husband, Brent, who was in the bedroom busily packing for his teachers' conference in Las Vegas.

Brent came into the kitchen and put his empty coffee mug in the sink. "Are you listening to those old hippy tunes again?"

Meggan pulled the earbuds out. "What?"

"You were just a baby when that pot music was popular. No one likes it anymore."

"My mom does."

"You probably heard it through her belly before you were born, when she was a hippy. That could qualify it as a prenatal addiction."

Meggan was used to Brent's sarcastic humor, but she still didn't like it. "My mom wasn't a hippy, and she wasn't a druggy. That kind of makes your theory suck, doesn't it, dear?"

Brent moped out of the kitchen without responding, and Meggan put the washed breakfast dishes away, letting them clink loud enough to annoy, but not hard enough to break. She slipped three paperback romance novels into a flimsy plastic grocery bag, knowing her mother would love staying up late to read them. Brent once said her and her mother's reading tastes were *banal,* and Meggan countered that they were more help to get through Minnesota winters than the dry, tragic tomes of *Hamlet* or *Ulysses* that he forced on his bored students.

Her mother's appetite for grocery store literature was more defendable than Meggan's, though. Having never married, her mom could vicariously surrender her love to any fictional hero she chose—without the disappointment of not having it returned.

Meggan took the bag of books from the kitchen counter, shouting "goodbye" over her shoulder, "have a nice time." She listened for a response on the way to the side door leading to the attached garage and stopped when she didn't hear anything. Maybe Brent didn't hear her. Maybe it didn't matter.

She had already loaded her overnight bag in her car, but when she got to the side door, she realized she had forgotten her car keys. She set the bag of books on the floor and went back to the bedroom to look for them.

Brent was squeezing his toilet kit into the already-stuffed orange carryon suitcase on the bed. "I thought you left," he said without looking up.

"Oh, then you heard me say goodbye?"

"Of course."

"I forgot my keys."

"Why don't you just keep your keys in your purse?"

"I do, sometimes."

"You better get going or you'll get caught in traffic."

"It's Saturday morning, Brent."

"Yes, and slippery roads will slow the people going up north for the weekend."

"Who's going up north in the middle of January?"

"You won't be the only one. Snowmobilers and ice fishermen—you'll see." He finally forced the zipper closed on his bulging suitcase.

She searched for her keys in a pocket of her jeans hanging by a hook inside the closet. "When's William picking you up?" she asked more to force a conversation than really caring.

"Around noon. We're stopping for lunch before going to the airport."

"Oh? I don't think you mentioned that." Meggan turned to him but he had already left the room with his bag.

She found her keys in the other pocket of her jeans and went back to the side door. Brent's bright suitcase stood ready near the front door, and he sat in a wingback chair near the front window with a travel magazine on his lap, gazing outside as if there was something interesting about the crusty snow and leafless trees.

After slipping on her snow boots, she turned to Brent and said, "Have fun on your Vegas weekend."

"You know it's just a boring teachers' conference, Meggan. Don't try to make it sound like a vacation."

"I wasn't trying to." After pausing for a response, she gave up and went into the garage to her car. She sluffed off Brent's rudeness this morning as normal behavior whenever he was nervous, and anticipating an airline trip always unnerved him. It would be better to just leave, she decided, and avoid any parting snipes, hoping sunny, warm Las Vegas will cheer him up.

While the electric garage door slowly groaned open, she watched a shiny red BMW sedan roll toward her on the snow-frosted driveway. When it stopped, Meggan walked out to see who the driver was. The tinted side window slowly recessed into the door, and Brent's friend, William, peered out. He wasn't wearing a hat over his perfectly coifed hair, and his

face was too pre-tanned for the dead of a Minnesota winter.
William was well prepared for Vegas.

"Nice car," she said, wondering how he could afford that
on a math teacher's pay.

"Brent said you'd be gone, at your mother's or something."

"Oh, goodness, and he told me you'd be here at lunchtime." She made a sarcastic tisk-tisk with her tongue: such a
big mix up for poor fastidious William.

William shook his head. "No, no, no, you must have misunderstood. We have to pick up another faculty member, and
we'll have barely enough time to eat after checking in at the
airport."

"Yes, I apparently erred. Could you please move your car
now, so I can leave?"

After William backed out of the driveway and stopped
next to the curb, Meggan backed out a little faster than usual
and sped past him without looking, hoping to leave a trail of
irritation in her wake. Everything about William seemed irri-
tating to her. She never understood why he and Brent were
such good friends: Brent, the mundane married suburbanite,
and William, a neurotic single urban dweller. She reasoned
that since they taught at the same suburban school, it was
some kind of professional bonding, like cops and soldiers
who bond regardless of their personal differences.

Meggan had always thought marriage would bond a husband and wife the same way. But now, seven years later, she
knew she had expected too much. Growing up fatherless had
ill-prepared her for what to expect in a marriage, substituting
reality with idealistic expectations about how married couples normally lived together day to day. As a kid, she used
to envy her friends for having protective dads to count on,
so when she first met Brent he seemed to fulfill that need,

bristling with self-assuredness, asserting command over even trivial matters. When she accepted his marriage proposal, she silently vowed to give her heart completely to him—except for one selfish holdout, something she planned to bring up at the right time, but the right time never seemed to come. Finally, one evening at dinner, she floated her idea.

"Brent, I was wondering how you'd feel if I kept *Mondae* as my last name."

"I don't care."

"It would mean a lot to my mom if I kept her surname. She's been like both a mother and father to me."

"Fine."

His nonchalant consent seemed uncharacteristically spontaneous and yielding for Brent. She would soon discover that he, too, had a prenuptial condition: Brent didn't want children.

He made that clear from the beginning. Whenever Meggan tried to tactfully resurface the topic, he carefully repeated, as if she needed remedial teaching, a reminder that as a school teacher his days were filled with the chaos of children, and he didn't want to come home to more of it.

Megan accepted Brent's condition of marriage, which meant forsaking any hope of ever having a child of her own. It remained to this day the greatest disappointment of her life.

***

After driving a few blocks from home, Meggan entered the freeway for her four-hour trip from Hopkins, Minnesota, to Marcell, a tiny town on the edge of a northern Minnesota wilderness. A few miles north of Marcell, she would arrive at her mother's small home on Turtle Lake, where her mother retired several years ago.

Meggan had been looking forward to this three-day weekend, relaxing and taking care of her mom, who was recovering from a sprained ankle she received after a fall. Her mom's doctor said that sometimes people get dehydrated during the winter, which could account for someone her age getting light-headed. Her mother accepted that as the only logical explanation for falling, but Meggan wasn't so sure. Her free-spirited mother always seemed younger than anyone her own age, and Meggan had never known her to get dizzy.

But Meggan was glad for the chance to care for her usually self-sufficient mom. The plants would need watering, no doubt, a chore her mother routinely neglected, always giving the excuse of not having a green thumb, something Meggan apparently inherited, according to her mom, from the father Meggan never knew, a man who grew up on a farm and could make just about anything grow.

Meggan planned to fix her mom's favorite hot dish, made with canned tuna, mushroom soup, shredded cheese, onions, and flat noodles, garnished with layer of crushed potato chips on top. While that was baking, she'd touch up housecleaning that would likely be even more neglected than the plants. They'd watch sappy movies in the evening, the predictable tearjerkers they both loved to feel terrible about. Sometimes she thought of Nancy as part mom and part older sister.

As soon as Meggan turned off the freeway onto the northbound state highway, she remembered leaving the books for her mother at home on the floor. Her mom was looking forward to them for a distraction while she recovered from her sprained ankle. Meggan couldn't remember any bookstores along the way but turning back would mean adding at least another hour to the trip. She slowed down while indecision nagged at her. If she showed up without them, her mom would dismiss them as just books, and don't worry, you can bring them next time. But Meggan knew she would be disappointed, and there was no hurry to get to her mom's house.

She made a U-turn at a traffic light and headed back home.

On her way, it started to snow. Frozen pellets crackled against the windshield, followed by big sticky flakes that kept her wipers busy. When she got close to home, she slowed down because new snow would lubricate the frozen back streets. She pulled around the corner to her street, and saw William's red car still in the driveway, covered with a thin layer of fluffy snow. Was something wrong? Is Brent making lunch for them? She decided they must have taken Brent's SUV because of the road conditions.

Meggan parked next to William's car, which blocked her side of the garage, and went to the front door instead of through the attached garage. She and Brent rarely used the front door, and she had forgotten how stiff the key lock was. She nudged the tightly weather-sealed door open with her shoulder and saw Brent's orange suitcase still sitting next to the door. She wondered how someone as well-organized as Brent could have forgotten it. After trotting back to her car, she fished around in her purse with cold fingers for her cellphone, then ran back to the house to call him from inside, thinking she could take his suitcase to the airport if he and William were almost there. She closed the front door and started tapping his cell number, until she heard what sounded like someone groaning with a muffled voice. Was Brent hurt? Could it be a burglar? She held her breath to listen, ready to bolt outside if necessary, almost hearing her own heart pounding.

The groan was louder this time. It sounded like it came from their bedroom, and was unmistakably human.

She started to call 911, but what would she tell them? There were no tracks through the snow, no sign of a break-in. She started removing her ankle boots, but stopped. She might have to run outside to escape, to yell for help, or pound on a neighbor's door.

Meggan pocketed her phone and crept toward the hallway. The groan again, a voice saying something this time, from the master bedroom.

The bedroom door was slightly ajar, and she slowly stepped toward it, holding her breath, trying to peek through the door's opening without moving it. She heard the voice clearly say, "Yes…" It sounded like pleading. She couldn't leave now, and she couldn't just stand there. She slowly, silently, pressed the door farther open. Brent's clothes were on the floor. He was in bed with his back to her, a sheet pulled to his waist. His naked arm was around the unseen person on the other side of him.

"Brent?"

When he rolled over to look at her, Meggan screamed. William got up on one tanned elbow from the other side and gawked at her. She bolted out of the room, slamming the door behind her, running out of the house on quivering legs while fighting tears and gulping quick breaths between sobs, wishing she was somewhere else, anywhere but here. She got to her car and tried to yank the door open, but her feet slipped out from under her. After lying on her back in the driveway, feeling stunned and helpless for a dazed moment, she began crying uncontrollably. She rolled heavily onto her side and started to choke, gagging, while struggling up on her knees in time to vomit into the white snow.

"Meggan, wait!"

Brent's alarmed voice shot through her. After hastily wiping her mouth with the back of her freezing hand, still trembling from what was happening, she slowly turned and glared at him. He stopped and looked quizzically at her, wearing only his red oriental bathrobe and sheepskin slippers. She didn't know what to say. There were no ready cliché responses to fire at him for something like this. She started shaking from the aftermath of panic, and stared at Brent as if he had just shook her out of a nightmare.

"Meggan, we have to talk."

She sat back heavily in the snow and leaned against her car, hiding her grimacing face in her hands. She could only nod agreement.

"Let me help you up."

She glared up at him and angrily shook her head. "No! Get out of my sight."

"I'll wait inside."

Meggan sat on the driveway and watched him step through the fluffy ankle-deep sidewalk snow back to the house. She took a moment to collect herself, wiping back tears with her numb fingers. When she heard the garage door grinding open, she stood up to look.

William was standing back in the shadows of the garage, dressed the way he came—tidy hair and all—with a craven glare on this face. She wanted to yell something awful at him, humiliate him. She wanted to hurt him. But Meggan now saw William as an emotionless beast, and she saved her outrage for Brent. After giving William a cold hateful squint, she trudged back to the house.

When she got inside, she stomped the snow off her boots and waited by the door. She didn't want to be there, she wanted to leave. She didn't want to talk to Brent right now, but knew she had to.

He was in jeans and a black sweatshirt when he came out of the bedroom. He stopped with his socks in his hand when he saw her. "Maybe you should sit down."

"Maybe you should go to hell."

"I've been wanting to talk to you about this, Meggan, but I kept putting it off."

"Well, now you don't have to tell me anything. I saw it for myself. I want a divorce."

"Alright."

"When did this other life of yours start?"

"Ever since I can remember."

Meggan gasped. "Our marriage has been bogus from the beginning?"

"No, I can be attracted to women; sometimes. I was attracted to you. I thought marrying you would help me make a choice."

"Oh, so I failed you somehow."

"I didn't say that."

"There's a lot you didn't say."

"I'm sorry—"

"I don't care about your sorrow, just get out of my house!"

"We own it together."

"I owned it before we were married, and I want it back—without you in it. Get your crap out of here before I get back from my mom's, and then I'm going to change the locks."

"Listen, we can sort this out when you've had some time to simmer down."

"I'll come back simmered down, but with my mom's shotgun. I mean it, Brent. I won't care what happens to either of us if you're still in this house."

Brent's blank expression said he believed her. "William already said I could move in with him."

She glowered at him with disgust. He had made her life nothing more than a cheap make-believe story with a bad ending. But the adrenaline fueling her rage was starting to wear down again, so she had to swallow hard to compose herself a little longer. Without another word, she turned and strode out the front door to her car.

All that was left of William was his BMW's tire tracks through the driveway snow. Besides the frozen pool of vomit, those tracks were her only tangible evidence that this nightmare had been real.

Meggan drove away gripping the steering wheel tightly, her way of keeping her nerves in check. But it didn't check her dejection. Shouted curses soon turned to sobs while she cruised absently down the freeway well under the speed limit. After a few miles, her exhausted anger and sadness drained into a cesspool of depression.

After almost an hour of mindless driving, she realized, with a tearful, relieving chuckle, that she again forgot the bag of romance novels for her mother.

CHAPTER 2

After knocking on her mother's door, Meggan heard her mom's booming "Come in."

"Hi, Mom." Meggan set her travel bag on the living room floor, unbuttoned her down-filled parka and started untying her ankle boots.

"Were the roads bad?" Nancy watched Meggan from the living room on a recliner in front of the fireplace. The footrest was up, revealing her left ankle's elastic wrap.

"Not really. Hardly any traffic."

Her mother pushed the recliner's lever forward to lower her legs. She picked up one of her crutches from the floor and struggled up on her good foot, watching Meggan pull off her boots.

"What's the matter?"

Meggan stood in stocking feet. "What do you mean?"

"I'm getting big blips on my radar."

Meggan tried to busy herself by carefully hanging her parka on a coat hook next to the door and making sure her boots were on the entry rug. After centering herself a bit, she faced her mom.

"I caught Brent in bed with his gay lover this morning, and they're moving in together. How's that for blips?" Her still-bloodshot eyes began tearing up again.

Nancy stared incredulously at her daughter for a moment, then hobbled toward Meggan the best she could on the one crutch. "Oh, sweetie…"

Meggan ran to her mom and embraced her tightly, not wanting to bawl like a baby, not wanting to let go. Nancy kissed her cheek and rubbed her back silently. Meggan breathed haltingly, trying to be brave, and then gently pulled away.

"There's something wrong with me, Mom. Why do I always end up with men who are such losers and liars?"

"You might not be the best guy-picker, but Brent misled you. You can't blame yourself for that."

"Maybe not, but I have a huge mistake to undo."

Nancy kept one arm around Meggan, and held the crutch under her other arm. "Why don't you put your stuff in the guest bedroom, honey, and we'll talk about it. I have a box of decent wine in the fridge."

"I forgot to pick up the stuff for the tuna hot dish."

"Let's just order a big pizza for supper, okay?"

Meggan gave her mother a quick hug and a brave grin. "I also forgot to bring the enlightening literature I had for you."

"I'll just reread some of the other lovey-dovey books you've brought. I'm sure they'll end pretty much the same way as the ones you left at home."

Meggan carried her overnight bag to the bedroom that her mother always kept ready for Meggan's visits. The bedspread was a wool Hudson Bay point blanket, white with colored stripes. Two throw pillows, one with a moose embroidered on it and one printed with a big yellow 1960s peace sign, were propped up at the head of the bed. The window was trimmed with short pine-green draperies, and a sun-yellowed blind rolled up at the top. One of the walls was cluttered with framed photos of Meggan at various ages and stages of life, from a bewildered chubby-cheek baby to a skinny high school teen valiantly holding a swim team trophy over her head. The photo next to it was a standard wedding pose at the altar with Brent. Meggan now saw his expression as merely being tolerant of the event, or maybe even bored with it. And then there was a faded coin-booth photo of a young proud-looking man in US Army dress uniform, the only photo she had ever seen of her father, who died just before she was born.

She set her bag on the small rocking chair next to the window and went back to the living room. Her mom put on a happy face, but Meggan knew she wasn't feeling it.

Nancy asked her to put a couple of split birch logs on the fireplace's smoldering embers, and invited her to relax on the overstuffed, over-throw-pillowed floral sofa across from her.

"Meggan, I've been thinking about what you said about picking men who are losers and liars."

"Mom, please, do we have to analyze this right now?"

Her mom was good at getting to the bottom of things, but Meggan wasn't quite ready for the bottom. Still, she thought, her mom was just trying to help the only way she could, by giving advice.

"Okay, what about it?"

"It's easy to understand why boys, and then men, were always buzzing around a pretty girl like you, but what attracted you to certain ones?"

"I don't know. I guess when I felt someone cared enough about me to look after me …where is this going?"

"Did you think Brent was looking after you?"

"He seemed able to, I guess. He had a secure job, and he was always so sure of himself."

"You had a good job, too, but you gave it up."

"I made good money managing the Emporium, but long late hours in the restaurant business made it impossible to be home evenings and weekends with Brent. That's why I quit. I hate my current boring insurance company job, and the pay is lousy, but between our salaries we've been living comfortably."

"Do you still pay the mortgage payments out of your own paycheck?"

"Yes, but I owned that house when I married Brent, and I wanted something I could call my own, that's all. Why do you ask?"

"I'm just bringing up financial matters because I can help with that if you decide to leave him."

Meggan slouched back into the sofa. "I told Brent I wanted a divorce, but I was mad and hurt. We haven't actually decided anything, though. But regardless, I don't want your money, thanks for offering."

"The money I'm talking about is already yours, Meggan."

"What do you mean?"

"I put it away years ago in an investment trust, with you as the beneficiary."

"Geez, Mom, can we please talk about something a little lighter? I'm not really in the mood to talk about my divorce and your death in the same conversation."

"I don't have to die for you to have those funds. It's not your inheritance, it's your birthright."

"And just how long did you save up this money? Which I still don't need, by the way."

"I didn't save it up. It was a gift from your father."

An emotional jolt ran through Meggan. She sat upright.

"From my father?"

"Before he was deployed to Vietnam in 1972, he took out a life insurance policy for $100,000. We were planning to get married when he returned, so he made me the beneficiary instead of his parents. It was a few years after the war ended, though, before the insurance company reluctantly paid me. Because of his official status as 'missing-in-action,' with no evidence of death, the insurance company refused to pay until I sued them. My lawyer, a Korean War veteran who represented me pro bono, made the argument to the court that wartime MIAs must be presumed dead after some reasonable period of time, especially after the war ended, all known POWs had been released, and official searches for MIAs had been made by US organizations. A sympathetic jury agreed. I put the money into an investment trust fund over forty years ago, and now it's worth quite a bit more."

"So, that's why you kept your maiden name. I always assumed you and my father were married. He intended that money for you, Mom, and it's your retirement fund now. I'll be okay, don't worry. I'm still healthy and employable."

"My social security income and pension dividends are all I'll need to live out my days, with money left over. I tagged that insurance money as yours from the beginning."

"But he would have named me as a beneficiary if that's what he intended."

"He couldn't name you because you weren't born yet, and neither of us knew I was pregnant when he left. When I found out, I wrote a letter telling him, but it came back unopened, marked as undeliverable by the Army Post Office. I was frantic because I thought he had been killed. I contacted the VA, the Red Cross, and even my district's congressman, but no one would look into it for me because I wasn't married to Peter. I had no legal relationship with him. I was just a girlfriend, as far as the government was concerned."

"If you loved each other, why didn't you get married before he left?"

"We did love each other, but Peter was going to be overseas for at least a year, which seems like forever when you're nineteen. He said he didn't want to tie me down in case I changed my mind about marrying him. I might meet someone else, he said, and the time apart would either strengthen or weaken our commitment to each other. I felt terrible. I thought he was saying he didn't trust my loyalty to him. But I now realize he was fibbing to me. The escalating body count in Vietnam was daily news at that point, and he didn't want to risk leaving me a widow. I'm sure that was his reason. We were so in love, it couldn't have been anything else."

Meggan's emotional tinder sparked again, and she dabbed at her moist eyes with a sleeve. She was learning about the origins of her life, her parents' love for each other, and their sad parting. That was big enough to distract from her own troubles, and she wanted to keep the conversation going.

"Why didn't you tell me this before?"

Nancy drew a deep breath. "I was afraid you might think you were an unwanted, illegitimate child, or that I was jilted by your father. That's why I always just said he died in the war."

"When did you finally find out he was missing in action?"

"A few months after my letter came back."

"Did the Army just send you a telegram, or whatever they did back then?"

"No, Peter's parents told me—reluctantly. I knew they owned a farm near Worthington, Minnesota, but locating someone back then without having a phone book for the area was almost impossible. I took a bus to the downtown

Minneapolis main library and looked for any kind of reference that might say something about Worthington. The only thing I found was a Minnesota travel guide that listed the phone number and address of a couple of motels. I cashed in my three dollars—the only money I had—for a handful of quarters at the library checkout counter, and then called the Worthington Inn from a payphone in the library's entryway. I hoped the town was small enough so someone at the motel could tell me if a family named McHillston lived nearby. I explained my situation to the kindly woman who answered the phone, and she paged through her local phone book, patiently reading the names and phone numbers of seven listings with McHillston as a last name while I quickly wrote them down on a scrap of paper. I had enough quarters left to call four of them long distance, which I did as soon as I hung up from the motel. No one answered the first call. After explaining my reason for calling to the woman who answered the second call, she told me her husband, Tom, lost his brother in Vietnam. My heart skipped a beat. Almost breathlessly, I asked what the brother's name was. When she said 'Peter McHillston,' I couldn't even speak. The woman asked if I was still on the line and I managed to say yes. The operator came on and said I needed to deposit fifty cents within thirty seconds, but the woman quickly gave me the phone number of her husband's parents, who owned a farm about a mile outside of town.

"I called them with my last quarters, praying someone would answer, wondering what I'd say if someone did. As soon as a man answered, I said I was a friend of Peter McHillston's, and asked if that was his son. After an uncomfortable pause, he asked who I was. I explained that Peter and I were engaged. I told him that my letter to Peter was returned unopened, and that I couldn't get any information from the army because I wasn't listed as his next of kin. The silence was longer this time, making me worry about my long-distance call time running out. 'Can you tell me anything?' I pleaded. The man's voice was softer, and halting, as he said Peter was missing in action in Vietnam. I could tell by his voice that was difficult for him to say. Then I made the mistake of telling him I was pregnant with Peter's child."

Meggan leaned forward. "Mistake?"

"Yes, because he didn't believe me, or didn't want to. He accused me of calling to press them for money, and warned me not to smear his son's name, now that Peter was unable to defend himself. I tried to say I didn't want any money, I just wanted to know what happened to Peter. But his father cut me off, telling me that Peter never said anything to them about being engaged, and his son would certainly not abandon a woman who was carrying his child because Peter was too responsible to do that, and then said he was going to hang up. I said, 'Wait…he didn't know—' but at that point I was talking to a dial tone."

"Geez, Mom…I made your life miserable from the get-go."

Without saying a word, Nancy picked her crutch up and shakily got to her feet, hobbling over to the sofa to sit next to Meggan. Nancy leveled her eyes at her daughter.

"Sweetie, you've never made me miserable. You've always been the brightest light in my life. I'll admit I was plenty miserable back then, but only because I was scared. More scared than I have ever been in my life. I had just found out Peter was probably killed, and only God knows how horribly or how lonely it might have been for him. I didn't know how to tell my super-religious parents in Iowa, and Peter's father had basically accused me of being a tramp and a con artist. I wasn't earning much money waitressing in a vegetarian restaurant back then, frequented mostly by hippies who were too short on cash to tip. I worried about how I could afford the time and money to take care of a baby on my own. The three girls I shared an apartment with said they'd help take care of my baby while I was at work, but one of them, my best friend at the time, said I should get an abortion. With the taboos against pre-marital sex blown apart during the early 1970s, waves of girls on the lam were getting pregnant from boys they barely knew. Abortion became acceptable, and was a growth industry."

"I'm glad you didn't listen to your friend."

Nancy tried to smile, but there was sadness in it.

"I did listen to her. I went to one of the free clinics that were popping up everywhere in inner cities, and the staff was really nice to me. They said the procedure would be confidential, quick, painless, and free. When I said I wanted to think about it some more, a nurse told me the longer I waited, the more difficult it could be for me, physically and emotionally. But I insisted on needing more time. They were apparently accustomed to young girls who were scared and confused, because the nurse was ready with a clincher: she said I shouldn't let this mistake ruin the rest of my life. That remark pierced my heart; but not for the reason she intended. I was pissed off at being manipulated like some strung-out dumb kid. I refused to think of Peter's child as a mistake. 'You're right,' I said. 'I won't let this baby, which you call a mistake, ruin my life. I'll make sure it becomes my greatest blessing.' The nurse rolled her eyes at me for being either stupid or belligerent, and said I had apparently misunderstood her. I said no I didn't, and I left."

Meggan lightly patted her palms together. "Yea, Mom! But you must have had second thoughts when you your anger wore off. You faced being alone for many tough years as a single mom."

Nancy took one of Meggan's hands and held it silently for a moment. "At nineteen, I didn't look very far ahead, and I've never looked back. Like I told that dumb-shit nurse, you'll always be my greatest blessing."

Meggan felt the strength of her mother's love flow into her; but she also felt sad because, in her mid-forties, getting past child-bearing years, she would never experience the motherly love her mom just described.

It was only a little past five o'clock, but the setting winter sun was already casting long twilight shadows from the snow-frosted pines across the lake. She told her mom she was emotionally and physically exhausted from the day and wanted to take a nap before dinner.

***

Memories continued flooding through Nancy's mind after Meggan went to the bedroom. She remembered the envy she felt for families and girlfriends of American POWs who were being released to the US. The newsreels showed crowds of people showering the haggard, grinning soldiers with sympathy and respect when they landed in the United States. But MIAs like Peter McHillston were not mentioned. Any sympathy, or even acknowledgement, for those still missing had not yet worked its way into popular discourse. Americans were exhausted by war news, and they wanted to stop thinking about it. But the MIA's loved-ones never stopped thinking about them. Nancy tried several times to find out more about Peter's disappearance but was always denied any official information.

While Nancy sat in her dark living room, lit only by dying flickers in her fireplace, she closed her eyes against sadness for Meggan, tried to find relief from grief and guilt—and from the burning pressure in her chest. Finally giving in, she hobbled quietly into the kitchen for a nitroglycerin pill that would soon relieve the angina pains, a secret she had kept from Meggan.

CHAPTER 3

Meggan woke before her mom did the next morning, and quietly made toast with peanut butter. She made a half pot of coffee and poured a cup for herself. While standing at the sink eating her quick breakfast, she wondered what she should do when she got home. She decided to talk to her mom about all that later, but she didn't want to wake her, and Meggan wanted some time to sort things out for herself.

After getting bundled up against the morning's freezing bite, she walked down the long driveway and crossed the highway, spotting a fresh deer trail into the wilderness of the Chippewa National Forest.

As a child, Meggan loved to wander through the wild woodlands around her mom's lake home, which was just a simple summer cabin before her mom retired up here and had it remodeled. She'd tag along when her mom hunted grouse on old logging trails in the forest, just across the highway from her mom's land. When Meggan turned twelve years old, her mother taught her how to use the shotgun, and when she was old enough to venture into the wilderness alone, her mom gave her a compass and showed her how to navigate with it. She taught Meggan how to bracket her position with known landmarks, such as the highway, or a river. If she ever got lost, she could simply trek west until she reached Highway 38, which ran north-south for miles. Meggan didn't bring her compass this morning, but the rising sun was the only reference she needed.

Meggan followed the deer trail until it ran into a willow thicket. After skirting around the dense stand of skinny trees, she hiked across an open area that lacked undergrowth because of a sun-starving canopy of towering red pines and white pines. She came out at a lake that was surrounded by federal land, so there were no roads to it, or cabins on it.

She sat on the trunk of a fallen tree and looked across the lake's dazzling white snow cover. Gusts lifted powdery tufts of dry snow, looking like white smoke sparkling in the morning sunlight. At any other time, this safe peaceful place would have calmed her. But her stomach ached this morning. She wondered if Brent had struggled at all while keeping the secret he said he was afraid to reveal to her. Did he ever feel guilty? Does he have any regrets?

Regardless, she knew the marriage was doomed. Now she just wanted her house back. With that decided, she suddenly felt chilled. Her mom would surely be awake and worried by now, so Meggan slogged through calf-high snow toward a more direct westerly heading, straddling over deadfall and pushing low branches away from her face. She couldn't see her footprints from coming in, but she trusted the rising eastern sun at her back.

She came out of the woods somewhere along the highway, and recognized a neighbor's mailbox. That would put her about a half-mile north of her mother's driveway, and it only took a few minutes along the plowed highway shoulder to reach it.

She let herself in without knocking and hollered "Hello."

There was no answer.

Meggan took off her boots and trotted past the kitchen to her mother's empty bedroom. She heard the outside door open and thump shut, and she rushed to see her mother standing there on crutches, her injured ankle covered with a thick rag-wool sock, the other foot in an old cowboy boot.

"Saw your footprints down the driveway."

"I went for a walk in the woods."

"I know."

"Sorry."

"Nothing to be sorry for." Her mother grinned. "That's what woods are for, to walk around in and gather your thoughts." Nancy sat on the bench next to the front door and pulled off her boot and wool sock.

"I don't know how settled my thoughts are, Mom. Like you said yesterday, I've made mistakes with men, but this one was a doozy."

"Well, I'm no expert about men, that's for sure, but let's get a cup of that coffee you made and maybe we can figure them out."

Meggan brought a cup of coffee to her mom, who was already settled into her recliner. She took her place on the sofa and set her cup on the early American style coffee table, after pushing aside scattered magazines and Nancy's reading glasses.

"I want a divorce, no doubts about that. But I did wonder if I was unfair to Brent yesterday."

"Why? Did you sleep with his lover, too?"

"Be serious, Mom. I just blew up and condemned him. I didn't give him a chance to explain what he's been going through."

"He's been unfaithful to you and deceived you for seven

years—that's what he's been going through. And I am being serious."

Meggan sipped her coffee, trying to collect words that made some sense. "Brent said he's been struggling with this sexual orientation and thought he might change if he married me."

"Well, I guess you didn't serve your purpose."

"Stop it, please. I don't blame you for being pissed off at Brent. I am too, but I think he at least deserves to be heard out."

"And I think there's a difference between being compassionate and being a pushover."

Meggan set her coffee back down and looked away from her mother. "Let's not talk about this right now, okay?"

"Oh, hell, I'm sorry, Meggan. Yes, I am pissed off at Brent, but I wouldn't worry about him feeling too bad about all this. The first time you introduced me, he seemed indifferent toward you. I thought you might have been blind-sided, but I kept it to myself. I also kept your father's insurance money in my name for a while."

Meggan shot a look at her. "Because I was marrying someone you didn't like?"

"No, because he was someone I didn't trust. If your marriage didn't work out, Brent would have been entitled to half of the money as a joint asset. I just wanted to give things a chance to sort out."

"You weren't protecting me, you were protecting the money."

"I was protecting the money for you, and for your children if you had any."

"I told you from the beginning Brent didn't want children." Meggan's shoulders drooped as she looked away again.

"Well, maybe you'll meet someone—"

"Mom, stop trying to fix my life, okay?"

Nancy's sad eyes showed defeat in them. "I know I can't fix you, I don't need to and I don't want to, but I let you down while you were growing up, and I feel guilty for it."

"Oh, please, Mom, how could any of this be your fault? I think you're running out of things to feel bad about."

"You grew up never having the security of a father, and that is my fault."

"I had plenty of security from you."

"I might have showed you how to be strong sometimes, or at least how to be bullheaded, but neither of us knew what it's like to live with a man. I think that left something missing in your life experience, Meggan."

"I doubt that, but it wouldn't be your fault."

"I read a magazine article about girls who grew up without a father, and how many of them became strongminded survivors from an early age. But they had also trouble relating to men. That's my fault. I stayed single without realizing how that would affect you."

"You once told me you stayed single because my father might come home someday. That was a lesson in loyalty that I will never forget."

"Yes, I did wait for him. But I eventually had to give up hope and accept that you and I were on our own."

"When did you give up?"

"April of 1975, when TV newsreels showed American helicopters rescuing the remaining diplomats and Marine guards from the roof of the US embassy. After that, I knew Peter would never come home."

Meggan swallowed hard. "I'm sorry, Mom. I'm the one who should feel guilty. Having me screwed up your life, not mine."

Nancy couldn't hold back her smile. "I'll make a deal with you. Let's both put an end to our guilt trips, okay?"

"Okay, it's a deal."

CHAPTER 4

The next two evenings with her mother helped distract Meggan from worrying about the trouble she'd have to face when she got home. They watched sentimental but uplifting movies while eating supper, and afterward Meggan would pull out her ball of burnt orange wool yarn and knitting needles and worked on the scarf she had recently started for her mom. They sipped wine and munched popcorn while talking into the late night, starting with questions like *what should I do with my life*, and quickly degrading into laughter about embarrassing and silly memories.

Sunday morning, Meggan made coffee and checked emails on her phone. She soon heard Nancy's crutches thumping along the hallway floor.

Nancy stood at the kitchen door in her tiny-flowered flannel pajamas. "You're up too early for a non-retired person. How about some bacon and eggs?"

"Toast would be fine, Mom. I want to get home around noon."

"I just remembered, I have something for you."

After more thumping and shuffling in the hallway, Nancy returned to the kitchen on one crutch, this time carrying a large white box under the other arm. She handed it to Meggan.

"This belonged to your father."

Meggan carefully opened the lid and removed a plaid wool shirt. She stood and held it open in front of her by the shoulders and examined the pattern of wide green bands crossed by smaller blue ones, and a thin yellow line running through the middle of both bands.

"It's beautiful."

"It's the tartan colors of the McHillstons, your father's ancestral clan in Scotland."

Meggan checked the label, which said it was custom-made in Edinburgh, Scotland. "Is that a purple flower embroidered above the pocket?"

"It's a Scottish thistle, the country's national emblem. You can also see one on each of the pewter buttons. Peter's parents had the shirt made for him as a high school graduation gift. He left it with me before going to Vietnam and said to keep it for him. It's your turn to take care of it."

"It's like new."

"I've never worn it. But you should."

"Why didn't you?"

"I always thought of it as a symbol of hope. But your father was a practical man, and I suspect he'd want a perfectly good shirt to keep someone warm. I also suspect he'd want that person to be his daughter."

Meggan snuggled the coarse wool against her cheek. She wondered if the aromatic scent was the Scottish wool, or the essence of her father. She decided it must be both.

While driving home Sunday morning, Meggan's worries came back like a migraine. What if Brent was still in the house? What if he wasn't? Would he agree to a divorce, or beg for another chance—and how would she respond? She finally turned the radio on to shut off the noise in her brain.

After two hours of driving and halfway home, snow began to drift down from the darkening overcast sky. At first, it blew off her windshield, but when wet flakes began to cling and stick, Meggan had to turn the defroster on all the way with the wipers flapping at full speed. While leaning forward to keep track of the road's increasingly disappearing edge, she spotted a car in the ditch ahead. She slowed and saw a young man outside already on his cellphone, so she kept going. Visibility worsened in minutes. She slowed again and gripped the steering wheel tighter, giving her a false feeling of more control. A sharp crosswind fought for control of the car, and shook heavy clumps of snow off towering bare-branched trees along the highway, a few bursting on her car like snowballs. A sudden stiffer gust grabbed her car and she immediately pulled her foot off the gas pedal, overcoming the reflex to jam on her brake, a mistake that could spin her small sedan out of control. It took Meggan almost four more exhausting hours to struggle home through the weather.

The street to her house had been plowed, perhaps less than an hour ago as evidenced by the inch or so of fresh accumulation since then. Her driveway was snowed over. If Brent had left, he did so before the snowstorm—or he was still inside the house. She pressed the button on her remote garage door opener and held her breath while the door slowly rose. It was empty. Before driving into the driveway, she got out of her car and kicked at the driveway snow to see how deep it was, estimating it to be about four inches, but wetter and heavier than up north. She felt too tired to shovel so she got in her car and backed up, careful to avoid hitting a car parked on the other side of the street. She carefully accelerated forward, just enough to avoid getting stuck from spinning the tires. She held her breath as she nursed the car forward, slowly, steadily pushing through the snow and into the garage.

After lowering the garage door, Meggan got her overnight bag from the backseat and went into the house. The first thing she noticed was the missing television. She dropped her bag and quickly pulled off her boots, unzipping her coat while she trotted to the bedroom. The closet door was wide open, and Brent's clothes were gone. She pulled open the drawers on his side of the chest of drawers, and they were empty. Meggan padded through the rest of the house. Her laptop computer, monitor, and laser printer were gone. The internet modem was still plugged in—it belonged to the cable company—but their Wi-Fi router was missing. Then a thought struck her: they kept about five hundred dollars in a small safe under the bathroom vanity. She pulled the vanity door open and sat on the floor while concentrating on the combination. It was empty.

"Shit," she yelled aloud, and sprang to her feet. When she got back to the living room, she noticed their antique rocking chair was gone, as was an original painting by a local, but nationally-known, wildlife artist, now worth several hundred dollars. Meggan grabbed the cellphone from her coat pocket and tapped Brent's cellphone number. She had been worried all weekend about talking to him, but now she could hardly wait. After several rings, her call went to voicemail.

After his happy greeting ended with *please leave a detailed message*, she said, "Damn you, Brent! You had no right to take things that belong to both of us. I bought that computer with my own money, and everything else we owned together, including all the cash you ran off with. You didn't get away with cheating on me, and you're sure as hell not getting away with stealing from me."

She hung up and paced around the house, gripping her cellphone and swearing, first under her breath, then aloud, wondering how to retaliate if Brent refused her demand, which he likely would.

She opened her cellphone's automated assistant and said "locksmiths close to me" into the microphone. Four choices popped onto the screen, and she tapped "Call" on the first listing. When a kindly man named Chuck answered the phone, she asked how soon he could come out to re-key her door locks. Chuck hedged his answer, starting with how slow traffic is, especially in this weather, and their full schedule. Meggan interrupted to say she was scared that someone apparently has a key to her house because she just got home and expensive things were missing, and she lives alone. He promised to be there sometime that afternoon.

She woke up several times during that night, wondering what to do if Brent didn't return her call. Confronting him by surprise at William's condo seemed to be the only possible way of rooting him out. She wasn't going to let Brent get away with his larceny, not without a fight.

Monday morning, she left a message on her boss's voice-mail, lying that she'd be in late because she had a sore throat and wanted to get a throat culture to rule out strep. The truth was that she needed time to call the school where Brent and William worked, and then try to find out where William lived.

When she called the school, she asked an administrative staffer for the last name of William, her son's English teacher. The staffer said, "Astead," and asked Meggan if she'd like to leave a message. Meggan said no, but asked for William's home address. She didn't think the staffer would tell her, and she didn't. Using her cellphone, her only access to the internet now, she did a search for William Astead. She found his occupation and age, but no address. Before leaving for work, she left another voicemail for Brent, less hysterical this time, but more to the point: if he didn't return the property he illegally took, she was going to call a lawyer—and maybe the police.

Meggan had trouble concentrating on her work that day. Her boss, Bill Champlin, asked for a database report by the end of the day, but at quitting time, Meggan said she didn't have time to complete it. Her punishment was a disappointed scowl from him.

The next day she forced herself to complete at least the minimum acceptable amount of her workload, constantly fighting back thoughts about how she could make Brent come out of hiding so they could have an unheated rational discussion.

When Meggan got home Wednesday, she heard her front doorbell ring within a minute or so after getting her boots and coat off. She hesitated, wondering what she would say if it was Brent. The doorbell rang again, longer this time. She peeked out of the front window, and saw a stranger in an olive-green waist jacket and black knit cap.

As soon as she opened the door, he said, "Are you Meggan Mondae?"

"Yes…"

"This is for you." He handed her an envelope and as soon as she took it, he said, "You've been served." He then turned and strode off down the driveway to his car, which was parked on the street in front of her driveway.

She closed the door against the cold and ripped the envelope open. It was an official-looking document from the Hennepin County Court, with the heading, "Summons and Petition for Dissolution of Marriage."

CHAPTER 5

Meggan found a divorce lawyer by doing an internet search for *family law*. She found a law firm not too far away, and chose a partner of the firm named Rhonda DuCrain. Her website photo showed that she wasn't very young, which might suggest sufficient legal experience, nor too old, perhaps indicating she wouldn't be too busy with a backlog of clients. Meggan called and scheduled a no-cost "assessment" meeting with Ms. DuCrain for the following afternoon.

Meggan left work after lunch, telling her boss that something she ate made her sick. When she arrived at Ms. DuCrain's law office, a young receptionist looked up from her computer and asked Meggan to have a seat, that Rhonda DuCrain was on a phone call. After a few minutes, Rhonda, a fiftyish woman, stockier and older-looking than her internet photo, swept into the reception room and introduced herself as cheerfully as if Meggan had come to pick out new furniture instead of discussing the collapse of her marriage.

Rhonda invited her into a private office, and Meggan sat in wood-backed chair in front of Rhonda's conference-sized desk, which was stacked with bulging file folders on one side, and a black plastic coffee carafe and red ceramic mug on the other. Rhonda sat heavily in her black leather swivel chair and put her elbows on her desk, leaning toward Meggan as if to get right to business. She asked to see the papers that were served.

Rhonda quickly read the summons and handed it back to Meggan. "Were you shocked to get served a divorce petition, or were you expecting it?"

"I didn't know what to expect. This is my first divorce."

Rhonda released a polite snicker as if Meggan was trying to be funny, and then apparently realized she wasn't.

"I meant, have you and your—is your spouse a husband?"

At first Meggan didn't know what she was being asked. "Oh, yes. He's my husband."

"Do you want a divorce, or are you contesting it?"

"Neither...I mean, I'm not sure what my options are."

"Any children involved?"

"No."

"A prenuptial agreement between you?"

"No."

"Okay, then you can either agree to the conditions of a marriage dissolution, in which case it will be fairly simple: negotiate who gets what, sign some forms, and you're done. If you contest the dissolution or the division of property, then the case will go before a judge. In simple terms, that means a court battle with an uncertain outcome, except that you can expect it to be prolonged, painful, and expensive. I'm not trying to talk you out of contestation, Meggan, but I want to be up front with your options and their possible consequences."

"I appreciate that. I'd like to work this out without the court battle."

"Understood. Working it out means negotiating for jointly held property. Do you own any real estate?"

"A house, but it's mine. I bought it before we were married, and I've made all the mortgage payments from my own paycheck. The title is in my name."

Rhonda sat back in her leather chair, which scrunched noisily under her weight, and she touched her fingertips together with a pensive stare. "The deed was granted to you when you bought the property, but now your husband has a half interest in the title. In Minnesota, real estate is considered jointly owned by married parties. It only takes one to buy, but two to sell."

Meggan felt sick to her stomach. "That's not fair. I made all the payments."

"Maybe it's not fair, but it is the law. Perhaps we could convince your husband that, as a matter of principle and fairness—and as a condition of the divorce—he should deed his interest to you."

"And if he doesn't agree?"

"A next step might be an offer to pay him half the equity in exchange for him deeding his interest to you."

"I probably have at least twenty thousand dollars or so of equity. I don't have half that much in cash to pay him."

"Then you would probably be looking at selling the house and splitting the net proceeds."

"Crap! So, Brent would get half the equity after I've made all the payments?"

Rhonda nodded solemnly.

Meggan slumped in her chair. "I know—it's the law. Damnit. Okay, what's next?"

"I'll have our secretary draw up our standard representation agreement. We'll need a retainer payment of one thousand dollars, which will go toward my hourly fee of $180 per hour, plus expenses."

"I'm on kind of a tight budget. I've been double-paying

the mortgage payments whenever I could—a stupid idea, as it turns out. Can I use a credit card for the retainer?"

Rhonda said yes, and then called her secretary to prepare an agreement of representation. When the secretary brought in two copies of the agreement, Meggan signed them, and then signed the credit card charge for the one-thousand-dollar retainer fee. Rhoda signed both copies of the retainer agreement and gave one back to Meggan.

"I'll contact your husband's attorney this afternoon and inform him of your desire to dissolve the marriage amicably, but only if your husband agrees to deed his interest in the house to you, and without any compensation."

"He'll probably refuse. Then what?"

"Then you can decide whether to split the equity, or make a fight of it. Do you have any valuable personal property that might be negotiable? Art, jewelry, antiques, that sort of thing?"

"We have a painting worth a few hundred dollars, which he took, and my wedding ring, which he can have back."

Rhonda nodded understandingly. "One last thing, Meggan: if your husband contacts you to negotiate anything directly, tell him he will have to go through me. It's difficult to negotiate when your emotions are so wrapped into this, and I need to consider how any binding agreements would affect your particular situation."

Rhonda escorted Meggan to the door, with the promise to contact her as soon as she hears about her husband's response to the real estate issue.

Meggan drove home in thick rush hour traffic that was further hampered by sporadic snowfall and slippery streets. As she crawled toward the approaching freeway entrance, cars were backed up as far as she could see, so she weaved through back streets to get home. Concentrating on the traffic helped distract her anger about Brent getting half the equity in her house—without ever paying into it. But the house payments, along with other living expenses, might become a financial burden now, and she fantasized about cashing out of it, quitting her job and moving away to a cabin in some remote wilderness, like her mom, swearing off men forever for a simple life alone. She used to feel sorry for her mom for living like that, but now Meggan thought she understood.

It took her two hours to get home on a route that would normally take thirty or forty minutes. She felt drained, partly from intense driving demands, but mostly from emotions knotting in her stomach. It was already getting dark, even darker inside her house, so she had to feel for the familiar light switch. She stomped her wet boots and pried them off with one foot and then the other, and stood a moment in stocking feet with her coat still on, looking around the silent house before going in. Brent had seemingly mocked her by taking the TV, computer and monitor, and Wi-Fi, her only connections, except for her phone, to the outside world. She felt like a fool for trying to love someone who couldn't love her, who apparently despised her enough to keep hurting her. She vowed to never trust love again.

Meggan hung her parka in the front closet, wondering what to do next. The patterns of her life the last seven years had been formed around accommodating Brent and his schedule, but she was free from that now. It struck her that if this was the pathway to freedom, it sucked.

CHAPTER 6

The next day Meggan again struggled to concentrate on her tasks at work, trying extra hard to make sure her statistical report was correct. When she got home, she took her vegetable soup recipe from a kitchen drawer, but she didn't have most of the ingredients on hand, and she didn't feel like cooking anyway. Instead, she ate a supper of corn chips, a granola bar, and three glasses of wine.

On the fourth day, Rhonda called Meggan's cellphone while she was at work. When Meggan saw the caller ID, she answered it and stepped out into the hallway with the phone to her ear, exchanging greetings with Rhonda.

"I heard from your husband's attorney," Rhonda said. "He's not willing to forfeit his interest in the house, but he will accept responsibility for future mortgage payments if you deed your interest over to him."

Meggan felt like someone had sucker punched her in the stomach. After taking a moment to regain her breath, she said, "He can go to hell. Now what?"

"If you want to keep the house, you'll have to pay half of the equity to him."

"I told you, I don't have that kind of cash sitting around."

"Yes, I remember. Can you borrow enough from someone to pay him off? Maybe a family member?"

She quickly considered her mother's offer to help her financially. "No, I don't have anyone to borrow money from."

"Then the property will have to be sold." Rhonda's voice then became less strident, almost sympathetic. "Meggan, I hate to tell you this, but the costs involved with selling the house will take almost all of the equity. I did a quick estimate based on your house's assessed tax value and normal selling and closing costs, and you'd be lucky to end up with a couple of thousand dollars to split with Brent."

"That's not even enough for a down payment on a crappy little condo. Maybe not even enough for an apartment's first month rent and security deposit."

"I fully understand your predicament, and I agree that none of the solutions are good ones."

"If I stop making payments, how long before the bank forecloses?"

"The lender's internal processes, legal proceedings, and redemption periods could give you a couple of years before they can physically evict you, but a foreclosure will ruin your credit, Meggan. A low credit score could prevent you from getting another mortgage for at least three years, and a lot of landlords check credit scores these days."

"It would hurt Brent's credit, too, right?"

"Did you add his name on the mortgage after you married him?"

"No."

"Then a foreclosure might not affect his credit."

Meggan pressed her lips together, waiting for a man to walk by and get past listening range. "Then I'm screwed, right? Why didn't you just tell me that up front?"

"Because I don't know what you mean by *screwed*, and we

needed to go through this preliminary round of negotiations before we talked about next options. Here's a suggestion: offer your husband the equivalent of what he would net after paying the costs of selling the property. For example, you could offer him a thousand dollars. Can you afford a thousand dollars?"

Meggan didn't know exactly how much she and Brent had in their savings account, but it was at least seven thousand dollars. "Yes, my half of our savings would cover that. When can you make the offer?"

"I'll call his attorney today. Because it's Friday, we probably won't hear anything until next week. This is a lousy situation, Meggan, but try to not let it ruin your weekend, okay?"

Meggan agreed bravely, but after hanging up she felt drained and leaned against the hallway wall. A woman with an armful of file folders got off one of the nearby elevators and gave Meggan a concerned look. Meggan forced a smile to reassure the woman, who made clicking steps down the tiled hallway with her high-heel shoes. It was almost noon, and people began leaving their offices for the lunch rush, heading for elevators to carry out whatever plan they had to fill the next hour or so. Meggan took a deep breath and exhaled, and then headed back to her tiny partitioned space in the middle of the insurance company's twelfth-floor accounting department. The room was almost deserted by now, but Meggan was in no mood to shuffle down a long line for a dull deli sandwich.

A coworker friend named Sandra stopped on her way out of the office. "Want to grab some lunch?"

"I'm not hungry, Sandra, but thanks. I think I have a touch of something."

"Maybe just a smoothie or soup? I could bring it back

for you."

"Well…" Meggan searched for another excuse but lacked the mental energy to create a believable one. "I guess I should eat something."

They rode down the elevator to the first floor, where the Green Meadow Deli served iceberg lettuce salads, predictable soups, and sliced meat and cheese sandwiches. Meggan chose chicken wild rice soup, served in a disposable cardboard bowl with a lid, and Sandra had a pre-made Italian hoagie. They found a small table near a window overlooking a bustling street that was further complicated by an electric city train honking and rumbling through over steel tracks and under a tangle of overhead wires.

"A little glum today?" Sandra asked, unwrapping her sandwich.

"Yeah, you could say that." Meggan sipped a spoonful of the warm soup. "I've found myself in the middle of a divorce that's gone from nasty to really nasty. It's a new experience for me."

"Wow." Sandra set her sandwich down and looked into Meggan's eyes. "My sister went through a divorce. It wrecked her life for at least a year."

"Thanks."

"Oh, I'm sorry, Meggan. On the positive side, my sister is better off now. She and her husband used to argue all the time, even at family gatherings. I felt so sorry for her. Tell me if you think I'm prying, but was your husband abusive?"

Meggan started to say no, but after quick reflection said, "He cheated on me, but he didn't beat me up, if that's what you meant."

"I don't know what I meant, Meggan. I'm so sorry. You seem so composed about this. I'd be a basket case if I found out my boyfriend had another girlfriend."

Meggan started to correct her gender assumption, but Sandra was something of an office busybody, prone to livening office life with dramatic rumors. Keeping the news at the level of a garden variety divorce would likely just cause enough buzz for a day or two of whispers and sympathetic glances.

"What really bothers me the most," Meggan said, "is that he's being a jerk about splitting what little property we own."

Sandra swallowed a bite of her sandwich. "That's terrible. Be careful; my sister's ex drained their savings account before saying he wanted a divorce."

They finished their lunch while Sandra complained about her tiny apartment in a lousy neighborhood and wished she could afford to move, and Meggan nodded sympathetically while worrying about her joint savings account with Brent.

When she got to her desk, she checked their savings account balance on her phone, and found it still intact. She made a mental note to ask Rhonda how to prevent Brent from withdrawing the money.

That night after a Chinese takeout supper, Meggan went to bed and streamed a movie on her phone. It was a comedy about a bank heist that went wrong, with a confused plot that depended too much on stupidity and pratfalls for humor. She deleted it after about twenty minutes, and then turned off her bedside light. Without the distractions of work or a bad movie, her mind began to churn again. She doubted that Brent would agree to deed the property over to her, so she needed a backup plan. Rhonda seemed to be on top of the negotiations, but Meggan knew she could never again depend on someone else looking out for her.

***

Soon after arriving to work the next morning, Meggan got a call from Rhonda.

"I've got good news and not-so-good news, Meggan."

Meggan started to say she'd call back from the hallway, but Sandra would have already made sure everyone knew about the divorce. Slinking away to the hallway would just heighten the drama for her bored coworkers.

"Okay, shoot."

"Your husband agreed to deed his interest in the house to you, but he countered your offer of a thousand dollars with a demand for two thousand."

"And would we split the rest of the money in our savings account?"

"Yes."

Yesterday's warning from Sandra suddenly returned Meggan. "What if Brent drains all the money from our account?"

"That would trigger a lawsuit by us that he couldn't win. His attorney would advise against anything that clumsy."

"What about the stuff he took when he left, like the painting and my computer. He also took five-hundred dollars in cash that belonged to both of us."

"We'll require credit for half of the cash he took, but do you want to counter his offer to get your share of the personal property back?"

"No. Let's just go for the deal he offered."

"I recommend that you get a title exam to make sure there are no liens against the property."

"How much would that cost?"

"Between three- and four-hundred dollars."

"The title was clear when I bought it, and we haven't had any work done to the house."

"Have you added any secondary mortgage loans since you've been married?"

"No…unless Brent did without telling me."

"He couldn't without you signing the mortgage application and the closing documents."

"Okay, then I'll skip the title exam."

Rhonda said she'd draw up an agreement, which would become part of the final divorce settlement.

Meggan returned her attention to the financial report that was overdue. Her boss would need it the following day for a presentation to the senior executive staff, and he would not be happy about receiving it at the last minute. She worked quickly, fighting back her own preoccupations.

She stopped after a few minutes, wondering why Brent, who always seemed so lackadaisical about financial matters, now seemed so greedy. Was this another side of the person she thought she knew so well, another secret that's boiling brazenly to the surface? More likely, she decided it must be William's influence coming into play. She never liked William, but now she hated him.

Meggan finished the report just before quitting time. After quickly emailing it to her boss, she rushed over to his corner office to tell him, apologizing for getting it to him so last-minute. He thanked her stiffly and added that he wouldn't have time to go over it before his presentation tomorrow morning, so it better be accurate. Meggan assured him it was, but worried about it on the way home. She wondered if she forgot to use the most current figures in her report. She couldn't check from home because she had no access to the company's internet network, and besides, Brent had her computer. That reminded her to ask Rhonda about getting her computer back from him, at least her files and photos. She made a mental note to ask Rhonda about that.

***

Meggan's ringing cellphone woke her the next morning. She groggily sat up on the sofa, noticing a couple of inches of wine left in the bottle sitting on the floor. The phone stopped ringing while she padded to the bedroom, where she found it on her bed. She tapped in her security code and listened to the voicemail. The message was from Rhonda, wondering if Meggan could meet at her office within the next day or two to sign the divorce settlement documents. Meggan tapped the "Call back" link, and Rhonda answered her direct line after a couple of rings.

"Hi, Meggan. I hope I'm not disturbing you at work."

"Oh, God, what time is it?"

"Almost nine."

"I've got to run, Rhonda. I'm going to be late for work as it is. I'll call you from there, okay?"

"That's fine. Drive safely."

Meggan mentally pushed through the fog in her brain to find her car keys, slip into yesterday's clothes—still draped on the bed—and ran to the garage door while pulling on her parka.

The morning sun was melting some of the street snow, which made it more slippery in spots. With her head throbbing in protest, she concentrated on racing to her company's office without losing control of her car.

She got to the office at 9:30 AM and sat at her desk a moment with her coat still on. Nearby coworkers would, of course, notice her tardiness, but she hoped none of them cared enough to report her.

Sandra walked over to her, showing concern her narrowed

eyes. "Everything okay?"

"I overslept," Meggan said, while slipping out of her coat and draping it over the back of her chair.

"Champlin called from the conference room. He was looking for you."

Dread flushed through Meggan. "Did he say why?"

"No, but he sounded pissed. Just tell him you were late because a crash blocked the road, or you were sick this morning. Geeze, it's not like he's always here exactly on time."

"I don't think it's about being late, Sandra. I might have screwed up that report I was working on. Champlin's presenting it to the executive board this morning."

"Oops."

"Yeah, no kidding."

A few minutes later, Meggan answered her phone to hear Champlin's perturbed voice asking her to come immediately to the tenth-floor conference room.

She walked down the two flights of stairs instead of taking the elevator, wondering if he was going to fire her. Through the open door, she saw Champlin alone at the end of the long conference table, writing something on a lined notepad. He looked up when she entered the room, clicked his pen closed and tossed it onto the notepad.

"Please close the door."

When the door clicked shut, he calmly met her frightened gaze. "I just had one of the most embarrassing experiences of my long career with this company, thanks to you."

"I'm sorry if—"

"Please let me finish." Champlin's face flushed bright pink. "Let me start by saying I don't care how sorry you are, okay?"

"Okay."

"When our top executives started drilling me about the

inconsistencies, errors, and obsolete data in this report, I sat
here like an idiot. Like you, I said I was sorry, but they didn't
care, either. I should not have trusted your report, I'll admit
that, especially given your recent job performance. I should
have either stayed late at the office or come in early to make
sure you didn't completely screw this up, which you most
certainly did."

"I'm sorry—I mean, I'm going through some bad things
in my life right now, a divorce, and my husband's...well, anyway, I promise nothing like this will happen again."

"I hope not, or you might add a job termination to your
list of 'bad things in life.'"

"Alright. I understand."

"Please shut the door on your way out."

After trying to busy herself with mundane projects the
rest of the morning, she remembered Rhonda's earlier call. At
lunchtime, Meggan took the elevator to the main floor, and
bought a granola bar and small plastic bottle of milk at the
tiny sundry store. With the sickening residue of last night's
wine, and today's humiliating reprimand from Champlin, her
stomach couldn't handle anything more for lunch. She sat on
a stone slab bench near the building's indoor courtyard and
called Rhonda on her cellphone. The courtyard was filling
with people on lunch break, with enough background chatter
to drown out her phone conversation.

Rhonda answered on the second ring, apparently noticing
the caller ID. "Hello, Meggan."

"Sorry I'm late getting back to you; I was busy getting
chewed out by my boss for screwing up an important project."

"Stress, no doubt, was a factor. But the good news is
that the terms of your divorce have been settled, and your
husband has signed all the dissolution documents, as well as

a quitclaim deed granting any and all of his interest in the house to you. You'll need to come to my office to also sign the dissolution documents and a document instructing your bank how to disburse your joint saving account to you and your soon-to-be ex-husband, crediting you with half of the cash he took from your house. Two thousand dollars will be credited to him for his willingness to deed the house to you. After that, it's over."

"Over legally, but I still have to deal with some emotional damage."

"You'll find a pathway to peace, Meggan, and when you do, have the courage to take it. That's the best advice I can give you."

Rhonda's advice, although vague, resonated with Meggan, helping her feel empowered for at least that moment. She agreed to meet at Rhonda's office at seven-thirty the next morning, which would give Meggan enough time to get to work before nine.

***

In the following days, Meggan began to reassemble her life, starting with removing any reminders of Brent. She donated his favorite living room chair to a charity and decontaminated his kitchen chair with an antibacterial spray. She put on her parka and opened all the windows for thirty minutes to replace the inside air with a crisp March breeze. She repainted the living room a subtle rose shade. Her share of the savings account was reduced substantially after paying Rhonda's fee, although she charged less than Meggan expected. She had enough money left over to buy a Scandinavian assemble-yourself rocking chair, a black floor lamp, an inexpensive tablet computer, and a new Wi-Fi device with a security code known only to her. The final touch was to restock the refrigerator with her favorite foods and beverages, and within a week, the house once again felt exclusively hers.

But Meggan soon realized it would take longer to get used to living alone again. She ate some of her evening meals at the kitchen counter, and watched movies on her tablet in bed. She called friends for get-togethers, but most of them were married with children and had tightly scheduled lives. She got used to living without a TV and enjoying just one glass of wine when she got home from work. She liked to relax on her rocking chair while reading, sometimes late into the night. But her new routines soon became more monotonous than refreshing.

Her job seemed even more boring, cranking out endless, seemingly pointless, spreadsheet reports, slogging through the workday grind instead of racing through it like her busy days as a restaurant manager. She started checking job postings online each day for restaurant management positions, even as a shift supervisor.

But she found those jobs to be scarce, so she prepared herself for a long wait. In the meantime, she tried to concentrate on meeting Mr. Champlin's expectations. She started having lunch the same time each day in the building's atrium with Sandra and other women, listening to gossip about coworkers, petty grievances about the higher-ups, and how working conditions should be improved. Meggan hoped that a routine, coping lifestyle like this would be the best balm for a broken life, at least for now.

CHAPTER 7

A couple of weeks later, Meggan's mother came to stay with her over the weekend. She arrived Friday afternoon, letting herself in with a key inside the combination lockbox Meggan had screwed into the front door frame. Nancy brought a cooler containing a glass bowl of beef stew she had made the day before, and the ingredients for fresh rolls. Both were in the oven when Meggan got home after work.

"Something smells yummy," Meggan said after coming in through the side door from the garage.

While Meggan slipped out of her snow boots, Nancy got up from the new rocking chair, struggling a little, but without crutches. "I put a box of chardonnay in the fridge."

"Thanks, I don't keep wine on hand anymore. I see your ankle has made progress."

"A little tender sometimes, but yeah."

"I'm going to change, Mom. Go ahead and pour a couple glasses of wine, if you like."

Meggan hung her coat in the front closet and went to her bedroom to change into pink sweatpants, a gray tee shirt, and wool slippers. When she got to the kitchen, her mom had the table set, and had two glasses of wine waiting on the countertop. They took their glasses into the living room, and Meggan sat on the sofa, leaving the rocker for her mom.

"How are you feeling, now that your divorce is settled?"

"Fine." Meggan gazed at her wine glass as if searching for something more to say. "I feel a little lonely sometimes. I don't miss Brent, but I haven't gone to bed alone for a long time. I still sleep on my side of the bed."

"I haven't gone to bed with anyone for a long time, but I've always slept on one side. It's easier to get out of bed and find the bathroom in the dark."

Meggan grinned, even though she knew her mom was serious.

"I'm glad you're getting over Brent."

"Sometimes I feel guilty for going crazy on him, though. When I told him to leave, I was beside myself, maybe even hysterical. But I didn't think he'd just turn and walk out of my life for good."

"No one, including Brent, can blame you for being beside yourself. So, bury your regrets, Meggan. You made a decision, a painful one, but one that was probably good for both of you. Brent had already replaced you in his life, so now you're free to replace him."

"Thanks, Mom, but thinking about another relationship right now isn't exactly uplifting."

"I could move in with you for a while, if you like."

"I've lived alone in this house before we were married, and I'll get used to it again."

***

When Nancy departed for northern Minnesota Sunday morning, Meggan's house suddenly fell quiet again. She caught up on cleaning and laundry, and bought asparagus, a sweet potato, sourdough bread, and chicken legs at the nearby coop grocery store, all of them things Brent never liked.

Not long after Meggan got home Monday evening, she saw a post office truck stop along the curb in front of her house. She watched a uniformed mail carrier walk toward the front door, and Meggan opened it just as he was walking up the steps.

"I have a certified letter for Meggan Mondae."

"That's me."

The mailman asked her to sign a slip of paper attached to the envelope, tore it off, thanked her and left. The letter was from her bank.

Meggan quickly tore the envelope open and removed the official-looking single page letter. It said that because of payment delinquencies, the bank was immediately calling the entire current balance of her mortgage loan due, to be paid in full, plus outstanding interest and late fees, within thirty days or the bank will commence foreclosure actions against her. It further stated that the bank will not accept any further installment or partial payments in lieu of the entire balance.

She read the letter again and gasped aloud: "Payment delinquencies?"

Since she had always made the monthly payments on time, sometimes over-paying so she could reduce the balance sooner, she assumed it was a mistake. Even so, why wouldn't they accept further payments? It all seemed so preposterous.

Meggan sat on the edge of her kitchen table chair and looked again at the name and address on the letter, making sure it wasn't for someone else. Perhaps someone with the same name got mixed up with her address. Or, maybe her payments were credited to the wrong bank customer, or... then she caught herself worrying about a mistake that could likely be easily resolved, and there was no sense in trying to guess at the reasons for it.

She called the contact number on the letter, and got a re-corded message said the bank's hours were from 8 AM to 4 PM. Remembering that the bank's local branch had an af-ter-hours drive-up window, she ran to the closet and pulled her jacket on without bothering to zip it, and then slid her shoes on. She drove to the bank, as quickly as traffic allowed, and waited behind someone already at the drive-up window. The wait seemed an eternity. Was the car just parked there? Was anyone helping the driver? Finally, the drawer slid out to-ward the car, and someone reached out of the car and took an envelope. More waiting. Is he sitting there counting the mon-ey? Studying the deposit slip? Meggan thought about honk-ing, but instead took a slow deliberate breath. The car finally rolled slowly ahead and Meggan pulled up to the window.

She hastily said "fine" to the attendant's standard hello-how-are-you, and said she wanted him to check her loan account because a terrible mistake had been made about delinquent payments. When he said he didn't have that in-formation at the drive-up window, she implored him to just look at the letter, that the account number and everything was on it. He said okay, and Meggan placed the letter into the sliding drawer. She watched him reading it over while biting his lower lip, almost imperceptibly shaking his head. He said he was sorry, but she'd have to see the bank manager during normal business hours, and then returned her letter to her in the drawer. She snatched it out without bothering to say anything more and drove off.

That night, Meggan struggled with sleep. She had to make sure this mistake was resolved fast, before it triggered some kind of legal action that couldn't be stopped. She had been dutifully making payments for too many years to have her credit rating ruined over a computer glitch or some clerk's screw-up. Even more unthinkable, she wondered if she could lose her house, the only substantial asset she's ever possessed, because of the bank's stupid mistake. The notice gave her a thirty-day limit to pay the balance, but that should be plenty of time for the bank's bureaucracy to correct the error.

When the cellphone alarm shook her sleep-starved brain awake at seven the next morning, she threw off her covers and sat on the edge of the bed while tapping her company's number into her cellphone. She told the answering service that she was taking a sick day.

She dressed and hastily brushed her hair enough to be presentable, and then backed her car out of the driveway just before eight o'clock. When she got to the bank, there were two other people waiting for it to open, and when they were let in, Meggan strode past them to the first desk she saw with a person sitting at it.

"I need to see the bank manager," she said.

A thirtyish rotund woman looked up from her computer, then remembered to put on her customer smile. "Is there something I can help you with?"

"Yes, you can get me in front of the bank manager right now, okay?"

The smile went away. "Oh, sure, of course. I'll be right back."

The woman waddled away hastily, disappearing behind a labyrinth of cubicles, and soon emerged behind an older woman with graying hair.

"I'm Cathy Masterson," the woman said with a cautiously pleasant expression. "How can I help you?"

"Your bank made a terrible mistake about my loan payments." Meggan presented the letter to the manager.

After looking it over, she said, "Could you please come with me to my office?"

After Meggan sat across from the desk on the edge of her chair, the manager closed the door, sat in her black swivel chair and leaned forward. "I'll make sure any mistake the bank might have made will be corrected, Ms. Mondae."

"You can call me Meggan."

"Alright, Meggan. Let me look up your account...okay, here it is." Masterson clicked her keyboard, and then scrolled with her mouse. The monitor was positioned so Meggan couldn't see the screen.

"As you can see, Cathy, I've been making my payments on time. I can't understand how this happened."

The manager nodded her head slightly, but was preoccupied with the monitor. "Yes, it shows you've been very good about making your monthly payments on the original loan."

"*Original* loan? There's only one mortgage, the same one I took out when I bought the house ten years ago."

"Yes, but there's also an outstanding line of credit loan balance of $10,000 that was due three months ago. That's a secondary lien on the property—the same as a second mortgage." The manager looked sternly at Meggan. "Ms. Mondae, you would have started receiving late notices thirty days after the first delinquency."

"I never received $10,000 from your bank," she said pleadingly, as if denying a crime, "and I didn't get any late notices. There must be a mistake."

Cathy nodded abstractly, as if agreeing to something. "The notices were sent as certified mail, and someone at your address would have had to sign for them."

"The notices might have been signed by my ex-husband, but I did not sign for any additional loans."

Cathy returned her attention to her computer monitor. "Three years ago, you and your husband signed a line of credit agreement with a $10,000 limit. You would have been given a checkbook to draw on those funds at will."

"But that wasn't a mortgage loan. My husband told me the line of credit was just in case we ever needed money in an emergency."

"Any checks written would trigger a mortgage lien against your property, with an obligation to repay the amount borrowed. In other words, you borrowed the money from the bank when the check for $10,000 was written."

"That's impossible. We kept the checkbook in our safe—I forgot it was even there. Someone obviously stole the checks. I didn't use them." Meggan suddenly felt helpless as someone falsely accused of a crime.

Cathy clicked a few keys on her keyboard. "The check was drafted by your husband eight months ago, payable to a BMW car dealership in Minneapolis. No repayments have been made."

A sick feeling washed through Meggan. Brent had been the thief, the betrayer she had lived with, a swindler who made her an unwitting contributor to William's new red BMW.

She tried to swallow, but her mouth was too dry. "How much are the delinquent payments?"

"I'm sorry," Cathy said, "but we can only accept the entire balance, plus interest, and late charges at this stage. If we accept any payments, it could legally constitute our withdrawal from a foreclosure action."

"But I don't have $10,000."

Cathy glared at her. "I'm sorry."

"You're sorry?" Meggan stood and raised her voice, "That's bureaucratic crap, and you know it. You're going to take my house from me, even though I've made all my loan payments on time all these years, and then you tell me I have no way of stopping you. Well, I'm going to call my lawyer, and we'll see how sorry—"

Meggan stopped shouting when she heard the door click open behind her. A husky security guard filled the open doorway. Curious bank staffers in the background were peeking over their cubicles.

He said, "Is there a problem?"

"I don't think so," Cathy said while glaring at Meggan. "I think Ms. Mondae was just leaving."

The security guard stepped aside when Meggan sulked silently out of the room, trying to ignore all the heads disappearing below the cubical partitions. The security guard caught up and followed her to the parking lot.

When Meggan got home, she called Brent repeatedly, yelling angry voicemails with every call.

CHAPTER 8

When Meggan collected herself, she called Rhonda DuCrain. The receptionist said Ms. DuCrain was with a client. Meggan tried to make an appointment for later, but was told Rhonda's schedule was full that day. Meggan then said it was an emergency, and that she couldn't take any more time off from work. After putting Meggan on hold for a couple of minutes, she said Rhonda could see her for a few minutes just after one o'clock.

When Meggan arrived, the receptionist ushered her to a conference room. Meggan paced the room until Rhonda came in with her legal pad.

"I understand you have an emergency," Rhonda said with a grave look.

They sat across from each other, and Meggan simply handed her the bank's letter. After Rhonda read and returned it, Meggan told her about the incident at the bank.

"Yes, you do have a problem," Rhonda said.

"You should have made sure that something like this wouldn't happen. Why wasn't it cleared up with the divorce? You're my lawyer, aren't you? Wasn't it your job to protect me?"

Rhonda took a deep breath, and said evenly, "I did try to

protect you, Meggan. I advised you to get a title search, which would have shown that secondary lien against your home. But you ignored my advice."

Meggan felt dumbfounded, not knowing whether to blame Rhonda or herself. After a moment to collect herself, she said, "Okay, what should I do?"

"Your options are limited at this point. You could try to negotiate with the bank, but I doubt they will be interested. You could sell your house and pay the loan balances, but you might not have enough equity at this point to do that. Or, you could borrow enough money from someone you know to pay off both loans and keep your house."

"That's not an option. Maybe I can refinance and pay off the loans."

"I doubt it. Your credit score will be adversely affected by the delinquencies."

"Then I'll stop making mortgage payments, and just live there for free until they finally throw me out."

"You might recall that we talked about that idea before. Yes, it would take a few months before the foreclosure process resulted in a physical eviction, but I'll repeat my previous recommendation against that course of action, for a few reasons. First, the bank could sue you for any shortfall after they foreclose and resell the property. They could use a court judgement for a garnishment of your wages, and they could put a lien on any other real estate you purchase in this state. It would also further trash your credit score, which would prevent you from buying another house or anything else on credit for at least a couple of years. And remember, even renting would be a problem because many landlords will check your credit score before renting to you."

"Can I sue Brent for taking that money?"

"What he did was underhanded, to be sure, but he was co-owner of the property prior to deeding his interest to you, and he had the right to draw on the line of credit that you both agreed to in writing. I'm sorry, Megan, but I must excuse myself now because I have someone else waiting in my office."

"Sure, run out on me now that you have my money. You shouldn't have let this happen. You gave me lousy representation and now you want to blow me off after you've screwed up my life. I'm going to plaster your mishandling of this all over the internet—and I know how, you'll see."

Rhonda rose ponderously from her chair, walked to the conference room door and opened it before looking back at Meggan. "Be careful, Meggan, because I'm perfectly capable of retaliating aggressively against any attempted libel, slander, or defamation of my character or reputation. As parting advice, I suggest you learn to control your temper."

Rhonda left the conference room door open, and Meggan sat stunned for a moment before getting up and stomping out through the reception area. She drove home feeling defeated, betrayed and humiliated from all sides: from Brent, the bank, and now her lawyer, and she felt powerless to do anything about it.

When she got home, she tried unsuccessfully to call Brent again, but left another angry voicemail with legal threats and a vow to get even with him, outside of the law, if necessary, because she had nothing more to lose.

Later that night, as she lay heavily on the living room sofa in the dark in her flannel pajamas, feeling helplessly drained but too agitated to sleep. She finally dragged herself to the bedroom and burrowed under the blankets, but it didn't help—until an idea flashed in her head.

She sat up and thought through the general idea: she'd somehow force Brent out of his hiding place, corner and confront him, hopefully in front of others, and then demand repayment of the money he stole from her. She'd show him that she could strike whenever she pleased, at the worst possible times for him, and if he continued to refuse repaying her, she'd continue making his life as miserable as hers, even if it meant risking whatever dignity she had left.

CHAPTER 9

Meggan rolled and tossed well into the night while planning her assault. Her phone alarm woke her an hour before needing to leave for work, and she threw off the covers, eager to put her plan to work.

She called the BMW dealership where William had purchased his car, and asked for the service department, knowing it would be the dealership's only department fully functioning that early in the morning, and, hopefully, not as privacy-conscious as an accounting department would be.

When a service manager answered the phone, she said she was William Astead's wife, and they were wondering when the next service appointment should be made on their new car.

"We recommend an oil change every seventy-five-hundred miles," he said. "How many miles do you have on the car now?"

"I'd have to run outside and check," Meggan said. "Can you tell when we last had an oil change?"

After checking the customer database, he said, "You had your first oil change just a month ago. Whenever you do need service, though, I suggest you schedule a week ahead."

"I'll do that…by the way, we recently moved. What address do you have for us in your database?"

The man gave her an address in the North Loop area of Minneapolis, and asked if that was correct.

Meggan felt a tinge of jitters: that seemed too easy. "Yes, that's our current address. What primary phone number do you have for us?"

After he gave her the phone number, Meggan politely confirmed that it was correct. She hung up feeling victorious, empowered, and on the offensive now. She was also nervous about the risk she was preparing to undertake.

On her way to work, she sorted through the realities and details of her plan. It had to be a seamless, foolproof way to corner Brent, both physically and psychologically. She'd agree that he embezzled her money legally, but legal or not, he had deceived her in every way. She had agreed to the divorce, but not to him taking her money. She mentally rehearsed quickly delivering that indisputable monologue, hoping to poke a needle into whatever sense of fairness he might have, hoping to make him bleed with guilt.

Of course, his first impulse will be his typical self-righteousness. He'd balk at repaying her anything and try to stumble through a case for that. But she'd twist an admission of wrongdoing out of him, making him realize he had been nothing more than a cheating swindler.

The brilliance of her plan dimmed somewhat by the time she got to work. The general idea felt satisfying to think about, but she started to see it wasn't anything close to airtight. Although she had sharp arguments memorized, she couldn't control how cornering Brent would play out. If she simply showed up at William's door, he and Brent could either refuse to open it or slam it in her face. And she wouldn't dare confront him on the school grounds, in front of surveillance cameras and mobs of students with cellphones to video the ordeal or to call the police. She needed to ambush Brent on neutral ground, where he'd be vulnerable, and she'd be safe.

Throughout that workday Meggan dabbled with minor computer tasks while obsessing with those details. But instead of solidifying a plan, she increasingly felt discouraged about coming up with a workable strategy instead of just a foolish fantasy.

During lunch, while absently eating a messy egg salad sandwich at her desk, she was struck by an idea. She put her sandwich down to concentrate, thinking through a scheme that wasn't exactly foolproof, but would certainly get Brent's attention and force him to at least listen to her, and maybe even get him to acknowledge her complaint. If nothing else, she could show him an example of how vulnerable he will be until he repays the $10,000.

***

Early the next morning, Meggan called her boss's direct line and left a voicemail message that she would be in late because her tire was flat, but would come to work as soon as someone came to change it. With nerves almost twitching, she dabbed on some makeup, combed through her hair, and got dressed. It was too early to leave, though, and the timing had to be perfect. She sat in her living room rocking chair and stared out the front window while composing herself. She needed to be ready for whatever happened once her plan was launched.

She checked her wristwatch more often than she needed to, hating to wait like this, wishing she could just go and get it over with. But timing was critical.

Brent always got to school at 8 AM, so she estimated that he would need to leave William's downtown condo no later than about 7:30. She had to be there ready to strike, and then it would all be over in a few minutes. She'd call him out while he was leaving the condo building, ruin his day in front of other residents with her demands and threats, and then drive to work. A simple plan. Strike, pull back, then see what happens after he swallows the reality that she can confront him whenever she pleases. She wanted it to be a quick confrontation, leaving little chance for much to go wrong.

When her watch showed 6:30, she got up from the rocker, put on her jacket, pulled on a knit cap, and headed for the garage. Right on time. Just as planned.

Meggan arrived in front of William's high-rise condominium building just after seven o'clock. She parked across the street from the main entrance and kept the engine running to keep warm. Most of the people coming out the glass door either had a leashed dog or a baby stroller, or both. People going in had to tap a code into the door's keypad. About thirty feet away, however, cars were leaving intermittently through the fast-rising door of an underground garage. Her plan seemed to be falling apart already: Brent won't need to expose himself to her confrontation. He'll be inside a secured building until he simply drives away. He wouldn't even notice her.

Meggan felt defeated, blaming her own lack of preparation. She put her car in drive and waited for a break in the stream of cars so she could pull out and go to work and try to forget her screwball idea.

She noticed the garage door popping up and down more frequently now, releasing more drivers with determined expressions, gunning their cars out onto the street to get somewhere on time. A pause in the traffic opened in Meggan's lane, but when she started to nudge her car onto the street, she spotted a shiny red car under the rising garage door, with a BMW logo on the hood. The two men who occupied the front seats stared ahead blankly while the door opened.

With the instant pounce of a predator, Meggan stomped on her gas pedal and made a screeching U-turn from the curb. Angry drivers from both directions leaned on their horns until she jammed on her brakes in front of the underground parking lot exit. William's car was already accelerating out of the short driveway, and he hit his brakes too late, crashing into the front corner of Meggan's car. William and Brent stared ahead wide-eyed as if her car was an apparition. In that moment of disbelief, she saw Brent's mouth say "What the...?"

Meggan got out and glanced at the damage. Her fender was smashed against her front tire. William's headlight was shattered and the hood was slightly buckled. She walked back to the street side of her car as if taking cover, and waited for one of them to make a next move. She knew her plan was already trashed. All the accusations and reasonable demands she had mentally rehearsed would sound ridiculous now, and she no longer had an ounce of moral authority.

Drivers inside the garage behind William's car tapped their horns, as if William could magically make the problem go away. He finally threw his door open and got out.

"What in the hell do you think you're doing?"

His scolding, condescending tone ran through her like fire. "I'm waiting for Brent to find enough guts to come out and listen to me."

She stood her ground and drew a deep breath while William glowered at her. The sidewalk was filling with gawkers, newcomers asking others what happened. The stress of the scene fed Meggan's anger and, aside from the money, she now wanted revenge. She wanted to attack Brent emotionally and physically, no matter what the cost. This no longer felt like a cockamamie drama gone wrong. It was a raw fight.

Brent got out and stood behind the car door. "Whatever you want, Meggan, this is not the way to get it."

"What I want is simple, Brent. You stole $10,000 from me, and I'm here to collect it."

"Let's talk about this after we get these cars out of the way, okay?"

She stared at him while he scanned the damage, exchanging frustrated looks with William, who was on his phone, looking around nervously at the crush of gathering bystanders.

Meggan sensed their fear and indecision. She had put both of them off balance, and that emboldened her.

"We'll talk about this now, Brent. You took money from my house's equity for your boyfriend, and I'm not moving my car until I get a check for it."

"How can you be so stupid to think I'd have that much in my checking account?"

William still had the phone pressed against his ear, with worry grooves streaking across his tanned forehead while he looked around. A few drivers behind William's car were still honking. Brent marched back and said something to William, and then walked around Meggan's car, stopping just close enough to lunge and grab her.

"You better get going, Meggan. The police are on their way."

It sounded more like a caution than a threat.

"Good, I'll tell the cops that William ran into me, which he did. I'll also tell them you stole my money."

Brent sniffed at her with a smirk. "Right. But if you don't want to get in trouble, you better get the hell out of here."

"In trouble for what? Calling you a thief, which you are?

Besides, I can't drive my car with the fender pushed into the tire."

"You purposely caused the accident, and that's a crime."

"You're a poor witness, Brent. Go ahead and try to lie to the cops, but they can see for themselves what happened."

More honking echoed from the garage. Someone on the sidewalk yelled to move the cars, and an elderly man on the sidewalk pleaded with Meggan to back her car up so people can get to work on time.

The reality of making a mistake fell on Meggan when a police car with lights flashing pulled up and stopped just past her car. Two officers got out with hands resting on holstered pistols, a burly female leading, and an overweight male officer standing off to her side.

"What's the trouble?" The woman officer made it sound more like an accusation than a question.

Brent stepped toward the policewoman. "That's my ex-wife, and her car is blocking ours. She's taking an argument between us too far, and my friend and I have to get to work."

"Ma'am, you'll have move your car. I don't care what your beef is, but I do care if you block traffic."

"I can't." Meggan pointed to William's car. "That guy crashed into me and I want to file a complaint against him."

The cop glared at her. "You can file whatever you want, ma'am, but first you need to try to move your car."

The other officer was looking at the point of impact, and said Meggan's fender was bent into the tire, and didn't look safe to drive. He used his shoulder mike to call for a tow truck.

The female officer said, "We're going to push your car back with our cruiser to let these drivers leave. Please step onto the sidewalk."

"No, you'll just do more damage. And you're not listening

to me. That man, my ex-husband, stole money from me, a lot of money, and I have the right to get it back."

The officer put her hands on her hips. "You'll have to get your money some other way, ma'am, because right now you're a public nuisance. Step over to my vehicle for me."

Meggan froze. "But I don't—"

Before she could finish her protest, the policewoman grabbed Meggan's arm and yanked her away from her car. Meggan stumbled and was forced face-down with a knee pinning her into the salted slushy street. She tried to breathe while the other officer roughly jerked her arms behind her back and clicked handcuffs tightly around her wrists. Both officers got up and pulled Meggan up to her knees by her shackled arms and then up to her feet. While the officers pushed Meggan toward the patrol car, she said they were hurting her, but her complaint was ignored. The female officer forced Meggan down into the backseat of the patrol car and slammed the door, trapping her inside. She turned her face away from onlookers, looked down and began to cry.

When she finally looked up, a tow truck driver was hooking her car to a winch cable, and then dragged it up onto the flatbed. The driver had taken Meggan's purse from her car and gave it to the female police officer.

William was able to drive his car out of the way of angry residents who were waiting behind him, and he parked in a no-parking zone to pick pieces of broken glass from his shattered headlight and to inspect the bent hood. Brent was saying something to the police officers on the sidewalk.

Meggan watched it all unfold, powerless to even wipe her running nose and eyes. When William and Brent got back into their car and drove past her, William flashed a sneering grin and gave her the finger.

The female officer opened Meggan's door and helped her out, then unlocked the handcuffs, telling Meggan she wouldn't be charged for a crime. She gave Meggan her purse and said the other driver told her it had been an accident, with both parties equally at fault, and that he would file his own insurance claim. The officer wrote the phone number and address of the impound facility where Meggan could re-claim her towed car. Before leaving, the officer scolded her with a warning to settle her future problems in a law-abiding fashion instead of with a temper tantrum. After the police car drove away, Meggan phoned for a taxi to take her to work.

CHAPTER 10

Meggan arrived at work just past noon. Most of the employees were at lunch, except her boss, Bill Champlin, who stopped by her desk before she could get her coat and hat off and sit down.

"What happened to you?"

"Did you get my message?"

"Yes…"

"Well, the auto club guy couldn't get my car started, so I had it towed to a repair garage."

"I meant all the salt stains on your jacket and hat. Did you fall?"

"Oh…yes. I fell. I slipped and fell at the end of my driveway." She cleared her throat, taking a moment to make sure she was stringing her story together logically. "After my car was towed, I was waiting at the end of my driveway for a taxi to take me to work, and I slipped on some black ice on the street."

"Your voicemail said you had a flat tire."

"Yes…that's right—but I didn't notice that until after I tried to start my car. A pushed-in fender had cut into it. Someone must have rammed my passenger side in a parking lot."

Champlin gave her a confused look. "Well, anyway, it sounds like you had a rough morning."

"Oh, just part of living in Minnesota in March," she said with forced bravado.

Champlin nodded a dry agreement. "Are you almost finished with that Kensington analysis?"

"Almost, yes. I'll have it to you by the end of the day."

"I'd appreciate that."

When Champlin returned to his office, Meggan sat at her desk with her coat and hat still on, telling herself she had to get through the day without falling apart. She hadn't even started the client's risk analysis that Champlin wanted, and finishing it by the end meant zero tolerance for distractions.

While she was taking off her coat, Sandra came into the office holding a plastic take-out food box and soft drink.

"What happened to you?"

Meggan stared at her monitor while the computer booted up. "Oh, gosh, Sandra, not much. I was just thrown onto the street this morning in downtown traffic by a brutish cop who knelt on my back and while another cop handcuffed me and they both dragged me to my feet and threw me into the back of their squad car while my crashed car was being towed to an impound lot. How's your day been?"

"Ha. I mean really. Your coat's all dirty."

Meggan buried her face in the palms of her hands.

"All that was true?"

Meggan nodded yes without looking up.

"We can talk later. Would you like half of my tuna salad sandwich?"

Meggan looked up with glistening eyes, shaking her head no and managing, "Thanks anyway." She was afraid that saying anything more could unhinge the little control she was clinging to.

She spent the rest of the day struggling with the analysis she had promised her boss. Pulling the necessary data together into a meaningful report was more complex than she had guessed. Emotional flashbacks of her horrible morning kept nagging her, so she had to constantly proofread her work to make sure she wasn't leaving a trail of stupid mistakes. She didn't need a scolding from Champlin to top off her day.

With an hour left before quitting time, she was barely half done. Champlin stopped by her desk.

"How's it going?"

"I ran into some questionable data that took extra time to sort out. I wanted to make sure it was perfect. Do you mind if I work late to finish this?"

Champlin exhaled disappointment through his nose. "Just email me what you've got so far before you leave so I can start going over it. You can finish it in the morning, that is, if you can be on time for a change."

Meggan had never heard open sarcasm like that from him. His usual management style was to disapprove with snide comments, sniffs, or eye rolling.

"I can come in early."

"Coming on time will do," he said, and walked away.

When Meggan got home that evening, she called the car repair shop she always used, and asked how she could get her car repaired. The manager said he'd arrange to have it towed to their garage, but she would have to meet the tow truck driver at the impound lot to get it released to him. He promised to have the tow truck there early enough for her to get to work on time.

She called the impound lot and was told she'd need to bring proof of insurance, current registration, and $180 for their towing and storage. She then called a taxi company and arranged an early morning ride to the lot.

The rest of the evening, Meggan tried to distract herself with asinine shows on the new television she recently bought over the internet. When that didn't help, she tried reading a novel, a usually-reliable diversion from life's troublesome realities, but the scenes felt contrived and improbable to her. The turkey sandwich she made for supper seemed tasteless. She couldn't sleep. She couldn't stop the flashbacks of today's blistering, humiliating experiences.

The sound of the doorbell the next morning woke her from a fetal clump on the sofa with the TV on, still in yesterday's clothes. When she opened the door, a taxi driver asked if he had the correct address. She invited him in and threw on her coat, grabbed her purse, and tried to straighten her hair while following him up the driveway to his car. They arrived at the impound lot within a half-hour.

Meggan strode into the waiting area, which was full of people sitting or milling around, waiting for their number to be called. She took a numbered slip of paper from the counter dispenser and joined the morose crowd of vehicle owners. The slow bureaucratic grind of releasing vehicles to verified owners took longer than Meggan had imagined. She kept checking her watch, and finally gave up any hope of getting to work on time.

When Meggan arrived at her office over an hour late, her computer had been removed from her desk. Sandra sheepishly approached her with a mournful expression.

"Meggan, I'm so sorry—"

Sandra was interrupted by Bill Champlin's fiftyish female administrative assistant, who brusquely announced that Mr. Champlin wanted to see Meggan in his office. A young woman and an older man stood outside Champlin's open door, with a partially filled black trash bag on the floor between them.

The assistant left and closed the door behind Meggan. Champlin told her to sit in the chair in front of his desk.

"I went over the report you worked on yesterday."

Meggan didn't even bother to conjure up an excuse for being late, but hoped he hadn't found any mistakes. "I should be able to finish it in an hour or so."

"No, you won't. I turned the project over to Sandra. You've botched it so badly, she'll have to start from scratch."

"I'm really sorry…I've recently had a lot of personal—"

"Meggan, I don't want to hear any more about your personal whatevers. As heartless as that might sound to you, I have a department to run, and I have to report to executives who expect results because, again, heartless as it may seem, they keep their high-paying jobs and big office suites only if staffers like you help them produce a service that will satisfy the company's clients. You've become a weak link in that chain. It will be better for both of us if you apply your energies elsewhere."

Champlin turned his attention to a paper he took from a file folder. He read a dated list of specific project errors, most of them insignificant, but adding up to an indefensible case against her for chronically unacceptable work performance. It also listed the dates and times she had been late to work, and it ended by informing her she was being terminated "with cause."

From her days of managing a restaurant, Meggan knew that *with cause* meant the company would dispute any claims by her for unemployment assistance.

Champlin took another paper from the file folder.

"This second document was prepared by our HR department. If you sign it, you'll be mailed a severance paycheck equal to two weeks of work. In exchange you'll be attesting to the fact that you are resigning from this position."

Meggan knew a voluntary resignation would make sure she could never file a lawsuit against them for wrongful discharge.

"I'll sign it," she said, and stood up, wanting nothing more now than to leave immediately and go home.

After giving Meggan her signed copy of the resignation letter, Champlin told her there were two human resource staffers outside his door, and they would escort her out of the building with her personal belongings.

When she left Champlin's office, the man standing outside the door handed her the heavy black trash bag, saying it contained the personal items they had removed from her desk. The two staffers escorted her without speaking or looking at her, as if marching her to the gallows, and Meggan avoided eye contact with staring, silent coworkers. She followed her escorts down the hall to the elevator, and down to the main floor security desk. She turned in her employment ID card to the security guard, and walked outside into the cold, overcast day, suddenly remembering that her car had earlier been towed from the impound lot to the repair garage.

Meggan brushed loose snow off a fake-stone landscaping wall near the building entrance and sat with her bag of belongings next to her. After calling for a taxi, she waited, flexing her shoulders against the cold, trying to look calm. She avoided the glances of people who walked by, afraid that, with her grimy stained clothes and bulging black trash bag, they would think she was a homeless person ready to hit them up for money. It all seemed too surreal to her, first being handcuffed and shoved around like a criminal, and William giving her the finger while she sat imprisoned in a squad car. Then having to bail her car out of the impound lot and spending most of what little money she had to pay for towing, taxi rides, and repairs. The final disgrace was being fired for the first time in her life, and thrown out like a tramp. All in one day. Too overwhelming to feel anything but cold right now while she watched for the taxi.

***

Over the next few days, Meggan pushed aside her miseries and looked for a job. She didn't want to work in another office. Instead, she looked for something she could easily handle, with less sitting and no mind-numbing paperwork.

She settled on bartending at a local bar named Reggie's, close enough for a short bus ride to and from work. It was a popular gathering place with a busy midday crowd, mostly regulars. Many of them returned later for happy hour, which is when Meggan's shift started, and ended when the bar closed at 2 AM. She welcomed the good-natured chaos and tipsy bantering from patrons who mostly lived in the neighborhood and wanted some relief from workday pressure or boredom. She didn't even mind the clumsy but good-natured flirting of fuzzy-faced guys who never took their caps off. The busy workload distracted her from her own problems, and made the time fly by. She always went home tired enough to sleep deeply through the night and into most of the next morning.

The bartending job brought back memories of her days as a restaurant manager, but with fewer responsibilities. The tradeoff was harder physical work, and a lot less pay, even with tips. Meggan made enough money to pay her next mortgage payment. She wanted to see how the bank would respond, as if in denial that keeping her house was doomed. A few days later the bank returned her check, with a terse letter saying the balance must be paid in full and no other interim payments would be accepted. She used the money for other expenses, like utilities and health insurance, but she cut luxuries like cable TV and take-out meals. She still blamed Brent for infidelity and ripping her off, but she now realized that carrying this nagging obsession around wouldn't pay her bills. She decided to forget about him and the money he took, and find a cheaper place to live.

She remembered that her lawyer had recommended selling the house and paying off the bank in order to avoid having her credit rating trashed. One day before going to work, she called a real estate agent named Carol Barns, who was a semi-retired friend of her mother's, and had owned a small real estate brokerage for many years. Carol come over the next morning to walk through the house and take room measurements, chattering away about how well the house had been maintained by Meggan, and reassuring her that, if priced right, it should quickly spark offers. She listened intently to Meggan's angry summary of how Brent had triggered the second-mortgage payment. Carol reassured her that she had helped free many house-poor divorced clients by downsizing. Meggan liked her right away and agreed to meet with Carol again the following day to go over Carol's researched analysis of the property's value, and an estimate of how much net proceeds Meggan could reasonably expect from a sale.

When Carol returned the next day, Meggan invited her into the kitchen and offered her coffee. After sitting at the table, Carol took a sip from her mug, and nodded approvingly. She took a stapled report from a leather handbag that looked too big to be a purse, and too small for a briefcase.

"Meggan, I have good news and bad news."

Oh, God, Meggan thought. "I'm so used to bad news, yours might seem good by comparison. Let's have it."

"After paying off the bank and selling costs, I don't think you'll have any net proceeds."

"Okay, yes, that's bad."

"You might actually have to pay the bank at closing for the shortfall, maybe a few hundred dollars." Carol grimaced sympathetically while waiting for Meggan to respond.

"I might have to shell out money to sell my house? You're going from bad to worse, Carol."

"Yes, probably. That second mortgage is what's hurting you. You had equity in your house a few months ago, but most of it was spent by your ex, and what's left goes for selling and closing costs."

"I understand all that, Carol, but having to bring money to the table to close the sale still pisses me off."

"No one could blame you."

Carol diverted Meggan's attention to recent MLS sales of nearby properties similar in size and style to Meggan's house. One-story houses like hers were typical of the area, so comparable sale prices formed a reliable pattern. After going through the expenses, ending in a worst-case negative net proceeds, Carol offered to shave her commission. Meggan thanked her but said no, the problem wasn't Carol's and she shouldn't have to pay into it.

Within two days of Meggan's house being listed on MLS, she received a call from Carol with the good news that three offers had already been received, all of them close to Meggan's asking price, but with all of them, there would be an equity shortfall of close to $1,000. Carol gave Meggan a summary of the offers' basic terms over the phone and said she had already emailed them to Meggan as electronic documents, but wanted to discuss details that could have a bearing on which one was the best choice. While still on the phone, Meggan pulled up the offers on her computer tablet, and Carol summarized and compared several key transaction details. After Meggan chose the best offer, Carol walked her through the electronic signing, and said the house was sold, but subject to the buyers' loan approval and final closing.

The closing was scheduled for thirty days later, so Meggan had very little time to find a place to rent, and not enough income to give her many choices. She found a walk-up second floor, two-bedroom apartment in a tidy-looking brick four-plex less than a mile from the bar where she worked, but the rent payment wouldn't give her enough left for even minimal living expenses. She remembered that Sandra had been looking for a new apartment, and she called Sandra to see if she wanted to move into the apartment and share the rent. Sandra said yes right away, and breathlessly added that she really, really loved that part of town. Meggan said she'd take care of the security deposit and sign the one-year lease, as long as Sandra committed to sharing half the rent that long. "Oh, at *least* for that long," Sandra said without hesitating.

Meggan paid fifty dollars to one of the guys who frequented Reggie's bar to help move her furniture with his pickup truck. Whatever furniture items would not fit into the apartment, she let the truck owner choose what he wanted. He chose a framed Monet landscape print and a dimmable table lamp, and Meggan sold the rest cheaply through a free internet website. She moved her three potted plants on the backseat floor of her car after warming the car for them. She thought of them whimsically as her little green children.

Sandra's boyfriend rented a trailer to help her move in a week later. Meggan overheard him complaining to Sandra about her having a roommate, because now he wouldn't be able to stop over whenever he wanted to, or stay the night.

***

At the final closing of Meggan's house almost a month later, she gave the closer a cashier's check for almost $900, the net proceeds shortfall. After that, along with paying the apartment rent and security deposit, she had just under $200 in her checking account. If it hadn't been for finally accepting Carol's offer to lower her commission, Meggan would not have been able to close on the sale of her house.

That night at Reggie's, the truck owner who helped her move came in with his wife and sat at the bar. His wife thanked Meggan for the pretty picture and the lamp, and asked if she was going to be alright living in an apartment after having such a nice house, which she said her husband described as "mint condition." Meggan said that paying rent without her ex's income would be challenging, but easier than a house payment. The woman went on about how some men are such jerks and should have their asses kicked, while her husband sipped his mug of beer and watched a noisy hockey game on the TV above the backbar. After the couple left, Meggan found a ten-dollar tip folded under the woman's empty beer mug.

Mid-March brought in one of the worst blizzards in Minnesota's history. Tree branches sagged heavily under sticky accumulating snow, and in rural areas, many trees split or uprooted under the strain of all that frozen weight, sometimes taking down power lines with them. Long stretches of freeways had to shut down until snowplow crews could push aside packed snow and knee-high drifts. In the Twin Cities, trucks constantly plowed and re-plowed day and night, barely keeping major streets passable. Residential side streets would have to wait, and their alleyways, with snowbound garages and full trash containers, were even further down the list. Many small business owners, especially those in small neighborhood commercial areas, locked their doors and stayed home until the snow-blasting gales finally spent their rage. A few neighborhood bars and restaurants, however, stayed open if there were any customers to serve, and if enough employees were able and willing to brave the weather.

Since Meggan's apartment was walking distance from Reggie's, she bundled up in her parka and trudged through snow-drifted sidewalks to work that afternoon, whenever possible walking under wind-snapping awnings that helped divert the snowfall. Even so, she barely arrived on time.

Reggie was tending the bar alone, chatting with three men who sat a few barstools from each other. They were staunch regulars who were determined to enjoy after-work libations with their buddies, regardless of bad weather or complaining wives.

Reggie brightened when he saw Meggan come in.

"You look like a lost Eskimo."

After Meggan peeled back her fur-trimmed hood and unwound the scarf from around her icy cheeks, she said, "I'm no Eskimo—just a barmaid dumb enough to go outside in this mess."

The three guys at the bar laughed, and one raised his highball to her. "Here's to the bravest, cutest barmaid in town!"

On her way to the backroom to hang up her things she said, "I don't know about the cutest, but I'm sure the coldest," which got another round of laughs.

When she came to the back of the bar, she started putting glasses and mugs in the dishwasher, wondering what it would be like outside when she had to walk home in the dark.

Reggie walked over to her and said, "Can you take over for a while? If I can catch up on some bookkeeping downstairs, we might be able to close early today."

She knew the guys at the bar were listening. "Sure, I can handle things until these guys get enough courage to go home."

That aroused a predictable round of laughter. After Reggie went downstairs, one of the men tossed a couple of dollars on the bar and got up, saying he was calling it a day. One of the remaining men ordered another bottle of beer, and the third man struggled off his barstool and said he'd see everyone tomorrow, unless the city was frozen over. Another man came in, stomped the snow off his boots, and sat next to his friend, the man who had just ordered a bottle of beer, and told Meggan to make it two. They compared complaints about how last night's pro basketball game was played while Meggan went back to loading the dishwasher.

The rest of the evening crawled on like that, one or two customers arriving, someone else confronting the storm to go home. Time ticked painfully slow for Meggan. She busied herself with dusting and straightening liquor bottles on the backbar, reloading the beer coolers, talking with patrons who wanted to chat. Just after 7 PM, she was down to one tipsy beer drinker, a painting contractor who always walked home after his daily three bottles of Grain Belt beer. After he shuffled out of the bar, she was alone except for Reggie, who was still working silently downstairs in his ramshackle little office.

This was the first time Meggan had ever been alone in the barroom. Rapidly-changing images from the barroom's three mounted TV screens reflected flickering splashes of light off opposing walls, something she had never noticed before, and now felt oddly irritated by it. The beer cooler's compressor motor seemed raspier and noisier than ever, like a growl above the blizzard's muffled moans and shrieks outside.

She thought about telling Reggie the place was empty in the hope that he'd lockup and let her go home. She went to the front door to see if the weather had let up any, but after opening it a few inches a frozen gust blew snow into her face. While she flinched and blinked her eyes, a blast of ice pellets stung her face. She pulled the door shut and wiped her face with her sleeve, and then carefully pushed it open with squinted eyes to see if any businesses across the street had lights on. The snow obscured everything that far away. Even the corner street light strained in vain to pierce through. Meggan wondered if being the only person left on Earth might seem like this. She started to close the door again—but at that moment, a pair of eyes seemed to stare through a swirling cloud of snow. The vague image of a face appeared to float toward her. She blinked and shut the door.

Her first intuition was to run downstairs for Reggie, but she'd first have to lock the entrance door: where did Reggie leave the door key? Then she wondered if someone outside was lost or needed help, but she was afraid to open the door again. She ran behind the bar and waited, ready to grab the sawed-off pool cue Reggie always kept underneath for protection, but never needed. Curiosity finally trumped her fear.

She crept cautiously toward the door and pushed it open a few inches against the howling wind pressure, then used her shoulder to force it open a little more—and gasped. An elderly man stood on the sidewalk with gloved hands buried in his woolen waist jacket pockets. His collar was pulled up around his neck, and a knit black watch cap covered his ears. He gazed at her passively, as if he had been patiently waiting for her to return.

"Are you open?" His calm voice barely penetrated the howling wind.

"Yes…" Meggan pushed the door open wider, letting swirling ice crystals and his presence take her breath away. "Come in if you like."

"Maybe to warm up a little."

The man took charge of pulling the door open the rest of the way and he followed her to the bar. Although his face looked old, he didn't carry himself that way. He carefully scooted two bar stools aside and stood between. Meggan walked around to the back of the bar and stood across from him while he carefully peeled off his gloves, setting them on a bar stool next to him and then making fists to warm his fingers. He removed his cap and set it on the gloves. His thin gray hair was damp and matted against his head. A day or two of facial stubble gave his tight cheeks an ashen, un-kempt look. He unbuttoned his thick wool jacket and care-fully draped it over the back of the stool that held his hat and gloves. He finally looked up at her.

Meggan reflexively took a half-step back. "Is there some-thing I can get for you?"

"Do you have red wine?"

"Is Merlot okay?"

"Sure, with a shot of brandy in it, please. In a highball glass, and no ice."

"You've had enough ice for one day, huh?"

"I never use ice in drinks."

Meggan took the gallon screw-top bottle of wine from the backbar. "I've never had anyone ask for brandy in their wine."

"Think of it as fortified wine."

She gave a polite chuckle at his presumed joke.

"That's basically what sherry is," he said. "Wine fortified with spirits."

"Oh…I didn't know that."

After pouring the wine, she returned it to the shelf and over-poured a shot of brandy into the glass. "Happy hour's over, but I'll give you a discount. How about two dollars?"

He took a ten-dollar bill from his wallet and slid it toward her on the bar. "Keep the overage."

Thinking that cashing in on a discounted drink would be unfair to Reggie, she rang up the entire ten dollars, and then tried to busy herself by resupplying the service area swizzle sticks and napkins, something she usually did after closing. As a further hint at her readiness to close the bar, she put the olive and cherry containers into the beer cooler.

She turned to the man when she heard the bar stools behind her being skidded back into place.

"Did you want another drink?"

"No, thanks." The man started putting his jacket and hat back on. "Like the wine, I guess I'm fortified enough to walk back to my son's house with his stressed-out wife always talking and my four rowdy, lovely grandsons adding mayhem with their not-so-lovely rambunctious dog. But I'm visiting for just a couple of days, so I'll survive."

"Did your wife come, too?"

He glanced at the wedding ring on his finger. "Her spirit is with me, but cancer took her body three months ago."

"Oh, I'm so sorry. I shouldn't have…"

"No, it's okay. You were nice to ask. My son's still a mess over losing his mom, and I got lonely moping around alone in my big Pennsylvania farmhouse. That's why I'm here. I needed time with my son, and he needs his dad."

That deeply touched something in Meggan, and she swallowed back the sudden tremble inside her.

"Your son's lucky to have a dad." She could barely speak, and sharing that feeling only made it harder.

The man looked kindly into her eyes, as if he sensed her emotional struggle. "What about your dad?"

"He was killed. In Vietnam. It was before I was born."

"So, you never met your father. I wonder what that's been like for you."

"Like there's been a hole in my heart." That slipped thought had never occurred to her, and she could barely finish saying it.

"Next time you visit his gravesite, tell him how you feel. It helps when I do that at my wife's final resting place."

"I would if he had a gravesite."

The man stopped buttoning his jacket and looked at her.

She guessed at the question in his eyes. "He was classified as missing in action."

"Do you know where he was last seen?"

"No, I don't." She reflexively glanced at the beer clock on the wall, but didn't take notice of the time.

The man slipped his cap on. "I only asked because I'm a Vietnam vet, and I served on an MIA recovery team back in the 1990s. We kept in close touch with surviving family members, and we had American forensic experts with us. We also had pretty good information of where individual MIAs were killed."

"The government wouldn't tell my mom that."

"The Department of Defense should have at least given her the general location and circumstances."

"They weren't married, so they wouldn't tell her anything."

"Oh, I see. But you're a surviving blood relative. If your dad's name is on your birth certificate, they have to give you everything they know."

"But no one saw him killed, and that's why he's still classified as missing. I only know that because if he had been classified as killed in action, my mom wouldn't have had to go to court to collect on his life insurance."

The man nodded deliberatively. "Last Known Alive," he said as if to himself. "That's what they label those rare cases when someone in the military just disappears. Almost all of them have since been confirmed as dead, but there are still a very, very few cases—maybe just twenty or so—that have never been resolved. Your father's disappearance is apparently one of those."

"So, is there any hope of me learning anything more?"

"There's always hope, miss, so never give up. The US still works with the Vietnamese government to find evidence of those mysterious MIAs, and if it's any comfort to you, the Americans working on this project will never give up until they've confirmed the status of every veteran and recovered at least some remains. Every foreign war veteran must return home, dead or alive. Until then, you'll see those black and white POW-MIA flags waving underneath many American flags."

After the man left, Meggan was again left with her lonely barroom vigil. But her thoughts stayed with the man. He talked about her father as if he was a real person, a flesh-and-blood man who had lived in Minnesota and died far from home, a man whose essence still remained somewhere, in some form.

Reggie startled her when he came up from his basement office. He said he was closing the bar for the night. After locking the door and turning off the neon window lights, they put chairs upside down on the tables and the stools upside down on the bar for the early morning janitor.

By the time she walked home, around ten o'clock, the wind had simmered to a gusty breeze, stirring only a few wisps of snowflakes glittered under the golden street lights. By now, the wind had drifted much of the snow into frozen waves, some too high to tread through, concealing the orderly layout of streets and sidewalks, and blocking traffic until snowplows showed up.

When she got home she noticed Sandra's chair and lamp were missing from the living room. A folded paper lay conspicuously on the kitchen table, and after kicking her boots off, she read Sandra's note.

Meggan, I'm really, really sorry, but I moved in with my boyfriend today. I just had to. We had a really bad argument and then made up and now I know how much he really loves me. Also, and no offense, but when you get home late from your bar job, it wakes me up and I have trouble falling asleep and I've had a really bad sleep deficit and headaches at work, but I didn't want to complain. I took my clothes and dishes, and you can have anything I might have forgotten. I hope we can still be friends.

Meggan scrunched the note in her fist, threw it onto the counter, and yelled, "Shit!"

She couldn't afford the entire rent payment on her own, and her name was on the one-year lease. Now she had to face finding an acceptable roommate who was willing to move this time of year.

CHAPTER 11

Meggan posted an ad for a female roommate on a free listing website. A few anonymous inquirers asked questions about privacy, whether the apartment is pet-friendly, rules for use of the kitchen, are overnight guests okay on weekends, is there room for a bicycle in the living room. Meggan responded through the website's anonymous email system to a "twenty-something" woman who said she just needed a place for a few months until she graduated from beauty school, but maybe longer if she didn't get hired right away. Meggan asked about her source and amount of income while going to school, and after three days still hadn't received an answer.

She received in inquiry from an advertising manager who needed housing for six months during a temporary assignment to Minnesota from her New York office, and needed easy access to downtown Minneapolis. After a round of emailed exchanges, Meggan felt her income and needs were satisfactory, and invited the woman to have a telephone conversation. The woman called shortly after Meggan sent the email.

"Hello, this is Meggan."

"I'm Donna Romain, the person who inquired about sharing your apartment."

"Nice to meet you, Donna. When would you be interested in moving in?"

"I've been staying in a hotel, so I could move anytime. Is your apartment completely furnished?"

"Yes, except the bedroom you'd be using."

"I obviously wouldn't be travelling with a bed."

"Maybe you could rent one."

"Maybe. Now, I go to bed early and sleep lightly. Television late at night could be a problem."

"I work from 5 PM to 2 AM, and I go right to bed when I get home."

"I also want you to know my partner plans to fly in sometimes and stay with me on weekends. Are you okay with that?"

"I guess it would depend how often…"

"And, don't take this personally, but do you have religious leanings?"

"What?"

"Not that I'm hung up on religion, but I had a roommate once who kept moralizing about her beliefs. I don't need that."

"I wouldn't, either. Now let me ask you a question: why should I accept you as a roommate?"

"I don't know."

"I don't, either. Good luck."

***

That evening at work, during the post-happy hour lull, Reggie said, "Meggan, are you feeling okay?"

"Sorry, I didn't know it was showing. I'll be okay."

"Anything you can talk about?"

"I'm worried about making my next rent payment. I was counting on my roommate, but she skipped on me."

"Maybe you can find another roommate."

"I've tried."

"Well, don't worry, because I can loan you whatever you need to get you through the next month."

"That's sweet of you, Reggie. Your offer already makes me feel better, but I think I can figure something out."

CHAPTER 12

Meggan withdrew her roommate ad from the listing website, and started floating résumés for a position as restaurant manager through an employment website. She told Reggie about this, and said she liked working for him, but she wanted to earn enough money to pay her living expenses without a roommate.

Emotionally, she was ready for a more challenging job, and was willing to work the long hectic hours demanded of restaurant managers. But until then, she stopped buying microwavable meals and deli meats, and bought her vegetables in cans, on sale. Her schedule at the bar and limited social life made her settle into a tolerable but dull existence, the lifestyle she thought her mom, for some reason, always seemed to enjoy.

She sometimes reflected on that Vietnam veteran who came to the bar during the blizzard a couple of weeks ago. He had talked about her lost father as if she could communicate with him, at least spiritually, and that stirred something inside her. The next Monday, which was her usual day off, she walked a few blocks to a veterans' club. The evening's patrons were beginning to fill bar stools and tables, an older crowd than she was used to at Reggie's. Couples sipped beers and wine at most of the tables, some eating their supper, and the barstools were dominated by men, some tearing off the pull tabs they bought at the enclosed pull tab booth by the front door. An American flag hung from the wall next to the bar, with a POW-MIA flag next to it, and military unit crests and prints of armed forces battle scenes scattered throughout the rest of the large noisy room.

Meggan stood next to the waitress station and caught the busy bartender's eye.

"Can I help you?" he said while prying the cap off a beer bottle and exchanging it for someone's empty.

"My father was a soldier in Vietnam, and I was wondering how I could get information about his service."

"Keith Henderson might be able to help you. He's the club manager, and very involved with Vietnam veteran affairs." The bartender scanned the room over the heads of those sitting at the bar. He waved to catch someone's attention, and then gestured for the person to come over.

When the man came to the bar, the bartender nodded toward Meggan and said, "Keith, this gal wants the service records for her dad, who's a Nam vet. Can you help her out?"

Keith turned to Meggan. "I'll sure try. You should start by requesting his records from the National Personnel Records Center. I can get you the address, but if you make your request through a US senator or your House representative, you might get a quicker turnaround."

"Do you think his service records would at least say where he was last seen alive?"

"He died in Vietnam?"

"Yes."

"I'm very sorry to hear that, ma'am. Yes, his military records should give the details of his passing."

"I don't think they'll give those details."

"Why not?"

"He's classified as missing in action."

"That might just mean the US hasn't been able to recover his remains. His commanding officer would have made a report of how he died, though."

"What if no one saw him die?"

"Well, I'd still start with requesting his service records. It'll tell you where he served, the last unit he served with, and you can do more research after that."

"More research?"

"Some units have veteran organizations, and if there's one for his outfit, you could ask them to post an inquiry in their newsletter or website. Give them the dates he was in Vietnam, and maybe someone who knew him will contact you. If that doesn't work, you could write inquiries to all the veterans' organizations. If none of those ideas work, come back and see me. I'll help you contact his army unit's official historian, and maybe I'll think of some other ideas by then. I won't give up if you don't, okay?"

"Okay, Keith. Thanks. My name's Meggan, by the way."

"Meggan, your father made the ultimate sacrifice for his country, and everyone in here honors service members like him. Wherever your search leads, you can always be very proud of him."

Meggan pressed her lips and nodded before turning away. When she got to the door, she turned and gave Keith a parting wave, which he returned with a happy grin.

She walked home deep in thought, almost oblivious to where she was. Keith gave her hope that she might possibly learn what happened to her father, and where his remains are resting; information her mother was denied all these years.

She thought about how her father's absence had sometimes affected her. Of course, Father's Days left her out, and she felt sad walking down the church aisle alone at her wedding. She wondered if there were less obvious ways it affected her, her relationships for example, or her personality and values. How would her life have been different if he had survived the war and came home to her mother and her? He would have been there for birthdays, her graduation, whenever she got hurt or sick. He would have warned her about dangers and foolish decisions, and comforted her during occasional catastrophes and when she needed his advice. Meggan knew she was idealizing his role in her life, but she still wondered. And then it struck her that he had been denied ever knowing what it was like to be a husband and father.

She arrived at the front door of her apartment and shook off her musing, realizing she'd never know the answers to those questions. But she could at least try to find out how he died, and where.

CHAPTER 13

That afternoon, Meggan called her mother, and after exchanging routine small talk she said, "Mom, I talked to a guy at a neighborhood veterans' club. He told me I might be able to get information about my father from the government if I could prove a blood relationship. Do you remember if my father's name is on my birth certificate?"

"Yes, it says Peter McHillston was your father."

"Do you have my birth certificate?"

"Of course. I'll mail the original to you. I should have given it to you years ago. Is there anything else I can do to help you?"

"No, but thanks."

"Did you find a roommate yet?"

"No, and I decided to get back into the restaurant business so I can earn enough to pay my own expenses. Depending on someone else hasn't worked for me."

After a pause, Nancy said, "I know. Being self-sufficient has always worked best for you. You've had to be strong, haven't you?"

"Yes, but don't start worrying about me, okay?"

"Okay. Love you, sweetie."

"Love you too."

***

Over the next three days, Meggan didn't get any responses to her restaurant job posting, but she received a priority mail envelope from her mother, containing Meggan's birth certificate. She scanned it into a PDF at a nearby library and emailed a copy to one of Minnesota's senators, Kendal Zattsman, with a request to help her obtain information about her father's service records. She received a stock-sounding email reply two days later, assuring her that he would look into that matter.

One night while Reggie worked the bar with Meggan, he said he was giving her a small raise, and would increase it when things picked up.

"Thanks, Reggie, but I can get by for now."

"That's good, but you deserve a raise and I can afford it. Any bites on your job search?"

"Not yet, but I'll give you as much notice as you need."

"I wouldn't need much notice. I can usually manage the bar myself and I can call a couple of part-time bartenders I know."

"Maybe you'll get busier in the spring."

"It's not about the season or the weather. Instead of coming to neighborhood bars like this, more people are drinking at home, thanks to cable TV sports and movies. And too many people are socializing on their computers instead of coming to joints like this to mix with old friends or meet new people."

Meggan suspected the problem was more likely competition from the new craft brewhouse and grill down the street. Most of Reggie's customers were beer drinkers, and the only hot food he offered was the kind of pre-wrapped sandwiches you find at gas stations.

"When I was in the restaurant business, I learned that any new bar or restaurant would syphon off some customers from the area, at least for a while. When the newness wore off, though, most of the regulars drifted back to the places where people knew them, where they felt comfortable. During that phase the new places had to really struggle to develop loyal customers, and most didn't make it."

Reggie just nodded and said, "We'll see" as if her cheery prediction was nothing more than kindness. He went back to customers waiting for him at his end of the bar.

***

Two weeks later, Meggan received a large thick envelope in the mail, with a return address from the United States Senate. The cover letter was from Senator Zattsman.

> *Dear Ms. Mondae,*
>
> *I recently received the enclosed response to my inquiry on your behalf from the National Personnel Records Center regarding the military service records of your father, Specialist 5 Peter McHillston. Although the records are inconclusive about the circumstances of his "Missing in Action" status, I hope these documents are what you are looking for and meet your needs. I appreciate and honor your father's sacrifice for our country.*
>
> *Please let me know if I can ever be of further service to you.*
> *Sincerely,*
> *Senator Kendal Zattsman*

Meggan thumbed through the enclosed official forms, letters of commendation, and official orders documenting such things as her father's assigned military posts and his rank promotions. It started with a record of his basic training at Fort

Leonard Wood in Missouri, then advanced infantry training at Fort Benning in Georgia, and finally, orders for Vietnam, where he was assigned to Company A, 32nd Infantry Battalion. The final form, dated 4 January 1972, classified his personnel status as Missing in Action. No circumstances or reasons were noted.

Meggan emailed the senator, asking why no circumstances were noted regarding her father's disappearance. A few hours later, a staffer replied, saying the senator had received all the official military documents available for Specialist 5 Peter McHillston. Meggan then searched the internet to find organizations for her father's infantry company, but found none.

She left for work early the next day and stopped at the veterans' club to tell Keith about her limited progress. As he listened, he nodded sympathetically.

"Okay, Meggan, let's try this: when you get home, email me your father's full name, unit, and dates of service in Vietnam. I'll include that in a locator listing in our organization's magazine to find someone who served with your father's outfit while he was there. If I get a response, I'll look it over to make sure it seems legit, and then I'll forward it to you. It's a long shot, but you just might be lucky enough to find someone who can give you firsthand information about your dad, maybe even about the place he was last seen alive."

Keith wrote what he asked for on the back of his business card, and gave it to her.

Meggan read it and said, "It was forty-five years ago. I wonder if anyone would still remember him."

"You can be sure that he's remembered by every living man who served in his outfit with him. An infantryman's life depends on his brothers, and those guys bond for life. Be sure to include your phone number when you email me the information I asked for, and I'll call you if we get a response. It'll take a while for the inquiry to go out, so be patient. Our organization still communicates with its members the old-fashioned way, a monthly snail-mailed magazine."

Meggan thanked him, and despite his caution about having patience, she walked out of the veterans' club feeling buoyant, hopeful that she might finally uncover something about the mysterious world where her father lived and died, where young men like him, mostly just out of high school, were thrown into terrible battles they had to either win or die. If she could talk to someone from his unit, she might even learn how her father died, whether he suffered very much, and if he knew he was being left behind. Meggan assumed that her mother must have struggled with those questions years ago when she was alone and carrying her unborn child. Now Meggan might be able to ask those questions, and she wondered how each of them would handle the answers.

CHAPTER 14

Each day Meggan noticed subtle signs that Reggie's business was slowly dwindling: a few regulars weren't showing up anymore, other customers left after the cheap happy hour drinks to get something to eat at the new brewhouse.

This migration made Meggan's work easier, but increasingly tedious. The long-time regulars could still be counted on to come in every day, order the same drink in the same quantities, and nurse them for the same amount of time before pulling themselves off their stool to go home. But any business needed new customers, and Reggie wasn't getting them. His bar didn't attract younger drinkers who liked glitzy bars with jazzy music, seemingly endless beer, wine, and whiskey choices, and fancy cocktails. Put simply, "workingmen's bars" like Reggie's were not a growth industry.

Meggan found herself increasingly checking the beer-sign clock on the back wall. Whenever business slowed to just a few customers alone on barstools or at tables, staring at endless TV sports games, or staring off with blurred worries or disappointments while nursing drinks to find relief, then Reggie would make excuses to leave the bar to Meggan, as if he needed her there while he checked the liquor inventory, ordered supplies, or caught up on bookkeeping. She wondered how long he could afford to find reasons for keeping her on his payroll.

***

Six weeks after last talking to Keith, Meggan still hadn't heard anything from him. She guessed that the veterans' magazine must have been mailed by now, but she was losing hope that anyone read those magazines, let alone the "looking for" inquiries, which were probably jammed together in small print in the back of the magazine. She was tempted to follow up with Keith, but didn't bother. He would have surely contacted her if someone had responded, so there was no sense in pestering him. She decided to give up on her failed long shot to find out more about her father, which started feeling like a useless obsession, just a vain curiosity that distracted her from her mundane, botched life. While walking home after her shift that night, she felt relieved instead of disappointed. Now she could just focus on getting a better-paying job and putting her life back together.

But her relief and resolve were temporary. After she got home, she wondered if she was giving up after just a meager effort, perhaps setting herself up for another failure. But what else could she do?

When she flipped on the switch to her apartment's light, she was surprised to see she had forgotten her phone, which was on the kitchen counter. After taking off her boots and coat, she checked for missed calls. A voice message from an unknown caller had been left shortly after she went to work. She touched the "play" icon, and heard Keith's excited voice saying, "Meggan, someone responded to the inquiry. Give me a call when you can."

She got into bed just past 2:30 AM, but being tired didn't

help her fall asleep. She replayed Keith's message in her head. Was the response from someone who actually knew her father? Maybe it was just someone who knew about Company A, or someone who wanted to wish her well in finding her father's whereabouts—or maybe it was just a mistake.

Some Minneapolis bars opened at 8 AM, but when Meggan called the veterans' club at 9, a recorded message informed her that they opened at 10:30 AM, and they served an inexpensive lunch until 2 PM. Rather than calling back, she showed up at the front door just before the bartender arrived to open for business. He said Keith usually arrived around eleven, but invited her in to sit at the bar with a cup of coffee. They chatted while the bartender organized bottles of the house's standard pours in the wells beneath the bar, and took a rack of clean glasses out of the dishwasher. While sipping her coffee, Meggan heard her name. She turned to see Keith walking toward her with a grin that deepened his eye wrinkles.

"I think we got lucky, Meggan. I got an email yesterday from a guy named Mike Sumner, who says he was with your dad's company during the time your dad was in Nam. I wanted to talk to you before responding to him."

Meggan stepped down from the bar stool. "I can hardly believe it. What's next?"

"I'll reply and introduce you, and CC you on the email. After that, you should email him and give him the name of your father—I didn't put your father's name in our magazine's locator posting, just the dates. Ask him if he knew your dad, and if so, what he knew about him. Let's see where that goes for starters. If you have any questions or reservations about what he says, call me. But if you feel okay with his response, go ahead and ask any questions you'd like."

Meggan's work shift at Reggie's wouldn't start for a few hours, so she walked home as quickly as she could without breaking into a run, and trotted up the stairs to her apartment. As soon as she got her coat and boots off, she opened her email on her computer tablet, and saw Keith's reply to Mike Sumner, introducing Meggan, and saying she would like information about her father, who served in his infantry company in Vietnam. She clicked Sumner's email address and composed a message to him.

> *Mike, my name is Meggan Mondae, and my father's name is Peter McHillston, who served in Vietnam with Company A, 32nd Infantry Battalion during 1971 and 1972. Did you know him?*

Within a couple of minutes, a replay came back.

> *Meggan, your father and I were good buddies. I knew Pete had a girlfriend back home, but he never mentioned anything about a daughter. The last time I saw him was during a North Vietnam Army ambush in January 1972. Please feel free to email me anytime, or you can call me at the number below if you'd like to talk with me about your dad. He was a very brave and upight man, and you can be proud to be his daughter.*

Meggan reread the message twice, slowly the second time to make sure she understood every word, looking for any nuance or possible subtext. The email made her father sound like a man who had loved her mother, and probably would have loved his daughter if he had survived. She nervously typed a reply, hoping Mike Sumner was still at his computer.

Mike, my father didn't know he had a daughter. My mother didn't know she was pregnant with me when he left for Vietnam, and when she found out, her letters to him were returned by the Army Post Office without explanation. She never learned what exactly happened to him.

After hitting *send*, she stared at the screen for a reply. Was he still there? Maybe he was reading other mail, maybe he turned off his computer for the day, or maybe...

Meggan, your news about you and your mother brought tears to my aging eyes. If Pete had known about you, he would have been excited beyond my ability to describe, except to say he was that kind of guy, a tough but sensitive farm boy from Minnesota. Devotion to your mother gave him an important reason to survive, something beyond just saving his butt, and knowing about you would have made coming home all the more urgent. But God called him one terrible day, and I saw where he fell. When you feel ready to know more, please let me know, and I'll do my best to explain whatever I know, to the extent you want me to.

She thanked him in one last reply and clicked off her tablet. She felt this initial exchange of emails had reached the limits of what can be expressed between one stranger to another about something that has so profoundly affected her and her mother. Meggan now needed to talk to Mike Sumner.

She microwaved some leftover vegetable soup for lunch and ate it with a buttered slice of bread while sitting on the edge of her chair at her small kitchen table. She wondered what she should ask Mike Sumner. He had let her decide when to call, but he might need some time to collect his own feelings and search his mind for long-ago memories, some that might be painful. She decided tomorrow late morning might be a good time to call.

She again had trouble falling asleep after returning from work that night. Sumner's words stirred heavily in her mind, phrases like *terrible day…God called him…I saw where he fell.*

Late the next morning Meggan quickly showered and dressed, as if she was going somewhere important before work. But she wasn't. She sat in a living room chair and stared at her phone for a few minutes, not understanding why she suddenly felt nervous about calling Mike Sumner. Without dwelling on it any further, she tapped his number into her phone.

A gravelly voice said, "Hello, this is Mike."

"Mike Sumner?"

"Yes…"

"I'm Meggan Mondae, Peter McHillston's daughter."

"Meggan! By God, I hoped you'd call me. How are you?"

"I'm fine. Is this a good time to talk?"

"Sure, and I'll give you as much time as you want. Your dad was a great friend, Meggan, and I often think about him."

"Can you tell me what happened to him in Vietnam, I mean, how did he die?"

"I'm not sure how much detail you want…"

"Everything you can tell me, Mike. I want the unvarnished truth about what happened to my father so I can think about him as a real person."

"Okay, here's what I can remember. The last time I saw Pete was January 1972, when our company was sent on an operation in the Central Highlands, just west of the remote mountain city of Dalat. A special forces outfit near there had been overrun by North Vietnamese Army troops pouring in from Cambodia, presumably to join forces with the local

Vietcong for a push south into Saigon. Our outfit was supposed to confirm the enemy's position and strength, and get out before being detected. Pete and I were two of the more experienced guys in our platoon, and we both thought the idea was a joke."

"A joke?"

"Yeah, but not a funny one. Sending in a swarm of noisy helicopters *and* avoiding detection—that was the joke. On top of that, the US was starting to shut down operations in Vietnam, so why send just two infantry companies into a huge area that dangerous just to confirm something they already knew? Anyway, Pete and I were in the first chopper to reach the landing zone, which was just a flat spot on the highest mountain in sight. Before it fully touched down, we were both out the door and running through a churned up cloud of grit to find cover. We dove in behind a fallen tree trunk just below the crest, and were soon joined by one of the newest guys, a scared private named Roger. He stared in the direction we were looking and asked if we saw something. Pete just shook his head while we looked for movement, a flicker of metal, anything unusual. After the choppers took turns dropping troops into the LZ, they high-tailed it back to the airfield near Pleiku. I told Roger to stay low and watch for Lieutenant Brakken to see where he was forming up the rest of the guys. It wasn't long before Brakken slid in next to us with four men in tow, including the radio operator. They crouched behind the deadfall tree trunk while the rest of the Alpha Company troops scattered into positions behind trees, into depressions, and in tall grass."

Meggan asked, "Did you see any enemy soldiers?"

"Lt. Brakken asked us the same question, and I said no. Pete wanted to know why Bravo Company was headed in the other direction. Was there a mix up? Bakken said no, Bravo Company would scout south along the ridge line, and we were going north. I reminded him that we'd never split up on an operation, but Brakken said this was just a quick in-and-out recon, then got up and hand-signaled the men to move out along the hillside, just below the crest. After almost an hour, the point man ran back to report that a guy in black pajamas was seen running down into the valley. Brakken mumbled 'A lookout,' more to himself, but loud enough for me to hear. After a couple more hours, Brakken said we'd spend the night in a small stand of trees ahead. He ordered Claymore mines to be set and aimed outward around our position, ready to be manually detonated. Pete volunteered for the first two hours of guard duty, and Roger said he'd take guard duty with him. I leaned back against a tree but couldn't sleep. After a while, I heard Roger whispering to Pete, asking why we didn't go after that lookout. Pete said if we got lured into an ambush down in that valley, we'd be screwed. We didn't have the firepower to hold off a division of North Vietnamese Army troops."

"I still don't understand why they sent you if they already knew the enemy was there."

"I overheard Roger ask Pete that same thing, and I thought *I wish to hell we knew*, but Pete told him we were just supposed to nose around for stuff you can't see from the air, and that we'd probably get picked up in the morning. After it got dark and my night vision kicked in, I saw Pete take the small photo of his girlfriend from his belt pouch and look at it. I knew he was mentally promising to return to her. He did that little ritual every night."

"Did he tell you her name?"

"Nancy."

"That's my mother."

"I know."

"Were you attacked that night?"

"No, but the next morning I was woken by a bullet cracking through the trees, followed by the distant gunshot sound. Two more shots, louder this time, sent all of us scrambling for our weapons. Lt. Brakken stood to yell orders and was immediately shot through the chest and neck. He dropped like a bag of wet sand. Men scrambled for cover and took shooting positions while gunshots popped all around us."

"Who took over after the lieutenant was killed?"

"A three-stripe sergeant named Shay. He got to his knees and yelled at the men to detonate the Claymores, but the mines had been turned toward us during the night by the enemy and burning shrapnel blasted into us. I still remember the clanking against steel pot helmets, seeing ripped clothes and torn skin. Three guys lie dead, including Sergeant Shay, and five more could no longer fight because of serious wounds. I was one of them. My leg was almost torn off the bones. The radioman was yelling frantically into his mic, begging for air support when the handset was suddenly ripped from his hands, and his body shuddered from more bullet strikes as he bent down to retrieve it. The concussion had slammed Pete to the ground, but he staggered up to crawl when a round glanced off his helmet. When he went down, I figured he was a goner."

"Is that how he died?"

"No, that wasn't enough to keep Pete down for long. Even though enemy gunfire kept dropping guys all around us, he struggled up and low-crawled toward the radio to continue calling for help, but just as he passed by me he came upon Roger. I could see poor Rog on his back, staring up into the brilliant sky with wild wide eyes. Blood foamed from his mouth with every strained gasp. Pete knelt over Roger and tore his shirt open, revealing the chest wound that I'm sure Pete hoped to not see. The bullet hole in Roger's lung that would soon drown him with his own blood if it wasn't patched. Pete ripped open a massive-wound bandage packet he always kept in his helmet band, tossed aside the gauze, and placed the plastic wrapper over Roger's chest wound, pressing down with his palm to stop the air from flowing in and out through the bullet hole. He put Roger's limp hand over the wrapper, and yelled directly into his ear over ever-louder blasts, telling Rog to hold the plastic wrapper down. I saw Roger's empty eyes roll toward Pete. His lips barely moved, releasing bloody drool but no sound. Your dad yelled at Rog to hold it as tight as he could. I can still hear Pete saying 'Come on, man, you can do it, okay?' Roger still stared into nothingness, but his hand showed life against the plastic wrapper. Pete said 'I'll get you out of here, Rog. We're getting out together, okay?' He had to take the chance that Roger would hang onto a thread of life for a few minutes, so he could crawl to the radio. I prayed it was still operable, that someone would hear him, because without immediate support and evacuation, there would soon be no one left to rescue. I twisted a tourniquet made from my belt around my leg, but knew I wouldn't last long."

"But you did survive. My father must have radioed for help."

"He tried, but when he finally got to the radio and tipped it up, I could see colored wires spilling out like a rainbow of guts from the ripped-open case. Deafening mortar rounds began thundering ever-closer to us about then, and the concussion from one shocked the air out of my lungs. Pete looked wiped out. I wondered if he thought he'd never again see his parents or Nancy. But his far-off stare passed with a blink, and he gathered enough energy to get back to Roger. He grabbed a dead soldier's rifle and squirmed across the ground on his belly like a beat-up lizard, right past me and around shot-torn tree debris and lifeless fallen brothers. I watched him draw a deep breath when he got back to Roger, who slowly turned his head toward Pete. 'We're getting out of here, Rog. The radioman called for an evacuation. We're going back to the LZ for a dust off and a trip home.' I prayed to make Pete's promise come true."

"But it didn't."

"No, but Pete sure as hell tried. He grabbed the gauze he had dropped next to Roger and formed a quick wad. He took off Roger's web belt and lifted him up enough to get it around his back and over his chest. Pete placed the gauze over the plastic and tightened the belt against it to hold the plastic wrapper in place. After pulling Rog up into a sitting position, he pulled an arm over his shoulder, carefully got to his knees, and grabbed Roger's leg with his free arm, slinging Roger's body over his shoulders into a fireman's carry. It must have taken all of Pete's strength to stand up while gripping Roger's arm and leg, half-trotting, half-shuffling back along the ridge toward the landing zone. I watched helplessly. A bullet grazed Peter's calf muscle but he just stumbled and fought to keep his balance and limped on, one heavy footfall after another. Another bullet punctured the back of his helmet on one side, almost knocking him down, but must have exited out the front after wounding him. Blood streamed down his neck while he made his way around the strewn bodies of Alpha Company troops, a few of them, like me, hanging onto life."

"What finally stopped him?"

"A grenade exploded just behind Pete. When I finally

gained my senses after the brain-jarring shock, I saw that Rog's body took the brunt of the blast, which would have partially shielded Peter, but it split Roger's back wide open just above his waist, finally finishing him off. But I couldn't see your dad anywhere. I figured the blast must have thrown him down the steep bank toward the valley, right into the enemy's hands. I never saw him again."

After a long silence that Mike didn't interrupt, Meggan asked, "How did you finally get out?"

"Bravo Company had heard the commotion and radioed for help. Air Force jets soon flew in with enough napalm and rockets to keep the enemy busy for a while. When the choppers arrived, Bravo Company troops piled as many of our guys into the bays as they could before the LZ got hot again. I was one of the lucky ones. All I lost was a leg. Your dad lost everything."

Meggan could barely speak. "And Mom and I lost him."

"I hope I haven't gone on too much."

"No. I'm okay, Mike. Was it hard for you?"

"A little maybe, but I'm fine. I've never talked this much about that day, though. I sort of felt like Pete was listening while I recounted this experience we shared. You're his daughter, after all, and part of your soul includes part of his. That probably sounds stupid…"

Another long silence passed between them.

Barely above a whisper, Meggan finally said, "No, Mike. Not stupid at all."

"Okay, good."

"Did any of the survivors go back to look for the guys left behind?"

"Company A had too many casualties and no replacements to carry out any more operations, but the day after the ambush, Company B sent a couple of platoons back in after the surrounding area was temporarily being secured with gunships. The troops were dropped at the original LZ, but they found no survivors in the little time they had. They collected a few bodies and dog tags for the rest, and then got the hell out. They found some of our guys headshot point-blank. It was later confirmed that the VC and NVA were amassing for a joint push to overthrow Saigon, and they didn't want to be encumbered by prisoners. I want to assure you, though, that Pete was not among those executed. When the final count was done, three men were still missing. The remains of two of them were identified years later, but your dad wasn't one of those, either. As far as I know, his status is still officially MIA."

"I got my father's service records from the Department of Defense, and it didn't include anything about this battle."

"That doesn't surprise me. Our guys didn't know it at the time, but that recon mission wasn't authorized by higher command, and it was classified as secret for many years."

"What do you mean?"

"Because the US started pulling out of Nam in 1972, we weren't authorized to be anywhere west of the city of Dalat, especially in that known VC hotbed near Bang Dia. So, officially, the operation never happened and we were never there. Years later, I tried to get official documents through the Freedom of Information Act, but there was nothing in the government records."

"I'm writing some of this down, Mike. Is Bang Dia near Dalat?"

"Yes, just a few miles west. Are you thinking about going there?"

"Oh, no. Maybe someday, but that's not possible now. I

just wanted to see where it was on a map. How about you, Mike? Any plans to go back?"

"I've thought about it, but my stiff bones and tight finances aren't up to that kind of trip. Anyway, that's what I tell myself. I know vets who've found some closure by returning to places where they got screwed up."

"Maybe it would help you. You might find a group going there. The area has probably changed a lot, and it would certainly be safe now."

"I guess so, but I think I'll just wait for you to go, and then you can tell me what it's like when you get back. That might be good for both of us."

The conversation ended on that note, and Sumner invited Meggan to contact him anytime she had further questions about her father or about their outfit. Meggan thanked him and invited him to call her, too, even if he just wanted to talk.

***

While Meggan was tending bar that night, she got a text notification that an email had been sent to her by her job search service. She opened the email and it was from a new downtown hotel she had never heard of, inviting her to schedule an interview for a management position in their restaurant. When she got home that night, she reviewed the restaurant's website. The interior showed it to be a classy traditional supper club, and the expensive menu apparently targeted the expense-account crowd. She emailed a request for an interview.

Late the next morning, Meggan found an email from the restaurant's general manager, inviting her to come in for an interview at one of three times. She chose the next morning at 10 AM.

When she arrived the following morning, servers with

white aprons were busily folding linen napkins and lining up hefty-looking silverware at the tables. Small vases of bright flowers were being carefully centered on each table. One of the servers approached her and said they would be opening at eleven. When Meggan said she was there for an interview, the server's official pleasantness relaxed a bit, and she asked Meggan to follow her to an office near the kitchen.

After the server's measured knock on a dark paneled door, a very thin man in a black tailored suit and yellow bow tie opened it, welcoming Meggan in while introducing himself as Pierre. His office was decorated with old-fashioned magic show posters that took up most of the wall space. Stacks of file folders covered the credenza behind him, but his desktop held only a laptop computer.

Pierre invited her to sit in the chair facing his desk. He sat behind his desk and opened his laptop.

"I see by your résumé that you have about five years of restaurant experience, most of that in a management position?"

"That's right."

Pierre searched the screen of his laptop. "I'm looking at your educational background, and it doesn't say what your degree was in."

"Most of my college courses were in business administration."

"So, your degree was business administration."

"I didn't finish college because of the long hours I had to work after becoming a manager."

Pierre looked up from his computer screen with a strained look. "You should have disclosed that. The job posting clearly stated that we're only considering degreed applicants."

"Oh. I missed that."

"Didn't your previous employer have similar minimum standards?"

"My previous employer was the insurance company, which I listed on my résumé, and right now I'm working as a bartender. But when I was in the restaurant business a few years ago, I worked my way up, first as a server, then as evening manager."

Pierre glanced back at his computer screen. "Bartender? There's obviously been a misunderstanding. But if you want an opportunity that could lead to advancement, we do have openings for table bussers, and then perhaps you could try to complete your education. Is that something you'd be interested in?"

"No."

Pierre closed his laptop. "Well, then I suppose our business is finished."

Meggan got to her feet. "I'm glad you didn't offer me the manager job because I would have turned you down."

"What are you talking about?"

"I'm talking about not wanting to work for a snooty overrated dive like this, and I resent you wasting my valuable time."

When she spun around to leave, Pierre commanded her with measured tension to please close the door on the way out.

Without turning her head, Meggan threw the door open hard enough to make it bang against the wall.

"Close it yourself."

She drove home with her usual nerve-settling grip on the steering wheel. When the steam in her temper cooled, she realized it would be more difficult than she thought to get a decent paying restaurant job without a degree, even though she knew she'd be good at it. In the meantime, she had to worry about next month's rent payment.

Before leaving for work that afternoon, Meggan called her mother.

"I feel like a loser for having to ask this, Mom, but I wonder if I could get a small loan—just enough to pay rent for a couple of months. And I'd want to pay you interest, at least the same rate you'd get from your investment fund."

"Sure, no problem. How's the job market?"

"It sucks. At least for me."

"Any luck finding a roommate?"

"I've given up looking."

"Did you try running a newspaper ad?"

"No one reads the paper anymore, Mom, except people your age—no offense.

"None taken. I'm proud of my ability to read and understand more than a one-sentence news story."

"I did try an internet posting, but I'd rather not have some goofball as a roommate, like the ones who responded to the post. I just need a job that pays more, and it looks like that might take a little longer than I thought."

"With your abilities, I'm sure lots of employers will want to hire you."

"Thanks, Mom, but I think it's going to be hard to find someone who cares more about my abilities than a degree."

Nancy was silent for a moment. "Oh, so that's it. But you're a survivor, Meggan. You'll land a good job."

"I'm sure I will."

"Of course. You're clever and feisty, like your dad. He could always turn problems around, and you will too. In the meantime, you can count on however much money you need—and forget about paying interest, I don't need it."

"Would a couple of thousand be too much?"

"No, not at all. Give me your checking account number and I'll make a transfer from my account to yours when the banks open tomorrow."

Meggan gave her the checking account number and bank information, and when she hung up, she had to grin about her mom thinking the bank had to be open for her to transfer money electronically.

The next day, Meggan received a text from her mom.

"I transferred your dad's life insurance money into to your bank account. It's not a loan because the money has always been yours. As you know, I had it in an investment fund for you. Your $100k grew over time. Love you."

Meggan logged into her bank account on her phone. A notification on her account page said funds had been received and deposited into her account. She clicked on the account balance link and held her breath while staring at the screen. She quickly logged out and then back in, thinking it must be a mistake. The same balance popped up: $467,933.65.

Meggan got up from her kitchen chair and went to the living room window, looking out in an unfocused daze while clutching her phone, as if it was the source of her new wealth. She wanted to return the money but knew her mother would stubbornly refuse it. Her mother would argue that she didn't need that much money, but neither did Meggan, and she wondered how it would affect her life. A windfall like that might even tempt her to spend it stupidly, the way some lottery winners supposedly do. But her mother had simply socked it away in an investment account and left it there, and that's what Meggan decided to do after paying her basic living expenses, until she found a good paying job. Putting a down payment on another house crossed her mind.

She sat on a kitchen chair and tapped her mother's number into her phone. After four rings she started to hang up, but then her mother answered.

"You're welcome, sweetie, and no, I won't take the money back and you know why. I guess that takes care of our financial business. So, how are you today?"

"I'm breathless, and grateful. But come on, Mom. I want you to keep that money. Keep it for me if you have to, but I feel like you're giving me an inheritance too soon. Besides, you're not getting younger, and an emergency or something might come up."

"I've got insurance for emergencies, and enough invested for the rest. Besides you're not getting younger, either, my dear—sorry to bring that up."

"Okay, but I'll only use enough to help for a while. The rest will be available in case either of us needs it. Okay?"

"Fine, but don't just bury it in your bank account. Make it grow and earn dividends. I'll email you the name of the fund I had it in, but do your own research, and double check any advice so-called experts give you. Most of them are quacks."

"You taught me to be careful a long time ago. By the way, quacks are bad doctors."

"Be careful of those, too."

***

Meggan had a lot to think about at work that night. After closing, while helping Reggie put the chairs and stools up, she struggled with the best way to tell him her decision.

"Reggie, this is difficult for me to say, but I have to leave."

He set the chair he was lifting back down on the floor. "I'd like to give you another raise or more hours, but I just can't right now. But if things pick up this summer…"

"It's not about the money. I just need to go away for a while."

"Where are you going?"

"Vietnam."

He gave Meggan a blank look. "Vietnam?"

"My father was a soldier there during the war and was killed just a few months before I was born. He's still listed as MIA because his remains were never found. I just found out where he was last seen alive, and I want to go there."

"And do what?"

Meggan tilted her head reflectively and looked past him. "I don't know, really. But I want to at least touch the ground where he died. I want to speak to his soul. Maybe I'll discover something about him, something deeper than my mom's recollections or his official service record. Sorry, Reggie. The way I'm feeling is clear to me, but the way I'm explaining it to you isn't."

"Some things don't need to be explained. How long will you be gone?"

"I don't know, maybe a couple of weeks."

***

Meggan called Nancy the next day, and her mother fell silent after the news.

"Mom? Are you still there?"

"Yes, but I'm stunned that you think going to Vietnam is going to make you feel any better. Those people are communists, you know, and they probably hate Americans."

"A lot of American tourists visit Vietnam. It's not like it was forty-five years ago."

"I get that, it just triggers a lot of bad memories of

those times."

"For you, but not for me. Can't you understand that I want to feel some tangible connection with my lost father? All I've heard about is the war that killed him, but I want to find some peace where he fell, like a returning veteran who wants to find healing where trauma once wounded his soul. You've given me the chance to try that. Right now, all I have is his favorite shirt and a photo booth picture, but that's not enough anymore."

"Maybe not, but you won't find anything more about him in Vietnam. I hope you're not setting yourself up for a disappointment."

"I'm not setting myself up for anything, Mom. I'll roll with whatever happens, but if I don't make this trip, I'll always wish I had."

CHAPTER 15

Ho Chi Minh City's Tan Son Nhat airport terminal was almost vacant when Meggan's flight arrived just before midnight. She followed the off-boarded crush of anxious, weary passengers to one of the customs lines. When it was finally her turn to step forward, the customs officer looked at her visa pre-approval paperwork, and said she had to bring that document to the visa counter to pay for the visa.

She registered her name at the visa counter and was told by a sleepy-looking girl in green military uniform that her name would be called when it was her turn. After waiting almost an hour, her name was called out by another female official at one of the glass-protected counters. Meggan slid her visa approval paperwork under the glass window, along with twenty-five US dollars, which the government website instructed visitors to pay upon arrival in Vietnam. The official gave her a frozen look and said the fee was fifty dollars. Meggan told her about the government website's instructions, but the official stiffly said her computer showed fifty dollars, and if she couldn't pay it, she would be put on the next flight out of the country. Meggan pulled her money belt out from underneath her pants waist, removed another twenty-five dollars, and slid it under the glass barrier while glaring at the official, who then told Meggan to take a seat in the waiting area while her visa was being processed. After almost another hour, Meggan was paged back to the counter, where her passport was returned with an official Vietnam visa label adhered to one of the pages.

Meggan was the only person left to pass through the customs counter, and the uniformed official studied her new visa while asking how long she intended to stay in Vietnam, and whether for business or tourism. Her answer of ten days for tourism seemed to satisfy him, and he officiously waved her through without looking at her.

She had a hotel reservation for her first night in Saigon and her travel agent arranged for a driver to pick her up at the airport. When she got outside in the hot muggy night, she looked around for someone holding a paper sign with her name on it. A man approached her and asked in halting English if she needed a taxi.

"No, a driver from my hotel is waiting for me."

"I don't see any drivers. Which hotel?"

"The Renoir Hotel."

"Oh, too bad Miss. That hotel closed."

"But I made a reservation just last week. I gave them a credit card deposit."

"They had very bad fire two days ago. I hope they don't keep your money. I can take you to a hotel better than Renoir, and cheaper. In best part of Saigon."

"I thought the city's name was changed to Ho Chi Minh City."

"It was, but most people still call it Saigon."

Meggan rode uneasily in the backseat of the taxi as the driver raced down lighted streets in the steamy night, passing other cars, going around trucks, and squeezing through small openings in motorbike swarms. On his dashboard, a small statue of Buddha smiled placidly, with a faded wreath of plastic flowers surrounding him. When they stopped for a red traffic light, Meggan rolled up her window to keep the taxi's billowing exhaust outside.

"Hotel very close," the driver said while staring intently at the stop light. When it turned green, he gunned his reluctant engine, but a crowd of nimble motorbikes lurched past him, some with a bored-looking female passenger balanced side-saddle on the back, and a few with drowsy children clutching the driver. Only the adults wore helmets. Some of the motorbikes carried baskets of vegetables or flowers, or bulging clear plastic bags of merchandise, like fluffy toys, clothes, sneakers—all apparently on the way to some marketplace.

The taxi driver turned down a dark side street lined with closed retail shops, all of them with locked iron shutters pulled across their windows and doors. The floors overhead appeared to be apartments, some with balconies, and all the buildings were strung together with tangles of black electric or phone wires that traced back to concrete utility poles.

The driver pulled up to a staircase that led to large double doors. The overhead sign said "Catinat Hotel" with something in Vietnamese below it. The driver turned off his puttering motor, jumped out of the car, and pulled Meggan's suitcase out of the trunk before she could get out of the car. She tried to keep up with him while he trotted toward the door with her suitcase on his shoulder. He pulled the door open and turned to her with a serious look. "Hotel very good. Every room with TV and minibar."

She followed him into the dimly lit lobby where two young men in white shirts were sleeping on their folded arms behind a long reception desk. One of them raised his head with a startled look, taking a moment to regain his senses, and then he stood and wiped his hair back into place. The other man, more a boy, groggily looked up to see what all the disturbance was about.

"Welcome to Catinat Hotel," said the standing clerk.

The taxi driver set Meggan's suitcase on the oriental rug in front of the desk and rattled off something in Vietnamese. The standing clerk replied to him sternly before returning to Meggan with a more pleasant look.

"We have a room available, with full bathroom and mini-bar. Very clean. Free breakfast from six to ten."

"How much for one night?"

"Two million dong."

The number took her by surprise. She struggled with jet-lagged drowsiness while pulling the phone from her purse for an app that could translate that staggering amount into US dollars. While tapping her money conversion app, she paused to realize the vulnerability of her circumstances: she was in a dubious hotel in the middle of the night with three strangers, and no options if she didn't like the deal or the room.

"Do you take US dollars?"

"Certainly." Dropping his perpetual grin for a moment, he picked up a small plastic calculator and tapped in some numbers.

"Ninety US dollars. Very good price."

"Can I use a credit card?"

"Of course, miss."

She was almost delirious with fatigue at this point and just wanted the privacy of a room and a bed.

"Okay," she said, handing over her credit card.

After processing her card, the clerk photocopied Meggan's

passport ID page, and he gave her the hotel's Wi-Fi code. She gave the waiting taxi driver five US dollars without asking his fare, and he seemed delighted with it. The youngest clerk picked up her suitcase and led her up the stairway to the second floor. He used a key to open the door and then gave it to her before taking in her bag. She gave him a dollar, and he responded with a stoic brisk bow before leaving.

Meggan slipped off her shoes and dropped heavily onto the bed. She connected with the hotel's Wi-Fi and used an internet phone app to tap out a message to her travel agent in Hanoi.

"The Renoir Hotel where you booked for me is no longer in business. I had to take a taxi from the airport to find another hotel. I expect a credit for the amount I prepaid. I hope your arrangements for the rest of my trip are more reliable."

After removing her socks, pants and blouse, she slipped under the bedsheet and drifted into a deep sleep.

***

Meggan awoke to roaring buzzes outside that sounded like a riot of chainsaws. She got up and drew back the window curtains, blinking against the brilliant sunlight, just able to see the nearby main street choked mostly with speeding motorbikes relentlessly competing with cars and trucks for space to move in, the entire scene making last night's traffic seem sparse and leisurely. She opened the window for fresh air and inhaled hot humidity laced with exhaust. After quickly shutting the window, she flopped back onto the bed and glanced at her phone. Her Hanoi travel agent had left a text a few hours ago.

Meggan, I am so very sorry that you had to stay in a different hotel. The Renoir Hotel is not closed and we book our customers there very often. Our driver waited for you for a few hours but when the airport terminal was empty, he gave up. You will, of course, get a credit card refund for the $55 room at the Renoir. Please tell me where you are staying now, and I will have a driver meet you in the lobby at 1400 hrs (2 PM) to take you to the airport for your flight to Dalat. If there is ever anything else I can do to make your trip more happy, please contact me ASAP. If you would like a short city tour before going to the airport, I will have the driver come at 1100 hrs. When you arrive in Dalat, a driver will be there with your name on a sign. His name is Vu, and he has a very good car.

Meggan tapped in "Catinat Hotel" as a response, and included the address, which she found on a hotel directory in the small writing desk's drawer. She asked to have the driver come 11 AM, which was checkout time.

After a quick shower, she went downstairs where a breakfast buffet had been set up in a room adjoining the lobby. A few Asians sat at various tables, engrossed in consuming their breakfast, most of them pulling drenched white noodles from bowls to their mouths with chopsticks, and ladling up the broth with metal soup spoons. Two soups simmered on hotplates, one labeled Miso and one Pho Bo, with bowls of lettuce and basil on the table next to them. On the next table, apples and oranges were piled on platters next to a large basket filled with small baguettes, and a bowl of butter packets scattered on ice cubes. Pitchers of orange juice and milk had cloth napkins over them, and a half-filled glass pot of coffee sat on a hotplate. Meggan poured a cup of coffee and took an orange and baguette to a table set for four people. No one seemed to notice her. She wondered about that, since she was obviously the only Westerner in the room. Were they being polite, indifferent—rude? She suddenly felt very alone. Did anyone here speak English? She hoped her driver did.

While checking out at 10:30 AM, she noticed a petite young woman sitting in one of the big square armchairs in the lobby. She had a black notebook resting on her lap. As soon as Meggan collected her credit card receipt, the woman sprang to her feet and cautiously approached Meggan.

"Are you Miss Meggan?"

"Yes, are you my driver?" Meggan wondered if she was really the one sent by her travel agent, or if this was an imposter set up by the hotel.

"No, the driver is with the car. I am your city tour guide, sent by your Hanoi travel agent. My name is Hanh." She gave the front desk clerk a scowl before turning back to Meggan, and whispered, "Renoir is much better hotel than here. This hotel is state run." She glanced at a young bellhop idly draped over one of the uncomfortable-looking reception area chairs. "Poorly trained workers. Are you ready for a city tour?"

"Yes, but I need to change some US dollars into Vietnamese money. Can you have the driver take me to a bank?"

"Exchange rate is better on the street. I will take you."

Feeling more assured about Hanh's legitimacy, she followed her out the door to the busy sidewalk, with the bellhop following at a distance with her suitcase. Hanh made a call from her phone and smiled at Meggan, assuring her the driver would be there soon, that he had to park a few blocks away because of morning traffic. A motorbike rider soon pulled up in front of the hotel, with the word "TAXI" printed in large letters on the back of his helmet. Meggan's reflexive unease was relieved when Hanh approached a white compact sedan that was pulling into the loading zone next to them.

A serious-looking middle-aged man jumped out and grabbed Meggan's suitcase while Hanh rushed to open the back door for her. After Meggan got in, Hanh gently closed the door and trotted around to the other side, getting in next to Meggan. After the driver deposited Meggan's suitcase in the trunk, he got in and sped away.

Hanh said something to the driver in Vietnamese, and then turned to Meggan.

"We'll stop to change money, and then start our tour."

The driver dropped them off at a corner jewelry shop with an open-air counter. People were lined up on the sidewalk holding foreign currency to exchange for Vietnamese dong, or wads of dong to exchange for foreign money. Four clerks were thumb-counting money like casino dealers, and tapping on small calculators to determine the exchange value. There was no negotiating. Hanh cautioned Meggan to exchange only what she'd need over the next few days because she would take a sizable loss converting it back for US dollars. Hanh said all hotels and most restaurants will take US dollars, but at a lower exchange rate than here. A clerk counted out sixty US dollars' worth of dong bills for Meggan, most in denominations of 500,000, each of those worth about twenty US dollars.

Their first tourism stop was a three-story Buddhist temple, where Meggan walked alongside Hanh while she recited fact after fact about the Bodhisattva who the temple commemorates, what the bowls of food on the altars meant, and why smoldering incense sticks were stuck in sand-filled containers. Hanh explained the meaning of various statues and paintings, and the monks' chants.

"Hanh, is there a toilet near here?"

"Yes, but maybe no paper." She took a few sheets of facial tissue from her shoulder bag and furtively slipped them to Meggan while looking away.

Hanh was waiting for her outside when Meggan emerged from the women's room, and Meggan followed her to the car, which was parked down the street. The driver popped out to open the back door for Meggan, while Hanh opened her own door.

"Are you a Buddhist?" Meggan asked when they were inside.

"I'm Catholic."

"You know a lot about Buddhism."

"It's my job, and I used to be a Buddhist. We have enough time left to see either the War Remnants Museum or the Independence Palace."

"Which would you recommend?"

"They are both very interesting about our history."

"Independence sounds more interesting than war."

Hanh said something to the driver in Vietnamese, who clicked on a turn signal without replying, and promptly drifted in between motorbikes in the adjoining lane. He turned again two blocks later and pulled into a long driveway to a large government-looking four-story building. They passed by two tanks displayed on tandem concrete slabs on the large grassy lawn.

Hanh looked through the window on Meggan's side. "Those are T-34 Russian tanks. The front one was the first to crash through the gates on April 30, 1975, the beginning of reunification."

"Why did it crash through?"

"This was the Presidential Palace back then." Hanh offered no further explanation, as if the rest of the story was common knowledge.

They spent almost an hour roaming through the building's commodious high-ceilinged meeting rooms, walked down stairways to stark underground war rooms, and strolled through elegant private offices on the top floor, one of them once occupied by Bao Dai, last emperor of Vietnam, and then taken over by President Diem, the Republic of Vietnam's first head of state.

Meggan dozed on the way to the airport. Traveling through thirteen time zones over the last three days was catching up with her, and she was further dulled by the monotonous press of traffic and Saigon's hot muggy climate, which was a drag on her senses after being acclimated to Minnesota's recent cold winter months. When her eyes drew open, Hanh was just finishing a text message she was tapping into her phone.

"My father was a soldier here during the war," Meggan said, more to break the tedium than to start a conversation. "Were any of your family members in the war?"

"My grandparents fought with the Vietcong."

Just before noon, they pulled up to Tan Son Nhat airport terminal. The driver deposited Meggan's suitcase on the curb with a slight bow, and Hanh gave Meggan her ticket to Dalat, wishing her well during the rest of her time in Vietnam. Meggan gave Hanh a five-dollar bill, and two ones to the driver. They both nodded politely and expressionlessly, got into the car and drove off.

At the airline check-in counter, Meggan was told by young woman in a blue and white traditional dress that her bag was too large to carry on, and it would have to be checked. When Meggan explained that all other airlines allowed her to carry a bag this size, the clerk merely smiled. She was soon joined by a uniformed older male who did not smile.

Meggan lifted her suitcase onto the scale, hoping she'd see it again when she got to Dalat.

CHAPTER 16

The flight from Ho Chi Minh City to Dalat took a little less than an hour. Meggan had an aisle seat assigned, but her row was empty so she slid over to the window. The green terrain below looked like an endless living blanket, with an occasional patches of different greens, which she surmised were fields or rice paddies. She strained to see any details, guessing that the occasional specks along thin roads and weaving rivers were villages.

After landing, she followed the small crowd of passengers hastily making their way to the baggage claim area. While waiting along the conveyor belt, her anxiety grew as each bag that wasn't hers was tossed intermittently through a hatch and onto a slide to the conveyor. After a few minutes, Meggan and a young Vietnamese woman in skinny black jeans and a pink shirt were the only ones waiting. Meggan's bag was thrown down the slide next, but after grabbing it she lingered to make sure the other woman's bag would appear. It finally did, and the woman nonchalantly wheeled her suitcase past Meggan toward the exit.

Inside the terminal, she saw a man was holding a sheet of paper with "Meggan" written on it. He watched her attentively while she approached him.

"I'm Meggan Mondae," she said.

He nodded eagerly. "I am Vu, the driver your travel agent sent to bring you to your hotel. Welcome to Dalat, my lovely home. I think you find it the most beautiful place in Vietnam."

She looked at the nearby parking lot, surrounded by a grove of tall pine trees just beyond. "It looks very nice, from what I can see so far."

"Come with me please, I'll take you to your hotel very quickly." He took her suitcase and carried it on his shoulder toward the parking lot. "I hope I can show you much more while you are here. We have a beautiful lake in Dalat. The 'Da' means lake, and the 'Lat' are the people who first settled here."

"What happened to them?"

"They are still here. They have farms on land at the edge of the city. When the city needs to expand, they sell their land and move farther out."

"That's too bad."

"Oh, no—too good. Each time they make more money to buy even more farm land."

"What do they grow?"

"Coffee, of course. Everyone with garden space grows coffee here, even me. And the Lat people have many greenhouses to grow flowers and vegetables. Truck drivers leave late every night to take their greenhouse harvests to the Saigon and Hanoi markets."

"It sounds like the Lat people have become modern."

"Their school is modern. The playground even has basketball hoops from America. But the Lat people have not changed their traditional ways. They haven't needed to. The communist government leaves them alone to govern themselves."

Meggan tried to sort that string of information into a meaningful pattern while Vu put her suitcase in the back of his white SUV, and then he opened the passenger door for her.

While driving into the city, Meggan said, "You have many tall red pine trees here, like in Minnesota, where I live."

"The French people brought pine trees here to help them remember France. The falling needles are poison, and kill everything trying to grow underneath them."

She then noticed the lack of undergrowth and tried to recall if she had seen that in Minnesota.

"Miss, the hotel you are going to, the Royal Tiger, is state run. If you like, I can call your travel agent and request a change to a privately-owned hotel."

Meggan rolled her eyes, believing Vu to be another hotel hustler trying to earn a kickback on the side. "Would you please just take me to the Royal Tiger Hotel."

"Yes, of course," Vu said cheerfully. "I will take you quickly."

When they pulled up to the hotel's lobby entrance, Vu ran around to open Meggan's door, but she was already stepping out so he shifted his attention to her suitcase. He carried it ahead of her past two uniformed staffers who showed no interest in helping. Vu opened the front door and escorted her past a similarly uniformed boy who stood in the reception area for no apparent reason, and Vu deposited her suitcase on the floor in front of the reception counter.

"I have my day free tomorrow. Would you like a tour of the city?"

"I don't think so, but thank you anyway."

"The Dalat Flower Garden and Zen Monastery are very lovely. One hundred percent of my customers love them."

"No thanks."

"Maybe a look at the countryside?"

"Vu, I'm tired, jetlagged, and not interested in hearing about touring right now, okay?" She pulled a dollar bill from her money belt and gave it to him. "Goodbye, and thanks for the ride."

Vu pocketed the dollar and took a business card from his shirt pocket. "Here is my phone number. Please call if I can help you in any way."

Meggan took his card and when he left, she waited for the cute receptionist to finish a transaction with the couple ahead of her. After giving them their keys, she turned to Meggan and said, "Good afternoon. How can I help you?"

"A room should be reserved for me. My name is Meggan Mondae." Meggan glanced back to see Vu leaving through the front door. Now that she could finally look forward to a shower and nap, she regretted acting so snippily toward him.

"May I see your passport, please? I just need to make a copy." When the receptionist finished making a photocopy, she returned it to Meggan.

"I think your driver is not a licensed guide. I hope he was good for you. How many days are you staying with us?"

"Seven or eight days. The driver was good, but a taxi driver in Ho Chi Minh City lied to make me change hotels."

"I am very sorry to hear that. Are you using a credit card?"

"Yes." After handing the credit card to the receptionist, Meggan said, "Do you know any licensed drivers? I'd like to see a place that's supposed to be near Dalat."

"Yes, I know licensed guides who help many of our guests." The young woman swiped Meggan's card and returned it. "They know everything about Dalat."

"What about areas outside of Dalat?"

"Licensed guides know all about the Central Highlands: the hill tribe peoples, the coffee visitor center, agricultural economic zones. You can ride an elephant if you want to. I know a guide with a very good car. His name is Duc. He will make your tourism very lovely if he's available. This is the busiest season except for Tet, but if all the guides are booked, I can arrange a ride on the back of a motorbike."

"No motorbikes, thanks, and no elephants. Can I have a meal delivered to my room?"

The young receptionist looked troubled. "We only have stir-fried beef right now."

"That's fine. Does it come with rice?"

"The cook can make rice for you."

The receptionist gave Megan a room key chained to a wood disk with the room number on it, and then waved palm-downward for the uniformed boy standing in the lobby. She said something to him in Vietnamese, and he picked up Meggan's suitcase. Meggan wondered whether anyone knew her suitcase had wheels, or if carrying it showed some kind of deference. She followed him up the stairs to her room, and after she unlocked the door, he set her suitcase inside on the floor, and left without a word, without lingering for a tip.

She looked around the austere room. A small humming refrigerator contained two cans of Saigon Special beer, two plastic bottles of water, and two cans of either soda or juice with a cluster of oranges on the label. The main attraction for Meggan was the cramped bathroom's shower, which she planned to indulge in after her late lunch. She set her suitcase on the bed and took out her indoor flip-flops, dropping them next to the bed. She removed her water bottle and hand-held ultraviolet water purifier. After filling her bottle from the bathroom faucet, she turned on the battery-powered purifier and stirred the water for two minutes, trusting it to kill any viruses or bacteria. After that chore, she lay on the bed and half-dozed luxuriously.

Her eyes popped open at a light tap on her door. She sat up groggily and slipped on her flip-flops, wondering if she had fallen asleep, and opened the door. The receptionist forced a smile while holding an obviously heavy tray of dishes covered with stainless steel lids. She walked past Meggan and carefully set the tray on the small writing desk next to the refrigerator.

"I hope this meal is good for you. I'm sorry it's all we have today."

"It'll be fine, thanks." Meggan quickly pulled a couple of dollars from her money belt and gave them to the girl, who looked at the dollars and then gave Meggan an astonished look.

"Breakfast is served from 6 to 10:30 AM. Please call the front desk if you need anything."

As the girl left, Meggan lifted metal covers off a bowl of hot rice and then a plate of sliced beef stir-fried with onions and basil in a fragrant sauce. She opened the paper sleeve containing disposable chopsticks and used them to pick pieces from the stir-fry and place them into the bowl of rice. Before coming to Vietnam, she had watched an internet video to learn how to properly handle chopsticks and practiced with a pair of pencils. Although there was a fork on the tray, an apparent courtesy for Westerners, she determinedly worked through the savory meal with just the chopsticks, using them to transfer saucy pieces of beef and vegetables to the rice bowl, and then raking the mixture into her mouth.

Meggan checked her watch, which she had set to Vietnam time when she changed flights in Tokyo. It was almost five o'clock in the afternoon, and although she was still sleepy, she wanted to recalibrate her jetlagged brain to local time by not allowing herself to sleep anymore until at least nine PM. She locked her suitcase, put her dinner tray outside her door, and then walked to the hotel lobby. The receptionist was doing something in the backroom and rushed to the counter when she saw Meggan waiting.

"Everything alright for you?"

Meggan handed her the room key to store it. "Yes, I put the tray outside my door."

"I will take care of it."

"Is it safe to walk alone around the hotel area?"

"Oh, yes, you are safe anywhere in Dalat. It's not like Saigon or Hanoi. Some people here even leave keys in their cars."

Meggan went outside and walked warily along the sidewalk, catching furtive glances now and then, but she saw no one gawking at her, even though she was obviously the only Westerner in sight. There were far fewer motorbikes than in Saigon, even fewer cars and trucks, and all vehicles moved slower and more cautiously—perhaps even more considerately—than in Saigon. Most of the motorbike riders, especially the females, wore white surgical masks that stayed in place with loops around their ears.

She stopped at an open-air stand that sold small plastic bags of fruits and nuts, canned beer, and roasted coffee beans in three clear plastic bins with a scale next to them. A man from a butcher shop next door was starting to move his sidewalk wares inside. He took bowls of chicken pieces, pans of whole fish on ice, and racks of beef cuts inside, where, presumably, they would be refrigerated overnight. She watched him then take in wiggling fat bullfrogs, all crowded into a large steel bowl with a screen over it, a cage with three colorful chickens inside, and a pan of sluggish softshell crabs.

The only shop sign not totally in Vietnamese was above the door of the Swiss Coffee House. She stepped inside for a peek. The wall menu showed four photographs of bowls of noodle soups, all of them looking the same to Meggan, and three baguette sandwiches that also seemed identical. After her late lunch at the hotel, she wasn't hungry, but she thought a cup of coffee would perk her up.

About half of the tables were occupied, mostly toward the back of the room. She sat at the first available table, and a waitress leisurely made her way toward her.

"What would you like, miss?"

"Coffee, please. I was worried that no one could speak English."

"This is a very good restaurant for you because most waiters speak some English. Do you want Vietnamese style coffee?"

"I've never had that before, but sure."

"Hot or iced?"

"Hot, please."

"Sweet milk okay?'

"Sure."

A few minutes later the waitress brought a tray with a can of milk, a glass carafe of steaming water, a glass coffee cup, and a small metal strainer. She set the coffee cup in front of Meggan and poured a small amount of condensed canned milk into it. She then set the strainer on the cup and added three tablespoons of ground coffee. She trickled in two teaspoons of hot water from the carafe, and while waiting a moment, the waitress said, "This wakes the coffee." She then filled the metal strainer with hot water from the carafe and put a metal lid on it. Dark coffee began dripping slowly into the glass.

The waitress took a saucer from her tray and put it next to the coffee cup, and then picked up the tray holding the carafe and milk. "After the dripping stops, about five minutes, you can take off the filter and put it on the saucer, and then stir to mix in the milk."

Before returning to the kitchen, she smiled for the first time, perhaps because she had performed this popular Vietnamese ritual for a first-timer.

Wondering if this was just a tourist thing, Meggan glanced around to see if other customers were drinking coffee this way. A few had identical metal strainers sitting on saucers, but most drank from white ceramic coffee mugs. She lifted the strainer's lid and saw the filtering process slowly progressing, making her realize that five minutes seemed longer when you're anxious for it to pass. She sat back in her chair and casually watched the drips and perused the wall menu photos again, trying to look nonchalant.

When the drips became excruciatingly slower, she lifted the strainer cover again to check the water level. While holding the lid off, a tall man in jeans and a blue-green polo shirt came into the restaurant and walked by her table, slowing a step while he exchanged glances with her. His neatly combed black hair looked almost dark brown, something she had not seen in Vietnamese men. At first glance, she thought he was a Westerner, but then saw a definite Asian influence in his striking looks.

Meggan self-consciously returned her attention to the final slow drips of coffee while the man strode up to the waitress's station. Two cheery waitresses were all atwitter when he approached the counter, and a third girl came out from the kitchen with a wide grin, saying something in Vietnamese that the other two considered laughable. After exchanging a few words, one of the waitresses poured coffee into a disposable paper coffee cup for him. He paid her, and without turning around nodded his head backward and said something quietly. The three waitresses glanced at Meggan and said something to him with earnest expressions. He took a sip of his coffee and turned to leave, smiling almost imperceptibly at Meggan on the way out. She stopped stirring her coffee and looked up, but he was gone before she could figure out how to respond: Did he really smile? If so, was it for her, or about her? She turned, but he was already out the door, and while taking her first sip of coffee, not thinking about the taste, looked back and saw a new-looking shiny black jeep slowly pass by the coffee shop's glass door, with him at the wheel.

When Meggan finished her coffee, she went to the counter to pay for it. The waitress who had served her helped Meggan choose which of the large-denomination dong bills would be best, and then gave Meggan several dongs for change. When she offered one of the 100,000 dong bills as a tip, the waitress shook her head and said, "Too much." She pointed to one for 20,000 dong and said, "This one better for a tip."

"Is the man who owns the jeep a Vietnamese?"

"Yes. His name is Tran Van Tam. His family is very important. They control many, many hectares of coffee and black pepper."

"Do they live in Dalat?"

"They have a villa on the edge of the city, and a family compound outside of the city near their coffee gardens."

Not trusting the availability of food at the hotel's restaurant, she pointed to a photo of a French baguette sandwich on the wall menu, labeled *Bahn Mi*, and asked to have it to go. The cashier barked something into the kitchen, and the cook soon brought her sandwich out on a plate. The cashier wrapped it in white paper and put it in a plastic bag.

The sun began to sink in the darkening sky, leaving tints of pink and orange on high thin clouds spreading off the surrounding mountain tops. Many of the shops were turning on interior lights and the traffic began to relax. Young people were beginning to cluster into small groups around the center of the city, many of them sampling street vendor snacks. The groups of girls continually giggled about one thing or another, while stoic boys, trailing at a distance in pairs or solo, pretended to not notice them. Most of people wore jackets or sweaters, but the cool evening air hadn't registered on Meggan's cold-climate sensibilities.

Although she had only ventured a few blocks from her hotel, she thought this might be enough of an adventure for her first day in Dalat. Back at the hotel, she stopped again at the reception desk and caught the attention of another front desk woman who was sorting papers. She brightened as Meggan approached.

"Yes, miss?"

"The receptionist last night recommended a licensed tour guide named Duc."

"Yes, I know him."

"He has a car and speaks English, right?"

"Certainly. He can give you a city tour or country tour."

"I'd like to go to the country, but not exactly a tour. I want to visit a particular mountain."

"There are many mountains all around Dalat."

"I know, but this one is near a village called Bang Dia."

The receptionist paused, but gave no other sign of possible confusion. "Of course, miss. Duc should know where that is. When would you like to be picked up?"

"Ten o'clock tomorrow morning, if that's possible."

"Yes, of course. I will contact Mr. Duc."

"Thank you."

The receptionist beamed. "I hope your mountain tour will be very lovely."

Meggan opened a can of Saigon Special beer from her room's minibar refrigerator and ate her sandwich, discovering that it was pork with pickled carrots, cucumbers, cilantro and a few slices of chili peppers, perhaps other herbs, and a hint of vinegar. After finishing the sandwich, she got her ball of orange yarn and knitting needles out of her suitcase. While adding rows to the scarf she was knitting, she wondered about the man in the coffee shop. She speculated that he was either the town playboy—given the way he flirted with the coffee shop waitresses, and maybe even with her—or just a tease; perhaps someone's husband, although she hadn't noticed a ring on his finger. Even if he was married, Vietnam might be one of those countries where married men, especially rich ones, could womanize freely and openly, without shame.

She caught herself speculating way too much about that stranger in the coffee shop, and wondered if this is how she had sized up other men in her life, first guessing about them and then believing her assumptions—only to later suffer from the blunders. She reminded herself that she had traveled to Vietnam for only one purpose, and she had only a few days to accomplish it. There would be no time for distractions.

CHAPTER 17

A ringing phone startled her awake the next morning. She looked at the watch still on her wrist: a few minutes after 10 AM. She answered the bedside phone, trying to sound calm while her heart raced. The reception clerk told her Mr. Duc was waiting in the lobby.

"Tell him I'll be down as soon as I can, okay?"

"Yes, of course."

She ran to the bathroom and then slipped on khaki cargo pants and a purple long-sleeved shirt. She remembered to bring her sunglasses, floppy brimmed blue cap, and her water bottle—and stuffed all of that into her shoulder tote bag, draped it over her neck, and padlocked her suitcase zippers together before trotting down the stairs almost out of breath.

The receptionist from yesterday was back on duty, calmly smiling at her as if she had nothing else to do. She escorted Meggan to the lobby exit and said Duc was the man on his phone, standing next to the black sedan parked in front.

Meggan stopped a few feet away from Duc while he finished his call. As soon as he saw her, he finished his call and shoved the phone into a belt case.

"Miss Meggan?"

"Yes, are you Mr. Duc?"

"Yes." His eyes showed lines that usually came with middle age. He wore a thin black mustache, and his somewhat darkened skin color suggested perhaps a life of working outdoors.

She walked closer to him. "Do you charge by the hour or by the mile?"

"By the day, miss. One hundred dollars for everything except meals and tour fees, but your special price as a Royal Tiger Hotel guest is only eighty dollars. How many days will you be in Dalat?"

"Just four or five; maybe less, depending on my success at finding a certain place."

"There are many good places in Dalat. Would you like to start with a city tour today?"

"I'm interested in going to a village called Bang Dia. There's a mountain near there I want to see, and I'd like to walk up it if I can. Do you know where Bang Dia is? I was told by someone who had been there that it was west of Dalat."

"I have heard the name."

He opened his car's trunk and took a map out. The well-worn creases where it had been repeatedly folded had been clear-taped to hold it together. He unfolded a section of it on the hood of his car. Meggan joined him and tried to see the names of areas and towns along a road he was slowly tracing with his finger.

"How long ago did your friend go to that place?"

"About forty-five years ago."

Duc looked up with dismay. "A long time. During the American war?"

She had never heard that name for the war. "Yes, that's right."

"Oh, now I remember that village. It was destroyed after

reunification."

"Destroyed? Why?"

"The people who lived there helped the Americans instead of supporting the Vietcong who controlled the area. After the war, many of the villagers were sent to reeducation camps or prison, and all the houses were burned. Many villages in the south were rubbed out like that."

"Can you show me on the map where Bang Dia was?"

Duc moved his finger around the map until he found Dalat again and slid it slightly to the west to a thin line, apparently indicating a minor road. "It was this area," he said.

Meggan strained to see if there were any names of villages, but the area appeared isolated and barren of any landmarks. "Can you take me there?"

"Yes, but there is nothing to see anymore."

"There's a mountain near there, right?"

"Of course. There are mountains everywhere."

"I'd like to see that area. Will there be enough time today?"

Duc stared at the map and tapped it lightly while looking up, as if contemplating the scope of the trip.

"Yes," he finally announced. "We will have enough time."

"Do I pay you when we return?"

"That's fine, however you like. Are you ready to go now?"

Meggan trembled with excitement. She would soon see the ground where her father fell, where he was denied any hope of rejoining her mother, where he was denied ever knowing his unborn child.

"Yes, I'm ready."

Duc stopped at an open-air grocery store to get extra bottles of water and "fast food," which meant baguette sandwiches, for the trip. Meggan paid for them and put the water bottles in cup holders between the front seats, and then set the bag of paper-wrapped sandwiches on the back seat for later. While doing this, Duc was on his phone a few feet from the car. He paced back and forth nervously, saying something forcefully in Vietnamese, pausing occasionally to listen intently. He finally slid his phone back into the belt case and checked his watch.

"Okay, we go," he said while striding toward the driver's side of the car. "I called to make sure the roads were clear. There is sometimes too much highway repairing."

While driving through an industrial section beyond the city's center, Meggan saw what looked like a derelict airport control tower. It was surrounded by one-level concrete buildings and a commodious round-roofed hangar inside a chain-link fence that was covered with wild leafy vines.

"Is this airport still used?" she asked Duc.

"Yes, mostly army helicopters. During the war, it was an American airfield."

"Are there any private airplanes here?"

"No, but sometimes an airplane comes from Hanoi to pick up a coffee businessman who lives near here."

"He must grow a lot of coffee."

"He's not a farmer. His family buys coffee from many coffee growers and exports it. Vietnam is now the number one coffee exporter in the world."

"Because of him?"

"Not just him. There are two other coffee exporters. One is another Vietnamese company in Hanoi, and the other is a company from Holland."

"What's the coffee businessman's name?"

"Con Rong. It means '*The Dragon.*' The second part sounds like 'zong' but it is spelled R-O-N-G."

"Is that his real name?"

"No one knows his real name, except his family and the highest people in Vietnam's Communist Party."

"Why is he called The Dragon?"

"Because he is very powerful and dangerous, but rarely seen. I know someone who thinks he saw him from a distance, but I never have."

Meggan wondered about this mysterious person while Duc concentrated on the narrow asphalt road, dodging potholes, some large enough to threaten a tire. She mused that the reputation of Con Rong made him sound like some kind of legendary fairytale hero or kung fu master. Then she remembered the man in the Swiss Coffee House. The waitress said he owned coffee and black pepper farms.

"Is Con Rong about my age?"

"No, he is very old."

"Does he live in Dalat?"

"He owns a restored French villa in Dalat, but no one knows where Con Rong will be at any one time. He lives in other places, too, like his research center on the way to Buon Ma Thuot. Everyone, like you, wants to know more about Con Rong, but he is always in the shadows."

"I'm not really that curious, but someone told me about a man around my age who owns coffee and black pepper fields."

"Many, many people in the hill country grow coffee and black pepper."

***

After just over an hour, the road climbed alongside mountains, with steep cliffs above them on one side and deep valleys beneath them on the other. Duc increased his speed along the short straightaways when he could. They passed a row of boxy concrete houses, all of them surrounded by white tarps covering what little level ground could be found. Duc said they were drying coffee berries.

After Duc rounded a blind corner, a policeman in a crisp khaki uniform stepped out onto the road and waved them over with a thick short baton with black and white stripes. Duc came to a gradual stop on a shoulder a few yards from the policeman.

Meggan turned around and saw two more policemen standing next to a patrol car.

Duc said, "This is very bad. Stay here, and if they talk to you, just say I am your friend. If they think you are paying me, they will want more money."

He got out of the car and walked back to the policemen. She saw him speaking to the man with the baton while the other two looked on. After a few minutes Duc came back to his car with a foreboding expression and opened the driver's side door without getting in.

"They said I didn't have my turn signal on when coming around that curve."

"You have to signal for curves?"

"It's not the law but they said so, and they are the police. They said they will have to escort us to Buon Mi Thuot for a hearing. It's about four hours from here, and we will be in jail until a hearing can be scheduled, maybe in a few days."

"Oh, my God! This is ridiculous. Why do I have to go to jail? I didn't do anything."

"I told them that, but we both must go. Besides, you would have no way to return to Dalat."

"Do they have an American embassy in the town we're going to?

"No, only in Hanoi."

"I would miss my flight home. This can't be happening. I want to talk to them."

"I don't think they speak English."

"You can interpret. Tell them I will report this to the American embassy."

"I don't think they will care, but I will tell them. Wait here, please."

Duc shut the door and went back to the policemen. After several minutes of conversation, Duc returned to the car.

"They will let us go free if we pay them a fine."

"You mean a bribe?"

"A fine. They will let us go and then share the money."

"How much do they want?"

"One thousand dollars."

"Wow! Do you have that much?"

"I have about fifty dollars' worth of dongs."

"I don't carry near that much cash. Will they take a credit card?"

"No credit cards. How much money do you have with you?"

"About five hundred dollars, but that's all I'll have for travel expenses, meals and transportation—and to pay you."

"Don't worry about me. I'll try to make a deal with them."

Meggan watched Duc saunter back to the policemen, and after another long conversation, he finally returned to the car. He opened his door and leaned in.

"I told them all we have is three hundred dollars. They agreed to accept that."

Meggan exhaled in relief and yanked her money waist belt out, quickly pulling out her US dollars before the policemen changed their minds. She counted out three hundred dollars and gave it to Duc.

"You should give it to them," he said. "They might arrest me for having that many US dollars. I will go with you."

Meggan zipped her money belt shut and stuffed it back under her pants waist. She opened her door with a shaky hand, took a deep breath and followed Duc back to where the policemen were waiting. Duc instructed her to fold the stack of bills and hand it to the policeman closest to her. While she did, another policeman took a photo with his cellphone. A souvenir, Meggan quickly assumed, to show their buddies how they swindled an American.

When they got back to Duc's car, Meggan bristled with anger.

"They must stop every car that comes down this road. Nobody's going to signal for a curve, for God's sake. The road curves every few feet on this mountain road."

"They wait for the cars with tourists because they know they have money."

"How could they have spotted me so fast?"

"They probably knew we were coming. The policemen reward spies along the route when they call ahead. Any of the people raking their drying coffee berries back there could have been a spy."

As she began to calm, Meggan reflected that she had once again, like at the Tan Son Nhat visa desk, been blackmailed by a government official—but with higher stakes this time.

"Duc, I think corruption will hurt progress in your country."

"It's a system we are used to. Policemen do not get paid enough to take care of their families, so they have to collect fines when they can. You don't have this system in America, but you might pay higher taxes. The cost could be the same."

"Do the policemen's bosses know what they are doing?"

"The policemen pay their boss for control over certain sections of the roads. Everyone has to earn a living."

"You know a lot about how this works."

"All Vietnamese do. Now you do."

After a few miles, Duc pulled into the gravel parking area of a dilapidated concrete building surrounded by scattered weeds. The building sat on the edge of a steep bluff. There were no other cars parked in sight, and Meggan wondered if it had been abandoned. Duc got out and headed toward the door, and Meggan caught up with him.

"This is the place," Duc said unceremoniously.

"What place?"

"The place you were looking for. I'll show you the mountain on the other side of the valley."

Meggan followed Duc inside, past a staring woman who sat on a blue patio chair. They made their way around scattered plastic tables and chairs to the back of what was apparently a restaurant, to a patio with a knee-high wall that overlooked a valley of small farmland plots, all of them separated by dense scrub forests. Duc pointed to a distant mountain that looked like any other she had seen along the way, with craggy rock outcroppings on top, and choked with wild bramble the rest of the way down. It was nothing like the woodland wilderness she had imagined after talking to Mike Sumner, the man who had survived and described the battle where her father was last seen alive.

"A veteran I know who was in a battle there said the mountain was covered by trees."

"Rains wash the loose soil over time, leaving only rocks and dirt."

"Are there any roads to the mountain?"

"No, entry to the area is forbidden by the government

because landmines from the war are still buried there."

"But what about all those farms?"

"They stay far enough away from the mountain."

Meggan stared at the mountain's rough reddish crest, rendering it uglier than the surrounding hills, a lonely derelict that deepened her already-low spirits. She couldn't imagine how soldiers could move across its steep ridges. She tried to accept that her father's decomposed remains had likely been rain-washed down to the foot of the dingy mountain, forever barricaded by live landmines.

"Let's go, Duc. I've seen enough."

On the way back to Dalat, they spoke very little. Meggan needed the silence and Duc apparently felt the same way. She surmised that he, too, regretted coming here. Not only did he have to put up with the hassle of driving over lousy, boring roads to satisfy her weird request, but he also had to suffer the humiliation of a bogus police shakedown—and then forgoing his fee from Meggan.

It had been disheartening for Meggan to see that ragtag restaurant as the only remnant of the destroyed village called Bang Dia. She wondered if Duc had just guessed which mountain was the correct one so he could just call it a miserable day and go home. She couldn't blame him. She finally realized this trip had been a harebrained idea from the beginning. It was time to go home, forget about all this, and find a job.

CHAPTER 18

After Duc let Meggan off at the hotel late that afternoon, she remembered that she had left the "fast food" sandwiches she had purchased in the back seat of his car. But she was too tired to walk around searching for a place to eat, and hoped the hotel had more than one choice for supper. While freshening up in her room, she thought about the Swiss Coffee House. The pictured menu on their wall showed only soups and sandwiches, but it was familiar, and the servers spoke English.

She took her time strolling the three blocks to the coffee shop, stopping to peek into clothing shop windows. They appeared to carry only Western-style garments, a surprise to her because the online tourist photos showed Vietnamese pedaling bicycles, clad in what looked like black pajamas, wearing flip-flops and traditional conical straw hats. Given the scene around her now, she wondered how many decades ago those photos had been taken. Most people now wore jeans and tee shirts or polo shirts, and either sneakers or rubber slip-on shoes. Men wore baseball-style caps, if any cap at all. Motorbikes are favored over bicycles now, except by a few elderly people, and Asian automobiles have replaced the aging French Citroens that Meggan had seen in those website photos.

The Swiss Coffee House was buzzing with activity, a surprise because it was about the same time of day that she first had coffee there. It appeared that soup was the most popular meal. Most people ate alone, using chopsticks to pull up the white noodles.

The same waitress came to her table, and Meggan asked about the soup.

"It is Pho Bo, which means beef noodle soup. It is our number-one specialty, and I think you will enjoy it very greatly."

"What kind of beef is it?"

"The best in Vietnam. Beef cattle are raised all over the lower hills near Dalat."

Megan ordered Pho Bo and a Saigon Special beer, her new regular brand. She worried about being able to maneuver the slippery noodles up with chopsticks, so she tried to watch other diners without seeming conspicuous. The idea, she decided, was to pull as many noodles as possible to one's mouth, which should be close over the bowl, and bite off a mouthful. Bite-size pieces of beef were also tweezered up with the chopsticks. A metal soup spoon lay next to every bowl, but she didn't see anyone use them for the broth.

The waitress brought the can of beer and a glass first, and a few minutes later she brought a large steaming bowl of the beef noodle soup. Meggan positioned the disposable wood chopsticks in her hand and practiced a few pinches before trying them with the noodles. No one seemed to notice her, but she suspected that everyone would notice if she failed to get the noodles to her mouth. On her first try, she captured several strands of fat noodles, but most of them slipped out of her chopsticks before her mouth reached them. She side-glanced, but no one was looking. She lowered her face closer to the bowl and tried again, concentrating this time on steadying her finger grip. More rice noodles and even a bit of beef made it to her mouth this time, and she bit off a victorious mouthful.

"Would you like a fork?"

The man's voice came from next to her. She turned and looked up at the man she had seen buying a cup of coffee yesterday. He looked worried for her.

"I can ask someone to bring you one." There was no discernable accent in his English.

"I'll be fine," she said, unable to think of something else to say, but wishing she could ask him about his fluent American English.

He came around and stood across from her so she didn't have to turn her head. "The noodle soup here is the best in Dalat, don't you think?"

"This is my first time to try pho."

"How long have you been in Dalat?"

"Just two days."

He acknowledged that with a thoughtful nod and an awkward moment of silence, and without another word he went to the cashier counter and got a cup of coffee in a paper cup, like he did yesterday. The waitresses were too busy to chatter with him today, so he paid and started to leave, pausing again at Meggan's table.

"How long will you be here?"

She was balancing an impressive load of noodles in her chopsticks but let them slide back into the bowl.

"I'm leaving tomorrow, if I can change my airline ticket."

"So soon?"

"Things haven't worked out very well for me."

A serious look tightened across his face. "May I sit for a moment?"

She started to feel a little uncomfortable. "Okay…"

He set his cup on the table and sat on the wooden chair across from her.

"My name is Tam."

She rested her chopsticks across her bowl. "I'm Meggan. Tam is a very common name in America." She still hoped to find out about his flawless English.

"I know, but my given name is spelled T-A-M. My full name is Tran Van Tam. Tran is my family name. Backwards from American names, right?"

"My family name is Mondae." She spelled it out, her habit to avoid misspellings.

"Tell me, Meggan Mondae, is there some way your visit to Dalat could be made better?"

"I'm afraid not. I had to spend almost all my money this afternoon. I can't afford to stay here any longer."

"How did you spend so much money? Dalat is not an expensive place."

"It is when the police stop you and threaten to take you to jail unless you pay them."

Tam narrowed his eyebrows. "What law did they say you broke?"

"None. I mean it was my driver who was stopped when he drove me through the mountains. They said he didn't signal his turn around a curve, and we would both have to go to jail."

"Why didn't your driver pay the police?"

"He didn't have any money. I hadn't paid him yet for driving me to a certain place."

Tam sat back in his chair and took a sip of coffee, never

taking his eyes off Meggan, as if studying her. He set his cup back down and folded his hands on the table.

"You were cheated."

"No kidding. The police have a nice little racket going here."

"You were cheated by the police *and* the driver."

"I didn't pay the driver. He even told me I didn't owe him anything."

"What's his name?"

"Duc. The Royal Tiger Hotel recommended him."

"I know who he is. He's a rascal who cheats tourists."

"He seemed very nice, and like I said, I didn't have to pay him."

"He must have called the police on the way to that trap, and told them he had an American tourist with him. They think all Americans are rich, you know. He will go back later and collect his share of whatever you paid the police."

"I paid the police three hundred dollars, and Duc did not charge me his daily fee of eighty dollars. If he had to split the money with the police, he would have been better off just collecting my fee. The math makes you sound unfair, Tam."

"Of course, he didn't know how much money you had, but..." Tam lifted his head slightly while considering this peculiar incident. He finally said, "I apologize. I have been no help to you." He grasped his coffee cup. "I hope you at least enjoyed the ride to your certain place."

"Not really. He took me to where a village called Bang Dia was destroyed. There's a mountain near there I wanted to see."

"What was unusual about the mountain?"

"Before I was born, my father died in battle there."

"You grew up without a father."

"That's right."

"I'm very sad to hear that."

Meggan studied his brown eyes, wondering if he really cared.

"Going to that mountain made me sad, too. So now I'll just go home and try to forget about it. At least I found the mountain I came here to see." She pushed her bowl aside a cue she wanted to leave.

Tam stood and said something in Vietnamese to a nearby waitress, and then turned to Meggan.

"And now I have to tell you more sad news. You did not go to Bang Dia. That village was untouched during and after the war, and now is thriving with many coffee and tapioca gardens. After reunification, the name of the village was changed to Bong Dung. I know because I grew up near there." Tam pushed his chair in. "I'm very sorry, Meggan Mondae. Never knowing your father, and now this terrible injustice when all you wanted was to touch the ground where he bravely fell. It cuts into my heart to hear that. After coming so far, I hope you take a little extra time to find the actual place where your father gave his life, and that you will find peace there. You would be honoring his great sacrifice and his soul."

She sat stunned for a moment after he left the restaurant. As she was getting up to leave, the waitress brought a tray with a bowl of steaming pho and another beer.

"This from Mr. Tam," she said while removing the other bowl of soup. "All paid for. He very good man."

Meggan ate most of the soup with her chopsticks, this time ladling up the tasty beef morsels and fragrant broth with the spoon while wondering about Tam. Was his story about Bang Dia being renamed Bong Dung true? If he grew up near there, was it on a farm? He didn't look like a farmer, and he spoke like an American.

When she got back to the Royal Tiger Hotel, a male desk clerk trotted around to her side of the counter and formally presented her with a sealed hotel envelope. Without saying a word, the clerk returned to his station behind the counter and busied himself on the computer.

She was afraid to open the envelope at first—she had enough surprises for one day. But she tore it open and read the message written in neatly flowing cursive.

Miss Mondae,

I have instructed my hotel staff to arrange any changes to your airline flights that you request, including any connections within or from Vietnam. The airlines will cooperate with your requests and will not charge you extra fees. All of your hotel charges are taken care of for as long as you care to stay with us.

Your servant,

Tran Trong Tri

General Manager, Royal Tiger Hotel

Meggan went to reception desk and held the note up for the clerk to see.

"Did you read this?"

"No, miss. It was addressed to you."

"It says my hotel charges are 'taken care of.' What does that mean?"

"It means you do not have to pay for anything; not your room, the bar, restaurant, or for laundry. Nothing."

"Why is the manager doing this?"

"I don't know, miss."

"Is someone else paying for all this?"

"I don't know that, either."

"I'd like to speak to the manager."

"Mr. Tri has just left for the day. Is there something I can do for you?"

Meggan shook her head no. She started toward the stairs but stopped and turned to the clerk. "Has anyone been asking about me?"

"Not that I know of, miss."

She flopped onto her bed, stone-tired and bewildered, wondering why the hotel manager would do something like this for her. Someone else must be paying her hotel bills, but she only knew three people in Dalat. Vu wouldn't have any reason to be her benefactor. He was obviously eking out a living and, besides, she had been rude to him. Tam had seemed sympathetic, but he had no reason to pay her bills. It must have been Duc. He had to stand by powerless while she handed her money over to the police. That must have humiliated him because of his responsibility and reputation as her guide. Maybe that's why he seemed so sullen and withdrawn during the rest of the trip. He had lost face, and he had no way to restore his pride—except, perhaps, to pay her hotel costs. She decided that it must be Duc. No one else would know that almost all her travel cash had been extorted from her.

CHAPTER 19

That evening, Duc visited the home of Khan, the policeman who took the photo of Meggan paying the other policeman a bribe along the mountain road. Khan answered Duc's knock at his door and invited him in.

"Not a good day today," Khan said, "especially after we pay you your split."

"Then you need better road spies. Weren't there any trucks to stop today?"

"None that weren't paying the Cobra syndicate. There aren't many unprotected drivers anymore."

"That's because Cobra protects them for less money than you take from them. Your greed is eating you now, like a swallowed tapeworm."

"Don't lecture me about greed, Duc. Unlike you, I have to collect enough money to pay our captain for a good stopping point. I'm caught in the middle. It's getting harder to make a decent living as a policeman."

Khan handed Duc seventy-five dollars, a fourth of the money collected from Meggan earlier that day.

Duc looked at it and sniffed contemptuously. "I would have made more from her if you hadn't stopped us."

"You gambled that she had more money, and you lost

your wager."

"I think she does have more money. Three hundred dollars wouldn't pay for her travel expenses, even for a few days."

"She uses her credit card, of course, like every tourist."

A sneer came to Duc's face. "Yes, that's the source of money I'm talking about."

"Her credit card is useless to us."

"I know. That's why I told you to take her photo today."

"You are confusing me, Duc. If you have some kind of plan, speak plainly about it."

"You have a photo of her paying a bribe to a policeman. You can show her how she committed a crime that would lead to a long prison sentence. Use that threat, and demand money to delete the photo."

"And charge it to her credit card? Have you lost your ability to think clearly?"

"You don't want her credit card. You want the money the bank will let her draw on it."

Khan's face went blank for a moment while he weighed Duc's scheme. "That seems too easy."

"It would not be easy if you acted on your own. She might panic and call the American embassy, or worse, the provincial governor. Without my help, you could end up in a jail filled with criminals who hate policemen, and your family would be disgraced. With me helping you, that will never happen."

"Keep talking, Duc. I'm curious about how you will make all of this easy and safe for me."

"Simple. You arrest her for corruption and then tell her you could let her go if enough people were paid."

"People like you, I suppose."

"Without her knowing, of course, and I will deserve half the money. I will negotiate the amount of payment on her behalf. She trusts me, and I will tell her she has no other choice than to meet your demand."

"We'd have to also pay my two partners."

"Why? They've already been paid for the only incident they'll know about. This bonus can be just between you and me. It could be worth hundreds of dollars, Khan, perhaps more than you earn in a year."

Khan pressed his lips anxiously while thinking. After drawing a long breath, he said, "How can I arrest an American woman without making bystanders curious? If this got back to my captain, he would punish me *and* demand the money for himself."

"Bystanders won't notice anything if you drive a civilian car and dress in street clothes. You can confront her quietly at her hotel room and show your badge. Tell her you are a police detective."

"She'll recognize me."

"No, she won't. You'll look different in civilian clothes and she'll be scared. Tell her to accompany you to your car."

"I don't own a car. I can't take her away on my motorbike."

"I'll borrow a car from a friend who owes me a favor. When you get her to the car, I'll happen to be walking by, and I'll ask what the trouble is. You can explain why you are arresting her, and I will intervene on her behalf to arrange the payment and her release. All you'll have to do is get into the car and sit there while I negotiate outside between the two of you. Then I'll ride with her in the car while you drive us to a bank where she can withdraw cash from her credit card."

"What if she refuses to pay?"

"I'll make sure she doesn't."

CHAPTER 20

Meggan ventured out after breakfast the next day, but kept close to the street that led directly back to the hotel, afraid that if she got lost, no one would understand English. She strolled past a shop that sold coffee beans, and the rich fragrance from their roaster lured her in for a look.

A young woman held up a small paper cup and gestured toward three large stainless-steel air pots, labeled in Vietnamese and English. The first pot was the highest price one, identified as "Weasel Coffee." Meggan had read about so-called weasel coffee in a guidebook, so named because the ripe sugary coffee berries are eaten by animals that look roughly like a cross between a weasel and a racoon. The animals digest the berries' sweet soft pulp, but defecate the undigested coffee beans. The animal's digestive enzymes are credited with imparting a rich earthy flavor. Meggan chose the air pot next to it, labeled "Arabica."

The coffee was rich, but not as strong as the Vietnamese-style drip coffee she had at the Swiss Coffee House. When she asked how much, the woman waved her hand and said, "Free." Meggan was going to drink the coffee on her way back to the hotel, but noticed other people sitting at small tables nursing their free sample. She sat alone at one of the tables and finished hers. When she got up a worker removed her empty cup and dropped it into a large trash bin.

While continuing her walk, she still felt troubled about the hotel manager's mysterious letter, although she was grateful for the relieved financial stress. She reaffirmed her guess that Duc must be the person behind it. Subjecting one of his customers to such a scary police shake-down could be devastating to his reputation at the hotel.

She also felt uncomfortable about leaving Vietnam after such a disappointing conclusion to her purpose for coming all this way. It did make sense to give up on what was probably an unrealistic idea and leave tomorrow as planned, but she wondered about at least trying to go to the village Tam had called Bong Dung, on the chance that he was correct about it being renamed. Tam had seemed so certain and insistent—and why should he lie? On the other hand, Duc, who was a licensed guide, and someone she knew better than Tam, was certain that Bang Dia had been destroyed after the communists took over.

Meggan gradually began to accept that probably no one, after all these years, knows for sure where her father's last battle was fought. If anyone pointed to some random mountain and swore that was the place, she'd have no way to confirm or deny it.

She finally decided it was best to claim at least a partial success, and go home. She had barely enough cash left to hire a driver for another possible goose chase, and she doubted any guide would accept a credit card. What's more, she didn't want to risk another highway robbery by the police.

Feeling more settled now, she turned around to go back to the hotel, but feared that she had been distracted from paying attention to her route. After taking a few wrong turns, getting disoriented and then reoriented, and with the help of people who spoke a bit of English, she found her way back to the Royal Tiger Hotel.

She collected her key at the reception desk and trudged up the single flight of stairs to her room. After kicking off her shoes, she flopped onto the bed, content to simply stare at the ceiling and restore her energy.

A knock at her door woke her up. Her watch showed that she had dozed for almost a half hour. She sat up and rushed to the door and opened it.

A man wearing a white shirt and black trousers glared at her. "Are you Meggan Mondae?"

"Yes…"

He took a badge from his pants pocket and held it out long enough for her to absorb the predictable shock of being confronted by a policeman.

"My name is Officer Khan, with the Dalat police. I have some questions for you about a police stop yesterday. May I come in?"

"Yes, come in. I'm glad you found out about this."

Khan took a phone from his other pants pocket, thumbed the screen a few times, and showed the image to Meggan. It was of her handing her money to one of the policemen who had stopped Duc's car yesterday.

"Is that you?"

"Yes. How did you get that photo?"

"Were you giving money to the policeman?"

"Yes."

"It was your money?"

"That's right. Why?"

"That's what I'm wondering. Why did you pay money to that police officer?"

"He threatened to take me and my driver to jail in some other city unless we paid him."

"So, you bribed him to let you go."

"I wouldn't call it a bribe; more like paying off a blackmailer. It wasn't my idea, either."

"I don't care whose idea it was. I do care about the fact that you admit to paying a police officer to get by with breaking the law. That's bribery in this country, and corruption is very serious here. I will have to place you under arrest."

"What! You're arresting me for giving in to the corruption of another policeman?"

Khan took a set of handcuffs from his back pocket. "Are you going to come with me quietly, or do I have to restrain you?"

"Oh, my God. This is a terrible mistake. Why don't you arrest the policeman who took my money?"

"Turn around and place your hands behind you."

"No, please don't handcuff me, I'll come quietly. Where are you taking me?"

"To the Dalat police station. You will undergo further questioning there, and we will decide how to handle your serious crime."

Meggan pulled on her shoes and grabbed her shoulder bag from the writing desk. She walked next to Khan while her heart raced on the edge of panic, trying to keep up with him down the stairs and through the hotel's lobby on wobbly legs. Khan opened the door, and she marched down the hotel's terrazzo stairs with him to the street. Khan told her to get into the back seat of his car and then went around to the other side.

She saw Duc through the windshield, hurrying toward them. He yelled something in Vietnamese, and Khan went to the front of the car. She couldn't understand what they were saying, but Duc's body language showed a combination of urgency and kowtowing. He talked nonstop while Khan listened stoically, glancing once toward the car. Khan shook his head about something Duc was saying. After what seemed like an excruciatingly long time, Duc broke away from the discussion and came to the car while Khan stood a few feet away on the sidewalk.

Duc opened the backseat door and leaned over to talk to Meggan.

"This is very bad trouble," he said.

"I want to call the American embassy."

"There is one in Hanoi. You might get permission to call later, but if this detective takes you to jail, your phone will be taken away from you."

"I need your help, Duc. Can you get me a lawyer?"

"Yes, but a lawyer will want money in advance."

"I have about one hundred dollars left, mostly in dongs."

"I'm afraid that would not be enough."

"Would a lawyer take my credit card?"

"I don't think so."

"How about ATMs? If you have those in Dalat, I could withdraw money."

"I don't know about ATMs, but a bank would let you withdraw money on your credit card. I'll ask the policeman if he will take you to a bank on the way to the police station so you can pay a lawyer."

Duc closed her door and resumed a discussion with Khan. Meggan prayed she could get money from the bank, and have Duc find a lawyer for her. After a few minutes of Duc doing most of the talking, Khan nodded agreement to something. Duc came back and opened Meggan's door.

"The detective said he would bring you to a bank, but it would be cheaper and less of a problem for you to pay him instead of a lawyer. If you agree, then this detective can easily make all the trouble go away."

"So, more blackmail."

"Yes, it's terrible. Should I tell him you refuse to make such an unfair bargain?"

"No, wait. How much would I have to pay him?"

"Five thousand dollars, and he will let you can go free. He can also make sure you will have no more problems with the police."

Meggan gasped. "I can't get that much. I only have about three thousand left on my card's limit. Can you tell him that's all I have?"

"As you wish." Duc went back to Khan, and after a quick exchange, he came back to Meggan. "He will accept three thousand, but he is afraid you might run away if he lets you go into the bank alone. I told him he could keep me as hostage to make sure you return with his payment."

"Thank you, Duc. I don't know what I'd do without you. And I appreciate you taking care of my hotel expenses."

Duc gave her a blank look. "I'm afraid I cannot pay your hotel expenses, miss. I earn very little money as a driver, and I have to support my wife and son."

"Oh, I'm sorry. I made a mistake. The hotel is not charging me for my expenses, and I thought it was because of you."

"No need to apologize," Duc said, still looking confused. "If you are ready, we should go and be done with this terrible business."

While riding in the back seat with Meggan, Duc explained that he would have to stay in the car as a hostage while she withdraws money from the bank, adding that if the policeman has to wait too long, he said he would take Duc to jail for arranging the bribe.

When they pulled up in front of the bank, her hands and legs were still trembling but adrenalin stirred her anger. Without saying a word, she threw the car door open and jumped out, leaving the door open as she strode along toward the cement stairs to the bank's wide glass door.

Inside, a man in a white shirt and tie stood up from behind his desk. "May I help you, miss?"

Meggan did her best to look nonchalant, as if this was about a routine matter. "I want to withdraw money with my credit card."

"Yes, please step over to one of the cashiers at the counter."

She went to one of the windows and asked a young woman with bobbed hair and bright red lipstick if she spoke English.

"A little," the woman said.

"I want to withdraw money on my credit card."

After getting a confused look from the woman, Meggan simply wrote $3,000 US on a slip of paper and slid it with her credit card under the counter window. The cashier bowed slightly, and then turned to say something in Vietnamese to an older man standing in the background, presumably her superior, who gave the cashier a quick answer, and gave Meggan a long look.

"May I see a photo ID, please?" she asked.

Meggan pulled her passport from her waist pouch and slid it under the window. She watched the cashier tap her computer keyboard for what seemed like several minutes, and then stared at the monitor even longer. She walked back to the older man, this time whispering something to him.

Meggan knew something was wrong. Her mind raced for

ideas about what to do if they didn't give her the money. Running away would put Duc in serious trouble. But if the policeman took her to jail, making her a prisoner with no available resources, and with no way of communicating to the outside world, she might be held captive in God knows what kind of conditions for days, or weeks—maybe months or years. She glanced around for another exit. There wasn't one.

She called to the cashier. "Is there a problem?"

"No, miss. Just a moment, please."

Meggan had called her credit card company before this trip, telling them she would be in Vietnam for a couple of weeks, but a withdrawal this large might have triggered an alert. She couldn't call the credit card company because she didn't have cellphone service from Vietnam to the US.

The cashier returned to her window with a relieved look. "Everything good now."

She wrote 68,310,000 VND on a slip of paper and slid it to Meggan. The cashier then opened a drawer under the counter and, placed stacks of Vietnamese dongs on the counter, most of them bound in neat bundles with rubber bands. She counted out additional dong notes to complete the total, and shoved all the money into a large mailing envelope. She slid the unsealed envelope under the window to Meggan, along with her passport and credit card.

Meggan thought about counting the money but realized that translating the currency conversion would take too much time, and she had no idea what the exchange rate was. Besides, the bank is more likely to be honest than the policeman outside.

She thanked the cashier and left the bank, hoping to put a quick end to this nightmare.

When she got to the car, Duc was sitting in the front passenger seat. He rolled down the window and looked around while telling Meggan to get in the back seat. Khan just stared out his closed side window as if idly watching traffic pass by.

When Meggan got in the backseat and closed the door, Duc turned to her. "Did you have any trouble getting the money?"

"No. Now what?"

"Put the money on the backseat floor. When we get back to the hotel you and I will get out and leave the money there. That way no one can say you gave money to a policeman."

"Very clever, Duc, but he is not honest, and I can't stand being in his car another minute. I'll leave the money, but I'm walking back to the hotel alone."

Khan turned around in his seat and barked, "No, you will stay in the car until we get back to the hotel."

Meggan opened her door and got out. "Khan, if you try to stop me, I will scream for help and yell to everyone around here that you are stealing my money."

Khan looked back at her with a smirk. "No one will interfere with police business."

"Dirty business, and everyone will know it; and they will try to help an American that has become crazy from a police bully. The bank will admit to withdrawing my money, and I will tell everyone you stole it from me. It's sitting in your car. How would you explain that? What would your superiors say?"

Before closing the door, Meggan pulled her phone and videoed the envelope on the floor, panning to Khan's face but avoiding Duc's.

"This is my insurance against any more trouble from you. I'm emailing this video right now to my American lawyer, and if I have more trouble from the police, she will send this to the American embassy, and they will complain to your government."

Meggan slammed the back door and strode off in the opposite direction, and then jogged for almost a block before daring to turn around and look. When she did, the car was gone. After a sigh of relief, she continued walking, hoping she hadn't put Duc in trouble.

CHAPTER 21

Meggan crossed the street and tried to retrace the route Khan took from the hotel. She had been so emotionally overwhelmed that she didn't think about keeping track, and everything looked new from the opposite direction. She stopped at what apparently was a beverage distributorship and walked toward a man maneuvering a forklift stacked with cases of beer, moving it from the sidewalk into the building's cramped storage area. He stopped when he saw Meggan run up to him.

"Can you tell me how to get to the Royal Tiger Hotel?"

The forklift driver said something in Vietnamese while shaking his head and with a palm turned up, as if signally *I don't understand you.*

The same confusion happened at the butcher shop next door, where hanging plucked ducks and a pan of iced fish were displayed in the front window. The woman behind the counter responded to Meggan's question with something in Vietnamese, and then gave Meggan an apologetic look.

She decided to trust her sense of direction and turned down what looked like a familiar street. Although the streets were seldom straight for very long, Dalat was not a huge city so she felt optimistic that she'd eventually recognize something. The sun was hidden by clouds, so it didn't indicate west from east, but she was, at least for that moment, free from immediate danger. Once safely back at the hotel, she planned to ask a staffer to arrange a flight to Saigon for the next morning, hoping there would be no extra charges for changing her flight to Tokyo, then for a connection to the US. She couldn't squander any money for a hotel in Saigon if she had to stay overnight, but she could sit in the airport terminal, for days if necessary. At least she'd be going home.

With that general plan in mind, Meggan continued wandering through unfamiliar streets for almost an hour. She started to worry about being outside alone after dark. It seemed safe now, but nighttime might change that, and her nerves were already at snapping point.

She came to what looked like an upscale suburb, filled with large deco-style villas well-spaced between manicured lawns and flowering bushes.

"Miss Mondae."

The voice from behind startled her.

She turned to see Tran Van Tam leaning toward the opened passenger window of his jeep.

"I'm on my way home. Are you lost?"

"I'm afraid so. I'm trying to find my hotel."

Tam got out of the jeep walked across the street to her. "You're going the wrong way. Your hotel is near the city center. I'll take you there."

"I'm sure I can find my way if you give me directions."

"Dalat is a tangle of delightful, but confusing, shortcuts. You'll have nothing to worry about if I take you. You already look a little unsettled."

"It would be nice to not worry for a while. Thank you, Tam."

"May I call you Meggan?"

"Yes, of course."

He stepped over to his jeep and opened the passenger door for her. Meggan paused a moment before getting in.

"Maybe you'd like to relax a little before going to the hotel. The city center market will be coming to life, with food vendors, shops, and coffee houses. It's just up the street from your hotel. We could stop for a snack if you like."

She got into his car. "No thanks, just drop me off in front of the hotel, please."

Neither of them said anything the first few minutes while he glided down the narrow streets, with pedestrians and other vehicles edging aside for him. When traffic thinned, he glanced at her.

"You hesitated about riding with me. I don't blame you. You only met me briefly at the coffee shop."

"It's not about you. Something terrible happened to me today." A tear started down her cheek but she quickly brushed it with the back of her hand.

"I hope you weren't harmed."

She wanted to tell him what happened, but could she trust him? "I'll be okay."

He broke the silence after a few minutes. "Is it because you visited Bong Dung?"

"No. I decided not to go there."

"I thought it's the reason you came to Dalat."

"I thought so, too, but I've seen enough. I'm going home tomorrow."

"I can understand why going to Bong Dung might be too haunting, and could spoil your trip. Sometimes I have difficult feelings when I go there. My father, like yours, fought in one of the many terrible battles near Bong Dung. He survived but almost died from his wounds. The mountain you wanted to see near there is officially called A-42, but local people, especially the older ones, still call it 'Massacre Mountain' because of the many American soldiers who were killed there one terrible night. I didn't tell you that before, because I didn't want to frighten you."

She stared out the front windshield without really noticing anything. "My trip is already spoiled. That's why I'm leaving so soon. It's not about what happened to my father, it's what happened to me."

"I can understand why that roadside police-stop scared you. Most people here are honest, and they are ashamed of that kind of corruption. It makes us all seem dishonest to Westerners."

"It wasn't the traffic stop, Tam. Today I was arrested by a police detective who made me drain my credit card limit. He took everything. I'm tired of feeling scared, and I'm going home."

Meggan pressed her lips together and looked out the passenger window. She didn't want to fall apart in front of Tam. They barely knew each other, and Tam was being kind enough—or carefully enough—not to press her for details.

They pulled up in front of the Royal Tiger Hotel and Tam turned off his engine. He took a business card from his wallet while Megan opened her door.

"If you have any more trouble, please call me at the number on this card. If you can't make local calls from your cellphone, have the hotel contact me. Would you do that, please?"

"Yes, thank you." She took the card, which was printed in Vietnamese, with a background photo of terraced fields stair-stepping down the slope of a lush green mountain. His name and something else in Vietnamese was at the bottom, with a phone number.

Meggan got out of the car without looking at him and closed the door. She suspected he was watching her, but hurried up the stairs to the hotel entrance, not looking back until she was inside the glass door entrance. He was just then pulling away from the curb.

She went to her room and got her ticket from Dalat to Ho Chi Minh City, and returned to the reception desk. She asked the young woman to change her ticket for a flight the next day. The woman took the ticket and made a call, speaking in Vietnamese for what seemed to Meggan like a long discussion for a simple flight change. The young woman put her hand over the phone receiver and said, with a regrettable look, that the only flight tomorrow was already full, and there were no flights scheduled for the next day. There was availability two days later, however. Meggan said okay, and the receptionists resumed her conversation with the airline.

Meggan wondered how she would spend two days with almost no money, but then remembered that the manager was taking care of her hotel bills. When the receptionist finished her call, she handed the ticket back to Meggan and said she was confirmed on a flight two days from now.

"Thank you. By the way, the manager left me a note yesterday that said all my hotel expenses are being covered. Is that still true?"

"Yes, that is correct," the receptionist said cautiously.

"Does he do that for other guests?"

"Oh, no. This is a special arrangement."

"Who arranged it?"

"I wouldn't know about that, miss."

"Is the manager in?"

"He is in Saigon the rest of this week for a business conference."

"Does he have a cellphone?"

"Yes, but I don't have the number."

"How would you contact him if there was an emergency?"

"I would leave word at his Saigon hotel, or email him. Would you like his email address?"

"No, thanks."

CHAPTER 22

Meggan tried to busy herself the rest of the day, first knit-ting—and missing stitches—then trying to get interested in her novel, giving up after too much melodrama for her heavy mood. The confinement of her room began to feel impris-oning, and she couldn't bear the thought of living like this for two more days. Besides, she reasoned, the police detective knew where to find her. She might be safer on the street, where she could at least run away from unexpected trouble.

Once outside, her spirits lifted. The brilliant sunshine was washing the sky into a pastel blue. A slight dry breeze cooled the air, but not enough to wear a sweater.

While walking down the sidewalk, she kept track of where she was at all times, frequently looking back for anyone fol-lowing her. At the end of every block, she turned to memo-rize what the return to her hotel would look like. After two blocks she came to the central market, where motorbikes, as always, outnumbered and outmaneuvered the cars and trucks, with all vehicles carefully processing around a huge roundabout to their respective exits. Merchants stood behind tables along the sidewalks, selling fresh fruits like strawber-ries, pineapples—and many others unfamiliar to Meggan— and vegetables like potatoes, onions, and artichokes. When motorbikers stopped to buy something, they often didn't bother to dismount, simply stuffing their purchase into back-packs and buzzing off.

She pointed to an apple at one of the produce tables, and a middle-aged woman wearing a straw hat handed it to her. Meggan held out an assortment of Vietnamese dong bills and let the woman choose which denomination would cover the cost. She took the 10,000 dong note and gave Meggan a few coins as change. The woman then took another apple and gave it to Meggan with a broad smile. Meggan thanked her for the bonus and bowed her head slightly.

This simple transaction gave Meggan a greater sense of peace than she had felt during the last few days. She was hungry and decided not to wait until she got back to the hotel to eat one of the apples. There were no trash cans along the street so she even ate the core, seeds and all.

When she got back to the hotel, she saw Vu carrying two heavy suitcases up the stairs to the hotel entrance, followed by a well-dressed Asian couple. When Meggan got to the lobby, Vu was accepting a tip from his customers. When he started to leave, he spotted Meggan.

"Miss Meggan," he said brightly. "I hope you are enjoying your time in Dalat. Did you become rested enough to see some of our city?"

Meggan felt more sympathetic toward Vu than when she first arrived in Dalat, when a blend of travel fatigue and stress left over from Saigon made her impatient with him.

"No, Vu. I haven't seen anything a tourist should see. I should have listened to you when you brought me from the airport."

"You were too tired from traveling to want more travel-ing. I should have given you more time to rest. Has this hotel been good for you?"

"They seem a bit disorganized sometimes."

He whispered, "Government-run."

"I know. You warned me."

"Have you needed a driver?"

"Yes, for a short trip. The hotel recommended a man named Duc."

Vu's cheeriness deflated like a flat tire. "Duc. Yes, I know who he is."

"Would you be able to take me to the airport two days from now?"

"So soon? Yes, I can take you because the Saigon flight leaves in the morning. I only have afternoon customers that day. I'll pick you up at 8 AM, in plenty of time. Would you like to see something before you leave, maybe a hilltop view of Dalat?"

"Thanks, but I think I'll just stay around here." Meggan wondered if Vu suspected that she planned to use Duc for touring instead of him. She stepped closer to him and lowered her voice. "The truth is that I have lost almost all my money, and I have to save what little I have for the trip home."

"Lost your money?" Vu whispered hoarsely. "How terrible! Don't worry, you do not have to pay me for taking you to the airport, or for touring tomorrow. I have no customers anyway, so I would lose nothing. How did you lose your money?"

Meggan now felt she could trust Vu, but wanted to make sure no one else was listening. "Let's go outside. I'll walk with you to your car."

Vu nodded almost imperceptibly, as if pacing her wariness. He opened the hotel's door for her, and when they got to the street, he stood next to his car and glanced around, as if checking the area.

"Did someone take your money?"

"Yes, the police."

"For what reason?"

"The first time, at a traffic stop. I paid a bribe because Duc didn't have any money. He didn't charge me for the ride, though. The second time a detective came to my hotel room and arrested me for bribing the traffic policeman. Luckily, Duc was nearby and negotiated my release, but I had to withdraw three thousand dollars, the limit of my credit card, to pay the detective."

Vu's faced grimaced with anger. "I told my teenage son that if he ever became a policeman I would disown him for eternity. The police like to stop tour drivers when they have Western customers, and they stop truck drivers who do not pay the mafia. They smell money like vultures smell blood. They disgrace Vietnam and I hate all of them."

Meggan was stunned by Vu's tirade, but it made her feel like she had an ally of sorts. "I'm worried they might arrest me again. They don't need much of a reason."

"Yes, they do need a reason—money, and then more money. Now you can no longer satisfy that reason, so they cannot profit from bothering you anymore."

"Thank you for being so understanding and kind. I wish I would have toured Dalat with you. I guess I just wasn't meant to be here."

"You were meant be in Dalat, Miss Meggan, otherwise you would not have journeyed so far. I am very sorry for what happened to you, and I wish I could have shown you our beautiful city. Do you still have my business card?"

"Yes."

"Please call me if you need anything. I will not accept any

money from you. I know many things and many people in Dalat, and I will find ways to help you."

"Thank you, Vu. Oh, there is something I'm wondering about. I met a man named Tran Van Tam. Do you know anything about him?"

"Yes, my goodness, everyone knows who Mr. Tam is. His family is very important in Lam Dong Province. They are coffee brokers and have helped Vietnam become the top coffee exporter in the world."

"Is Tam a good person?"

"You met him? What do you think?"

"He seemed very nice, but I've made mistakes about people, especially men."

"Mr. Tam is a very good man. I know that his family supports an orphanage near Dalat and they privately do other good things."

"I heard his father is secretive."

"Mr. Tam's father is called Con Rong, 'The Dragon,' because his power is great, but he is never seen. But his son, Tam, is very lively in Dalat. I think Tam is running the family business now because Con Rong must be very old."

Meggan stood on the sidewalk to watch Vu drive away in his white SUV. These few minutes with him recast an entirely different feeling for her about Dalat. If she could wish away her dreadful experiences, and had some money left, she'd like to see more of the city. She'd like to know more about Vu, too. And about Tran Van Tam—and his mysterious father, Con Rong.

CHAPTER 23

After Vu left Meggan at the hotel, he drove home feeling agitated, not because of traffic or lateness or any other personal reason, but because he knew Duc had cheated Meggan. Vu was never able to get a tour guide license because his father had been a soldier for the South Vietnamese. Duc, however, had a license, which is why the government-employed hotel receptionist could recommend him—for a kickback, of course. While Duc relied on his license to cover up his scams, Vu built an honest business through unofficial sources and returning customers.

It annoyed Vu that Duc had easily obtained his tour guide license without any experience. But Duc had another asset: connections at the provincial governor's office, thanks to the wartime service of his father, a low-ranking North Vietnamese Army soldier who had tortured American and South Vietnamese prisoners during the war. In 1973, when American POWs being released told the world about his sadistic deeds in front of international newsreel cameras, Duc's father became obsessed with the fear of ancestor humiliation and of painful retaliation from phantom spies. When even opium couldn't help him stand it any longer, he took his life with a makeshift rafter noose.

Vu knew Duc's usual trick of arranging police stops, and later receiving a share of the bribery payment. Vu thought it was clever of Duc to not charge Meggan, so he could deny a kickback to the hotel receptionist. But Duc's relentless greed had apparently spilled into cruelty when he and the policeman kidnapped Meggan with a false arrest, then ransomed her release. It was a bold, lowly trick, even for street dust like Duc. In Vu's opinion, Duc was worse than the police. At least the police do not hide their corruption; Duc cloaks his evil with clever plans and false friendships.

What made Vu angriest, however, was knowing that Meggan was being forced economically and emotionally to abandon her purpose for coming to Dalat. She would always feel bad about coming to the hill country, and she would take home terrible misperceptions about Vietnamese people. He wished he could help her understand that she had been a victim of a scam worse than anything Vu had ever heard of. He wished for something in his power to help Meggan know the real Dalat, the beautiful, safe, and happy place where Vu had lived all his life. But with her decision to leave, that hope would remain just another powerless wish.

Then he remembered that Meggan had met Tran Van Tam. There was no greater power in Lam Dong Province, except that of Mr. Tam's father. Telling Mr. Tam about Meggan's catastrophe might inspire him to help in some way.

But this was an audacious idea. Vu only knew Mr. Tam as many others do, enough to say hello, but nothing more personal. And Meggan might resent Vu repeating something she shared with him in confidence. Vu decided to stay out of Meggan's private affairs, but as a good Catholic he prayed for her.

On the other hand, who else would care about Meggan?

She might trust Duc again, and a man like Mr. Tam would certainly care about preventing terrible things from happening to her. Vu felt this realization was the answer to his prayer.

Vu drove to a hilly upper-class Dalat suburb where restored French villas built during the 1920s and 1930s were scattered throughout a peaceful wooded neighborhood. He drove through the winding narrow street to one of the largest homes, built on the highest ground and owned by the Tran family. Walking self-consciously to the front door, he noticed a gardener alongside the house pruning a palm bush. The man wore jeans, a green tee shirt and baseball cap, and glanced sideways at Vu while he kept working. Although Vu avoided looking directly at the gardener, he thought the man did not look Vietnamese, perhaps he was a Filipino or Malaysian.

Feeling deeply out of his element now, Vu carefully tapped a brass knocker on the wall next to the glass-paned front door. He hoped Mr. Tam would not be angry by this uninvited visit from someone overreaching his station, presuming responsibilities beyond his authority. He began to hope no one heard the knock, and if no one came in a few seconds, he would quickly leave, being sure to smile politely at the gardener as if everything was fine. But this plan was spoiled when a hill-tribe woman wearing a brown shirt and black loose trousers padded toward the door in bare feet, and opened it for him.

"What do you want, sir?"

"I was hoping for a word with Mr. Tam, but if he is busy, I can come another time."

"May I tell him your name?"

"I am Vu. He doesn't know me. I came to tell him something about an American he knows. Her name is Miss Meggan."

"Please come in and sit in the living room. I'll tell him."

Vu sat in one of two white upholstered chairs that faced a bowed wall with five large windows across its length, overlooking a lush lawn bordered by flowering shrubs, all protected by a tall privacy hedge. A flood of sunlight brightened a white crescent-shaped sofa that fit exactly under the windows, decorated with neatly placed orange, green, and white throw pillows.

After a few minutes Tam walked in from a back room and crossed the large adjacent dining room's gleaming wood floor. Vu stood as soon as he saw him.

"Sir, my name is Vu. I apologize for intruding."

"Not at all, Vu. Please sit down." Tam sat across from Vu in the matching white chair. "I recognize you. I've seen you driving tourists."

"Yes, sir. That has been my business for nine years."

"Mai said you had something to tell me about Miss Meggan?"

"Yes, sir. Miss Meggan came to Dalat because her father was killed near here during the war, and she wanted to see where he died."

"Yes, she told me."

"But policemen have made such terrible trouble for her that she now only wants to go home. Her reason for coming to Dalat has been denied to her."

"She told me about the roadside police stop, but that alone didn't seem enough to scare her away. If something worse happened, she didn't tell me."

"She told me, sir. She didn't ask to keep it a secret, so I feel a duty to tell someone who might be able to help her."

"I appreciate your confidence in me, Vu. Please continue."

"Miss Meggan was arrested this morning for bribing the

traffic policemen. The policeman who arrested her agreed to let her go if she paid him three thousand dollars. It was all the money her credit card allowed."

"My God. That's awful. It must have happened just before I found her wandering through the streets. She was lost and looked scared. Now I know why."

"Yes, and she was still afraid when she talked to me."

"I'll visit the police chief about this today. A bit of corruption here and there is one thing, but I doubt very much that he would tolerate this kind of larceny, especially against a tourist, and in particular, an American tourist." Tam gazed out the window while thinking this through, then turned back to Vu. "This could cause great trouble if she reports it to the American embassy, especially with hinted trade talks going on with the Americans. I'll press the chief to restore her money, Vu, but I need the name of the policeman who arrested her."

"I didn't ask his name but he probably didn't give it to her, and she probably wouldn't remember it if he did. She did mention a tour driver named Duc."

"I know this man, Duc. He works with police friends to swindle tourists. How did she say Duc was connected to this?"

"She said that he was her driver during the roadside stop. He also happened to be outside her hotel when the arresting policeman took her to his car. Duc negotiated Miss Meggan's freedom both times."

"He, of course, would take a split of both payoffs."

"Of course."

"Does Meggan connect Duc with any of this treachery?"

"I don't think so, sir. These kinds of tricks might be unusual for Americans."

"They should be made unusual for Vietnamese, too. Our

people have struggled for years, for centuries, to build Vietnam into a great country, but to grow we must first earn respect beyond our borders instead of hijacking tourists."

"Yes, sir."

"I'm sorry about making a speech to you, Vu, and you have been polite to listen to me, but I like Meggan Mondae, and hearing about her terrible experiences angers me."

"It angers me, too, sir. That's why I came to you. I hope the police chief will get her money returned."

"I'm not going to the chief." Tam got up and paced back and forth in front of the window. "We're unable to give him any names, except Duc's, and we have no proof of Duc's connection with the policemen. The chief might help us if he could, but I don't think he can."

"But Duc must have conspired with the policemen."

"Of course, Vu, but if Meggan gave the money to the policemen, then Duc did not participate in the bribe in any way that can be proven."

"You understand these matters much better than I do, sir."

"You flatter me, Vu, but I still don't know how I can help Meggan. I need to think more about this."

"Yes, sir. Thank you."

"Please leave your phone number, in case I have other questions."

"Thank you, sir." Vu stood and took a card from his wallet, then handed it to Tam.

"And if something else comes to mind, please tell me."

"Yes, sir, right away."

Tam stepped outside to watch Vu drive down the driveway and disappear behind a bend in the street. He wondered how he could find some way to help Meggan. He understood why she would want to go home after such frightening threats against her, and then being swindled out of so much of her money. Of course, she would want to feel safe again, return to her predictable life in America, be with family members, friends—perhaps her lover.

While walking across the lawn to the side yard, he noticed a palm shrub that had been freshly pruned, and the nearby flower garden was already weeded. Tam had to smile to himself: such effort from someone who didn't need to do this work, but found such joy in using his talents, like an artist, to make living things bloom, especially some of the flower species that existed nowhere in the world except in this little patch of suburban yard, thanks to countless patient cross-breeding experiments.

A shiny black Audi sped up the driveway and parked in front of the villa. Tam opened the back door, lifting smiling little Anh from her car seat, while her mother, Bien, opened the car's trunk to reveal today's shopping bounty.

Tam held squirming Anh in his arms and said, "What treasures did you find today, Bien?"

"My computer watch finally arrived from Saigon." Bien held up a package wrapped in red paper with gold ribbon for Tam to see.

"What do you need a computer watch for?"

Bien left the trunk open and walked toward the villa's front door. "I don't need anything, Tam, if that's the point you are trying to make. Just a bowl of rice and some water. And air, of course."

"Okay, I'll change the question. What purpose does a computer watch serve?"

"It syncs with my phone."

"I didn't ask what it syncs with."

"Leave the trunk open, Tam. I got a nice lake fish for supper and fresh basil. I'll send Mai out for it."

Tam followed Bien into the house while tickling Anh's tummy, who said *More* as soon as she could stop giggling. He was tempted to go back for the groceries after he planted Anh firmly on the foyer floor, but decided against dusting up Bien's apparent edgy mood, so he let it sit in Bien's car trunk for Mai, who wouldn't think anything about carrying out such a routine errand.

Bien sat at the large dark-wood rectangular dining room table and unwrapped her package. "I thought you were going to the gardens today."

"I was, but a visitor came by. I'll go tomorrow."

"A visitor?"

"A man named Vu. He's a tour driver."

"Are you going on a tour?" There was a sardonic lilt in her voice while she worked at releasing the computer watch from its complicated packaging.

"I might take a tour, perhaps with a pretty American girl who, unlike you, is friendly."

Bien stopped fussing with the box and looked at Tam. "Okay, I'm sorry. My stomach is giving me problems today and it's making me witchy. What about this driver named Vu, and the American girl are you talking about."

Tam pulled out a dining table chair and sat across from Bien. "Vu knows an American woman who the police shook down for money, a lot of money—in fact, all the travel money available to her. She came to Vietnam to see where her father died as a soldier during the war. She has never met him, and now she has to go home without even seeing where he died."

"Okay, that's sad. But how does it involve the tour driver, and why did he come to you with this problem?"

"He wondered if I could help her."

"You told him no, didn't you?"

"I told him I'd think about it."

Bien set the watch's box on the table and glared at Tam. "You should think about your family instead. She might be a spy."

"She's not a spy."

"She could be, and if you get too friendly, she'll try to find out more about us and our business."

"Credit me with enough wisdom to manage that."

"You are very wise, Tam, but matters of the heart can betray wisdom."

"You would know."

Bien went back to unpacking her watch. "Yes, I would, and you may wash my face in a past mistake if that gives you pleasure."

"I'm sorry, Bien. That slip was not from the wisdom you credit me with."

"I know marrying my ex-husband was a mistake, but Anh is the blessing from it."

"Yes, we're all lucky to have Anh, and she's lucky to be rid of her scoundrel father. Forgive me for forgetting that."

Bien merely nodded and removed the computer watch from its box, holding it to her wrist to test its attractiveness, then looking away and setting it on the table to wipe back a rolling tear.

Tam got up and slowly pushed the chair back under the table while watching her. He walked through the French doors to the adjoining balcony and rested his hands against the wide daffodil-yellow cement railing while trying to unravel his thoughts. He regretted hurting Bien, prodding an old wound that has been so hard for her to heal.

He wondered if his attraction to Meggan might be fogging his judgement, distracting him from responsibilities for his family. This question helped him understand Meggan's passion for learning more about her own father, for wanting to see where he fell in battle.

When he heard the door open behind him, he turned to see Bien standing at the doorway.

"If you can help the American woman," she said, "then I suppose you must. We both know that father would agree to that, regardless of the danger. And maybe you'll uncover why she's really here."

CHAPTER 24

Later that afternoon, Tam called a friend who worked for the city government, and asked him to find out where Duc lived. Tam recognized the name of the controversial street, located in a newer settlement near the railroad tracks where hastily developed homes were erected within in a few weeks, all without permits. Its residents, with the help of Buddhist monk demonstrators, ignored the government's edict to evacuate. Because of overwhelming public support for the residents, the city's officials eventually agreed to a small fine to save face, and allowed the occupants to stay in their cheaply built dwellings.

Tam pulled up to one of the row of houses and went to the door. To soften the look of stark construction framing, the front porch showed a female's essence: a delicate wind chime, a ceremonial miniature ancestor's house with an offering of a full rice bowl and a plate holding three persimmons.

He knocked at the door, and was welcomed by a shy forty-ish woman who appeared too stooped over for someone her age. She invited Tam in without asking who he was or what he wanted. He removed his shoes and stepped in, assenting to her invitation to sit in a small Chinese sofa ornately embroidered with colorful flowers and pine trees, an obviously prized piece of furniture to impress and comfort visitors.

The woman left the living room and soon returned from the back room behind Duc.

"Mr. Tam, I'm honored by your visit," Duc said, sitting in a red plastic chair across from him. His wife sat at the kitchen table and looked away, as if disinterested.

"What brings you to my humble home?"

"I came to discuss some business."

"My business is driving as a tour guide, as you might already know. How can I serve you?"

"I won't need your service, Duc, just your cooperation. In return I will leave you and your peaceful home."

Duc stiffened. "I would like to know more about this business."

"I will tell you, but first I will explain why I am making this my business. You have seen Vietnam change since Doi Moi in 1986, when people like you and me were allowed by our government to start, and profit from, farms and businesses."

"Yes, opportunities have opened since then, and you have prospered far greater than most."

"My family has been lucky, Duc, but we've also worked hard and we've been honest in our business dealings. That is why we are able to trade with foreign business people. We are trusted, and without trust, a people cannot grow with the modern world."

"I think you are telling me something, Mr. Tam, but I don't know what it is."

"I will put it as plainly as sunshine, Duc. When Americans and other Westerners come to Vietnam and are robbed by greedy thieves, they go home and paint us all as dishonest barbarians."

Duc's breath shallowed. "Who are these thieves you

talk about?"

"I'm looking at one."

"If you believe that, remember that I did not ask you to come, and I will not ask you to stay."

"I will go when our business is settled, and not before. You and your crooked policeman friend have taken a lot of money, far too much, from an American who is my friend. I am here to reclaim it for her."

"I know who you are speaking about, and you misunderstand what happened. I only negotiated a fine for her. You cannot blame me for doing the best I could."

"Now you insult me, Duc."

Duc straightened in his chair. "How?"

"Your clumsy lies tell me that you consider me a fool. Everyone knows how corruption works, and not in the least, me. It's the very problem I've been talking about."

Tam stood and looked down at Duc. "But I won't waste your time trying to explain things you don't care about, like how Vietnam should become an economic power. I'll stick to the business at hand, which is the return of Miss Meggan's money."

Duc got up from his chair and took a step back. "I'll talk to the police detective if you want me to. Miss Meggan gave the money to him."

"Yes, and he split it with you later. No more insults to my intelligence, Duc, just get the money. If you don't produce it immediately, I'll tear your house apart to find it. And go ahead and call your police friends if you like. You should know—and the police will certainly know—that I have powerful friends and political alliances from Saigon to Hanoi. Don't expect the local police to throw their careers away to help dust like you."

Duc glared at Tam, like a weasel cornered by a wolf. "I only have half of the money."

"Alright, then stop testing my patience. Bring it to me now, and I'll take it to Miss Meggan. That will complete our business."

Duc went to the kitchen and took a jar from the top shelf of a cupboard. His wife stood and pleaded in whispers for him to stop. When Duc removed the money from the jar, she grabbed his arm and repeated her plea, louder this time, and then started yelling at him while he shuffled toward Tam, handing over a thick stack of dongs tied into a bundle with rough twine. When Tam took the money, Duc's expression turned from a drained defeat to a blushing rage.

"Now get out of my house," Duc said from the back of his throat. "And be watchful, because this business, as you call it, is not over."

Tam slapped Duc across the face with an open hand so hard that Duc almost lost his balance. Duc pressed his palm against the cheek, his eyes wide with disbelief. His wife screamed curses at Tam for being an overly-rich capitalist who treads on the backs of little people like them.

"I'll ignore your wife's ignorance, Duc, but any further threats from you will always be answered. Don't ever make that mistake again. I am not one of your gullible, frightened tourists, I am the son of Con Rong."

***

Tam drove to a tailor shop near Dalat's center, parked along the curb, got out with a news magazine that he used to conceal Meggan's money. His Chinese tailor, a man named Zhang Wei, made everything from men's trousers and shirts, and women's skirts and blouses, to wedding apparel and school uniforms for Dalat's business and professional families. He was also the fairest and most resourceful money changer in town.

A springy bell clattered when Tam entered the tailor shop. There were no clothes for sale on racks because everything was custom made by Zhang Wei and his wife. His two teen-age daughters also worked there after school, and during the summer his son, who attended university in Saigon, also worked with them.

Zhang Wei drew aside a sheer linen doorway curtain that concealed the clutter and activities of the backroom, and formally positioning himself behind his counter with a genuine hint of pleasure on his face.

"Mr. Tam, I am honored by your visit. I hope your family is lucky with health and prosperity."

"I am grateful for my blessings, Zhang. And I hope your family is healthy and your business is prospering."

"Yes, yes, thank you, Mr. Tam. How may I serve you to-day? By the way, I just received a bolt of the finest silk from Chiang Mai in Thailand, a very lovely weave that would make an impressive business shirt worthy of a man like you."

"Perhaps another time, Zhang. Today I need to exchange dong, a lot of it, for American dollars."

Zhang Wei's pleasant look took a more ominous turn, as if bracing for a serious transaction. "American dollars are dear, as you well know. I will give you the best exchange rate I can."

"I have no doubts about that, Zhang. Can you handle just over 34 million dong?"

Without any sign of emotion, Zhang Wei pulled a drawer out from behind the counter and removed a small calculator. He tapped in a few numbers, deleted the answer and did the calculation again to make sure.

"Almost one thousand five hundred US dollars. I'm embarrassed to say that I do not have that much right now. I could get it in a few days, perhaps even two days, if you can come back then."

"How much can you exchange right now?"

"I will look."

Zhang Wei flipped aside the linen curtain and disappeared into the back room. While waiting, Tam went to the large front display window, scanning for any obvious spies. As soon as he had left Duc's house, the humiliation, pain, and financial loss would have erupted into a full rage, especially if fueled by Duc's hysterical wife who was chiding him as a coward. Duc might have called the street lice that Duc called friends, and they would have no problem locating Tam—there was no other vehicle in Dalat like his American jeep.

When Zhang returned, he said, "Mr. Tam, I have a little more than one thousand US dollars. I could make up the difference today with European euros."

Tam thought about whether to come back, but Meggan might leave Dalat before Zhang could get more dollars, and she'd have a hard time converting dong when she got back to her home in America. Euros, on the other hand, would be easily converted at an American bank, or even at an American international airport.

"Okay, Zhang, I'll take what dollars you have and the balance in euros."

Tam didn't ask Zhang what his exchange rate would be; he knew it would be fair and certainly the best, or at least among the best, in Dalat. When Zhang went to the back room to get the currencies from whatever secret stronghold he stashed them in, Tam took the wad of dong bills out of the news magazine. Within a minute or two, Zhang reappeared, and with machine-like precision and speed, counted Tam's dongs, and then dealt the US dollars and euros in separate piles, counting the cumulating balances aloud.

After he placed them inside his magazine, Tam thanked Zhang, promising to tell Bien about his fine silk shipment. Zhang said he looked forward to making Bien something beautiful and stunning, perhaps a magnificent white ao dai—the traditional Vietnamese dress seldom worn anymore except for special celebrations—and the men exchanged goodbyes.

Tam drove from the tailor shop directly to the Royal Tiger Hotel. He hurried up the stairs to the lobby, and asked the young receptionist which room was occupied by the American named Meggan Mondae. The receptionist gave the room number without having to look it up, and without challenging Tam, a familiar friend of the hotel manager.

He tapped lightly on Meggan's door and waited, listening for any sound that indicated she was in her room. He didn't hear anything. He began to feel anxious, a side-effect of the adrenaline still in his blood from dealing with Duc and his wife, and then the hasty money exchange with Zhang. He wondered if he should have crossed into Meggan's private world so presumptuously, making bold decisions on her behalf, and he now worried that she might resent it. But he couldn't just leave. He had her money.

After a harder knock at the door, he heard, "Just a minute, please." There were footsteps, a stumble, her voice softly saying "Shit" to herself, and then louder, "I'll be right there." The door chain rattled while she hastily unfastened it, and then the metallic sound of the doorknob twisting open. Meggan peeked out.

"Oh, Tam," she said, opening the door wider with one

hand, flipping her hair back with the other hand. "I was just getting up from a nap."

"I'm sorry I woke you."

"No, that's okay. It's time for me to get up." Meggan glanced at the Vietnamese magazine he was holding, and then noticed something hesitant about him. "Would you like to come in?"

"Yes, if you have a minute."

"Of course." He stepped in and waited for her to close the door.

Meggan sensed he had something important to talk about, hoping it wasn't more bad news.

"I have some good news."

She released a held breath. "Oh?"

Tam took the stack of money from inside the pages of his magazine and handed it to her. She stared at the wad of money as if Tam had just handed her something alive. She took the stack of bills with both hands and gazed at him with a bewildered expression.

"What are you doing?"

"Returning your money. At least part of it. I couldn't get any more American dollars, but euros should be easy to exchange when you get home."

"No, I mean how did you know I was conned out of my money today? How are you involved with those people? You're scaring me, Tam."

"No need to feel scared. Vu, the tour driver, knows me and told me how you were swindled. He asked if I could help you. I went to Duc's house and demanded your money back, that's all."

"That's all? How was Duc involved?"

"He set you up, but his share was only half. The policeman kept the rest, and probably had to pay others to keep them silent. I'm afraid this is the best I can do."

Meggan flipped through the bills—not to count them but to weigh the reality of this surprise.

"I'll go now, Meggan, but first I want to tell you that I know some police are corrupt, and I know there are a few con men like Duc who prey on tourists. But I also want to tell you that most Vietnamese and hilltribe people are honorable. They want the same things from life as you do, to live with their families in peace and good health, with enough money to be comfortable."

"I believe you, Tam. Can you stay awhile? Maybe I can find something for you in the minibar."

"I'd share a sweet drink with you."

"Sure." She set the money on the bed and took an orange beverage can from the refrigerator, pouring it into two glasses and handing one to Tam. She sat on the end of the bed. Tam sat on the small wood desk chair.

She took a long sip, and said, "I'm surprised Duc admitted cheating me."

"I didn't ask him to admit it. I told him I knew and he believed me."

"Did he just hand the money over? I can't imagine him giving in so easily."

"He gave in quickly, but not easily. I left him suffering a little, but not enough to change his ways. People like Duc are snakes; they never forget how to strike."

"We have people like that in America, too. Criminals can be anywhere."

"It's hard to think about America that way."

Meggan picked up the wad of bills. "I'd like to give you part of this money, Tam, to show my appreciation."

"You've already shown your appreciation. You gave me a nice sweet drink."

She laughed and said, "I only gave you half of it. Seriously, how about letting me take you to dinner tonight?"

"I have a better idea. Let me take you on a picnic tomorrow to a beautiful place near some of our family's coffee gardens. We'll take a good road through forests and green mountains where the hilltribe people live. If you let me show you this lovely side of Vietnam before you go home, I will feel fully compensated for reclaiming your money."

Meggan clicked her glass of orangeade against his. "Okay, you've got a deal."

CHAPTER 25

At the appointed time of eight o'clock the next morning, Tam arrived at the Royal Tiger Hotel. Meggan had been watching for him through the glass door, and she stepped out with her cloth tote bag before he got to the entrance.

"I hope you're not bringing your own lunch."

"No, just a long-sleeved shirt and a bottle of water—and a couple of granola bars in case you showed up empty handed."

Tam grinned to himself while they walked together to his jeep. "Vietnamese call those American food bars *fast food.*"

"We call hamburgers and French fries fast food."

"Food bars are faster."

"Yes, but we call those a snack, more like instant food."

"Our lunch will be Vietnamese fast food. You'll see that we are not very fast when it comes to enjoying a meal."

Tam opened the jeep's passenger door for Meggan. After she got in and tossed her bag onto the back seat, he started the engine and drove through Dalat's city center, and then through an industrial area, passing by the dilapidated airport she had seen with Duc.

"Duc told me that airport is still used by the military."

"That's right. It's always been a military airport. After the Americans abandoned it in 1973, there was panic and chaos everywhere. During that time, my father was able to scrounge many supplies and parts the Americans left behind."

"What did he do with the parts?"

"He used them for his garden. For instance, he took a ceiling fan from an office, a pump from a fuel truck, and many spools of flexible tubing. Can you guess what he did with those things?"

"The pumps and tubing might have been for watering your gardens. The ceiling fan to keep cool?"

"Very close. He removed the motor from the ceiling fan, and then made the blades work like a windmill. He got the idea from the Moulin Rouge, the name of a bar in Dalat. The name means *red mill* in French, and it had a miniature windmill on its roof—but a smaller one than at the Moulin Rouge in Paris or the one in Saigon. He attached metal braces and gears to the windmill, and the fuel truck's rubber fan belt was used to turn the pump. After much tinkering, he finally made it pump water from a small pond up to his garden, where the water flowed back down between small channeled ditches between the rows."

"Did other gardeners make windmills like his?"

"No, he had to keep his invention a secret. He only used the pump at night, and the tubing was buried underground. During the day he turned the windmill on its side in tall grass, and covered it with a green canvass army tarp he found at the airport."

"So no one would steal it?"

"No, he was afraid the new communist government would put him in either prison or a reeducation camp, either of them almost a death sentence. The government was arrest-ing anyone accused of capitalist activities back then. After reunification, all the privately-owned land was taken from the farmers and made into collectives. Every worker was paid the same small wage, regardless of their tasks or how much work they did. Many people only came to the fields one or two days a week, and nobody worked hard. The crops all over Vietnam, even the rice paddies, began to fail, and no one felt responsible. They thought it was the government's problem, and that only the government could fix it. Famine began to show its fangs, and that's when my father began planting his illegal gardens. He kept them small and scattered, and the pump and mountain streams brought water to all of them."

"And you remember that?"

"Oh, yes. When I was a small child I worked with my father at night by candlelight, planting, weeding, or harvesting. That kept us alive. I also remember one scary night when he accidently dug up a buried Vietcong weapons cache near one of our secret gardens. It had five Chinese AK-47 automatic rifles, greased and wrapped in a canvass tarp to preserve them, and lots of ammunition in clay jugs sealed with waxed rags. Father reburied them and marked the location by planting a tapioca bush nearby."

"Your father was a resourceful man."

"And a natural planter. His father and grandfather had been farmers, and he learned much when he was a boy. He is still happiest when working in the soil, making things grow."

"He still farms?"

"Mostly as a hobby now, but he still oversees research and education for our coffee growers. After it became legal to own land, we kept needing more and more coffee to sell, so he taught hilltribe families to grow it for us. They supply the land and labor, and we supply them with plants and fertilizers. Father taught them ways to grow better crops, like pruning and using irrigation during droughts."

"Did you inherit your father's green thumb?"

"Green thumb?"

"It's an American expression that means being able to grow things well."

"Then I don't have green thumbs. My father taught me much about coffee growing, but it is not my talent or my passion. I'm better at the business side of our family's coffee company."

"You must be good at that. After I met you at the Swiss Coffee House, a waitress told me your coffee business was important to the area."

"I hope so."

"Do you sell your coffee in America?"

"No, mostly in Europe—and much of that is made into instant coffee, I'm sad to say. I pray trade relations will soon allow us to sell in the USA. It's a large, rich market, and I know that Americans, like the Vietnamese, appreciate quality coffee, and they even brew it in their homes. We are also growing more organic coffee now. At first, our farming families resisted the extra work of organic growing, but many of them have gotten used to it, and they like the extra money from higher prices."

Tam drove past a deep valley that stretched almost to the horizon. Large fenced fields were separated by narrow dirt roads, with small houses clustered at the edges. There were also dozens of long, clear plastic-covered greenhouses in the adjoining foothills, all of them broadside to the sun for the greatest exposure.

"Is that a corporate farm?" Meggan asked.

"No, it's an economic zone, established by the government. Some hilltribe people were scattered throughout the forests after reunification to stay clear of the new communist government, especially the tribes that helped American soldiers. But they couldn't grow enough food in the forest, and they were starving. They even had to bury their dead in the forest instead of at their traditional homeland. The government eventually made them leave the forest and gave each family land to farm. They also receive some rice and other necessities."

"What are they growing?"

"Mostly coffee, but also black pepper and tapioca, and some fruits like persimmons and jackfruit. They grow vegetables in the hot houses.

"Is your coffee farm this big?"

"We only own a few coffee gardens, and those are mostly for research. Coffee must be picked by hand each day to choose only the ripe red berries from the clusters of green ones. They ripen at different times, so machines cannot replace the farmer with a good eye and careful hands. We guarantee a few farm families a small monthly payment to tend our gardens, and then give them a share of the annual harvest income. In a few minutes, we will be near a few of the gardens we own. Would you like to see them?"

"Sure."

After a few more miles through steep mountain passes, Tam slowed down over a stretch of damaged roadway. He called the medium potholes buffalo holes, and the largest, elephant holes. He downshifted and pulled alongside the road overlooking a sunny green valley that stretched between two protective mountains. Terraced green fields looking like giant staircases had been planted almost halfway up one of the mountains, each level planted with tidy rows of small trees.

"Do you see that little blue house at the bottom, next to the river?"

Meggan scanned the valley's center and found the narrow curvy river, and then spotted the building. "Yes, I see it. How do people get all the way down there?"

"You'll see."

Tam drove a few yards to an opening in the dense roadside brush. Meggan didn't see it until he slowed enough to turn off the asphalt road onto a rough trail barely wide enough to let his jeep through. The transmission whined in low gear as he groped his way around bends and over washouts. Bushy branches scraped the sides of the jeep while it waddled down the bumpy hard clay path, splashing through streamlets that merrily tumbled and spilled toward the valley's bottom.

Meggan gripped the dashboard's handhold with a combination of holding her breath and the urge to giggle. "Do the people who live down here use jeeps?"

"No, something even better for this road—a motorbike."

After what seemed to her as longer than it probably took, they arrived on the other side of the river from the bright blue building. Tam rolled down his window and shut off his engine. The building looked much larger than Meggan had estimated from the road high above, and now she could see flowers and small shrubs neatly planted around it. Although in good condition, it was nothing more than a metal shed with a small window on the side and another one next to the white front door. A single electric wire ran down from the roadway, like a tether to the world above. A rope footbridge about fifty feet long with a wood-planked walkway crossed the expanse of the peaceful flowing water.

While they were getting out of the jeep, an elderly woman came out of the front door, wearing black working pajamas. She said something to Tam in Vietnamese that made him laugh. He replied in Vietnamese, and looked at Meggan.

"She asked if you are my mistress."

Meggan restrained her grin. "I hope you cleared that up. I have a reputation to maintain."

He laughed with more abandon this time and closed the jeep's door. Meggan was already out and smiling back at the woman, who bowed slightly and said something to her in Vietnamese.

"She welcomes you to her and her husband's home, and she's offering you coffee or tea."

"Do we have time?"

"Of course, and it would make her very happy."

"I'd like some tea."

After Tam interpreted Meggan's answer, the woman rushed back into the house.

Meggan eyed the slim footbridge. "Is this safe?"

"I hope so. They ride their motorbike across it. Hold onto both rope handrails and walk with one foot in front of the other so it doesn't swing too much. I'll wait until you're across."

Meggan stepped onto the footbridge tentatively and took a couple of steps. She looked back at Tam who nodded encouragement, and then she kept going. The bridge slightly swayed back and forth when she got near the middle, and she stopped to steady it.

Tam said, "Keep going, the middle moves the most."

She stepped quickly to get to the other end, and then turned and raised her arms victoriously. Tam sauntered across as though the bridge was made of concrete, and raised his arms, too.

"You were very brave," he said, "and a good bridge walker."

"You're teasing me."

"Yes, but it's still true. Let's visit Mrs. Hoa."

Tam knocked on the open door and the woman invited them in, motioning for Meggan to sit at the table. Tam removed his shoes, and Meggan did the same. Three china teacups with saucers had been positioned in front of chairs at the table. Tam pulled a chair out for Meggan, and then sat next to her while Mrs. Hoa poured steaming pale-yellow tea into each cup, starting with Meggan's. She said something to Meggan in Vietnamese, which Tam interpreted as an offer of canned milk. Meggan smiled at Mrs. Hoa and shook her head no. While Mrs. Hoa put the teapot back on the wood countertop, Meggan looked around the combined kitchen and living room. A motorbike was parked in the sitting area, next to an eclectic combination of wood and plastic furniture. Intense midday sunlight made the rooms bright and cheery. The kitchen was austere but tidy, with a freestanding two-burner gas stove sitting on the countertop, and next to a shorter counter, was a refrigerator smaller than Meggan's hotel minibar.

Mrs. Hoa joined them at the table and said something to Tam. He took a sip of his tea and Meggan followed his lead. Meggan said it was delightful, and so fresh tasting. Tam interpreted this to Mrs. Hoa and that success seemed to make her relax.

"This is uncured tea," Tam said to Meggan. "They pick a few leaves each day, and keep it fresh in the refrigerator. I wondered if you'd like it. You can be candid with me because she doesn't understand a word of English."

"I do like it. It's a little like an herbal tea."

Tam interpreted this latest comment to Mrs. Hoa. She nodded with pleasure and took her first sip, as if first needing to make sure of Meggan's approval. Mrs. Hoa got up and took a metal can that was brightly illustrated with Chinese-looking figures from one of her three small cupboards, opened the lid and set it on the table close to Tam and Meggan.

"Try a cracker if you like," Tam said. "They are made from rice flour, black sesame seeds and some chili paste. I call them *fire* crackers in English, but they aren't really very hot, not like Thai food—or Texas food."

"Have you been to Texas?"

"No, I've never been to America, but I saw a television show about Texas barbequing. I think all Texas people must be wild cowboys at heart. They are always ready to ride horses with their special riding boots and wide sun hats."

"The way you drove down that steep trail, I'd call you a wild cowboy."

Tam gave her a quizzical look.

"I meant that as a humorous compliment."

"Oh, thank you."

Meggan took one of the crackers and tested a nibble. She nodded agreement. "They're good. A nice balance with the soft tea."

Just as Tam finished interpreting that for Hoa, they heard the noisy chug-chug-chug from an engine. Tam got up and opened the door for Meggan to look out. She saw a sun-cured man wearing a dirty tan baseball cap, sitting behind the long handlebars of a two-wheeled knobby-tired tractor, an oversized version of an American garden tractor. A trailer filled with stacked plastic bushel baskets was attached to it. The engine sputtered in protest when the man shut it down. He jumped off the trailer and walked toward Tam and Meggan.

"I saw you coming, Mr. Tam. I was working in garden number five, so I had a long way to come."

"You didn't have to hurry, Viet. Your charming wife was

taking good care of us. I would like to introduce you to my American friend, Meggan."

Viet quickly pulled off his cap. He came to within a few feet of the doorway and after a shallow nod, said, "I am pleased to greet you, Miss Megan."

Viet's English was not accent-free like Tam's, but clear enough for Meggan to understand.

"I'm pleased to meet you, Mr. Viet. That looks like a good tractor for these hills."

"Oh, yes, to be sure. This kind of tractor is used by almost all hilltribe farmers. The big growers can buy bigger tractors, but they are not as easy to fix and they are not as good on steep hills."

Tam turned to Meggan. "There are thousands upon thousands of these tractors throughout the hill county."

"I've noticed."

Viet followed Meggan and Tam back to the kitchen, removed his boots and placed his cap on a hook next to the door. "It's nice to come inside and enjoy some comfort from the sun."

Meggan and Tam returned to their chairs, and Viet sat next to Hoa. She went to a cupboard to get a cup and saucer for her husband, and then poured his tea.

After Viet took a short sip, he said to Meggan, "I have thought Americans only drank coffee. We have good coffee if you want that instead of tea."

"Thank you but I'm enjoying your delicious tea."

Viet said something in Vietnamese to Tam. Tam repeated *delicious* followed by an apparent explanation.

"Oh, yes, tasting it is most delicious. We grow it in back of this house, just for us and our guests. I think it's better than coffee in the afternoon."

Tam turned to Meggan. "Our company owns these gardens to experiment with different growing methods, and Viet and Hoa manage the operation for us. Viet studied agriculture and English at university in Saigon as a young man, but he learned the best ways to grow coffee by working with my father."

"Our two sons found jobs in Saigon after graduating," Viet said. "After that, my wife and I moved here from our village and we have found a good life in this valley."

Tam said, "Meggan, have you ever seen coffee growing?"

"No. I've only seen roasted coffee beans."

"We call them beans, too, but they are actually seeds inside a sweet berry. Viet, would you like to show her what they look like?"

"Yes, of course."

The three of them put on their shoes and Meggan and Tam followed Viet across the footbridge to the nearest garden, the only one at ground level.

"This is garden number one," Tam said. "No climbing needed."

Meggan shielded her eyes from the sun with her hand and looked up, counting nine terraced gardens staircasing up the side of the mountain. Only a narrow reddish clay pathway connected them.

"Are all the beans—I mean berries—carried down by hand?"

"Yes," Tam said as they walked to the garden. "Some of our company's contract growers come from the nearby village early every morning to pick the ripe berries. They bring them down in baskets that fit on their motorbikes, and they take them home to dry. After twigs and leaves are picked out, the berries are spread out in the sun on tarps and are turned regularly for two or three weeks to dry evenly. After the seeds are removed, we grind the berry pulp and let it decompose for fertilizer."

They followed Viet, and Tam pointed to a tree about eight feet high. "This one is Arabica. It gives the best coffee and sells for a better price than the other types, but it is smaller and fussier, like a spoiled child. During a drought we need to irrigate the plants to keep them alive. Robusta is not as good as Arabica, but is heartier, so we grow them in higher fields. Robusta trees want to grow taller, but we cut the tops off so workers can reach the berries."

From a low-hanging cluster of round berries, Viet pulled a bright red one, a little smaller than a cherry tomato, and gave it to Meggan. "You can taste it if you want to but be careful of the seeds inside."

She took a small bite. "It's sweet."

"Now," Viet said with a grin, "look for the coffee seeds."

She pulled the berry apart and found three seeds.

"Three seeds are rare," Viet said. "There are usually two. I think this means you will find good luck today."

"How about starting your new luck with some lunch?" Tam said.

"Sure, I'm hungry."

Tam thanked Viet for showing them around, and he and Meggan walked back to the jeep.

"Where are we going for the picnic?"

Tam pointed up the top of the green mountain on the other side of the river. "Up there."

Meggan looked up and gasped, not just because of the height, but because of the steepness. She assumed he was teasing her.

"You're going to make me earn that fast food lunch you

brought."

"You've already earned it by coming here with me. Now I'm going to carry you to the top of the mountain."

"Oh?" She wondered if his grin was a sign of playfulness.

"In my jeep, of course. First, we'll cross farther downstream where the river becomes wide and shallow, then we'll take the road to the top."

She looked up again and spotted the thin dirt slit zigzagging back and forth across the face of the grassy mountain to the top. "That's a road?"

"Well, almost a road."

He opened her door and she climbed in, worrying about the safety of this bizarre plan. Was Tam just foolishly showing off? What if the jeep rolls over?

"I don't need a scary adventure."

"It won't be. I promise."

After driving the length of the coffee gardens, she saw that the river did, indeed, widen and become shallow enough to see gravel and stones just beneath its rippling surface. Tam shifted into low gear and pulled the short four-wheel-drive lever on the floor between them. He eased the jeep into the water, which came almost to the middle of the front wheels while he worked his way across the river slowly, patiently letting the tires find traction. Meggan held onto the grab bar in front of her while the jeep wobbled over the larger stones, some the size of coconuts. She could see tire marks where vehicles, perhaps this one and Viet's tractor, had scaled over the low riverbank across from them, and she allowed herself to enjoy the fun of off-roading.

After the jeep pawed its way up and over the opposite riverbank, Tam stopped. "Are you still with me?"

"I'm still sitting here."

"I mean for the climb. I'll go slowly."

She tightened her seatbelt. "Okay, I'm ready."

Tam drove down a worn trail until he came to a wider red dirt path that began up the side of the mountain. Meggan reconsidered how safe this was going to be, but Tam seemed unperturbed while the jeep whined ahead in low gear. He shifted up a gear on the short straightaways and downshifted to a crawl around hairpin switchbacks and over washouts. As they made their way back and forth across the face of the mountain, gradually ever higher, Meggan began to relax and notice the lush, rounded mountains around them. They would be called big hills by anyone who had been through the craggy US Rockies or Sierras.

"These must be older mountains than those in America," she said above the jeep's laboring engine noise. "They're shorter and rounder."

He nodded with a playful look. "Then God must have made Vietnam first."

As they got closer to the top, Meggan saw that the vegetation, which had looked so uniform from below, was actually hip-high grass mixed in with bramble, brush, and scattered trees. At some point near the top, shorter grasses and bushes began to dominate, and when the rough little road finally petered out on the mountain's flat crest, only short grass grew, its green blades pulsing wildly in wind gusts that poured over from the other side.

They got out of the jeep at the same time and Meggan walked a few feet away, turning around and around in the breeze, pulling together all the breathtaking beauty around them.

"There are hundreds of mountains," she said.

Tam stood watching her. "Hundreds you can see, hundreds more beyond."

"Is this one the tallest?"

"Yes, the tallest within sight."

While he took two canvass folding chairs from the back of the jeep and set them up a few feet away, Meggan started noticing little details. The highway they came down from was now lower than they were, and she saw a village farther down it. The blue house of Hoa and Viet appeared even tinier than from the highway, and the river below was nothing more than a flickering silver thread. This mountain's flat wide crest meandered for perhaps a few miles, looking ever-narrower as it disappeared from view. Then she noticed what looked like a wood cross only a few yards away.

She rejoined Tam rubbing her arms. "It's chilly up here."

"I'll get your shirt from the jeep."

Tam handed her the Scottish tartan shirt from her bag. She buttoned it and rolled the long sleeves up past her wrist while he brought a square canvass tote bag from the jeep, set it on the ground between the chairs, and unzipped it.

"Your picnic fast-food?"

"Yes, but I confess that I can't take the credit for it. Our housekeeper, Mai, made this for us. She gave us both fried shrimp and pork spring rolls, and sticky rice with mushrooms wrapped in leaves. She also included cans of orange-flavored water."

Meggan sat in a folding chair and crossed her arms to stay warm while Tam served her one of each spring roll on a plate, and a squared leaf package containing a mushroom rice cake. He opened a can of orange water for her and placed it in the chair's cup holder, and draped a linen napkin over her knee. They ate in silence for a few minutes, while Meggan glanced at the magical vistas around them. She noticed how comfortable Tam looked while eating his meal, as if he was having lunch with an old friend, no pretenses or expectations, just the joy of sharing a meal on a beautiful sunny day.

"This is delicious. Thank you, Tam."

"I'll deliver your compliment to Mai. She'll be very happy because she was worried that you might not like her Vietnamese food."

"Do you come here often?"

"Not anymore. I used to come up here on my motorbike when I was a teenager, to watch the Americans working. They came to help the Vietnamese government put in this road."

Meggan got up looked at the curvy roadway below. "Why did they want a road here?"

He joined her and studied her eyes. "To find the remains of American soldiers killed in a terrible battle here, just below the crest."

Meggan started walking toward the wooden cross. She had to stop. Her breathing became tight and she turned toward Tam, not wanting him to say anything more about this place, not wanting him to spoil the peace she found here, yet she desperately wanted to understand more.

As if sensing her feelings, he said, "See that village farther down the highway we came on? That's near where I grew up, Meggan. It's Bong Dung—the village that was Bang Dia before reunification."

She saw the tiny village and then looked plaintively at Tam.

"Yes," he said, understanding the question in her eyes. "You are standing on the same ground your father walked on."

Meggan suddenly felt overwhelmed with conflicting emotions: anger at Tam for not telling her sooner, while wishing he hadn't said anything to spoil her enjoyment here. She looked around with new eyes and suddenly feeling weak, afraid of the great height of the mountain, the steepness of its overgrown slopes, and the wind that seemed to push her away. She dropped to her knees and then sat on the ground looking away from Tam, wondering with dread how her father must have felt while he lay on this mountain dying. She covered her face with her hands and wept uncontrollably.

Tam came over and knelt next to her. He put his arm around her, and she rested her head on his chest while sobbing a while longer. She finally pulled away and dabbed her eyes with a shirt sleeve.

"I'm sorry, Meggan, if I handled this clumsily but I thought we should come here for you to understand the peace and beauty of this place without fear. As you were able to see, this is no longer a place of suffering. It's a sacred place of peace. The horrors of war have long passed, and this beautiful mountain is now a memorial to the brave men who gave everything they had. Everyone who lives around here sees it that way."

She got up and said, "I'm not upset with you, Tam. I don't know what's wrong with me."

Tam got up and touched her shoulder. "Can you accept that there's nothing wrong with you?"

Meggan looked into his eyes and nodded yes, not sure about what she was agreeing to, but it made her feel better. When he offered his hand, she took it and they walked together back to their impromptu picnic area. Tam started folding up the chairs.

"So, the people in Bong Dung know about this battle?"

"Oh, yes," Tam said. "The older people still remember the explosions from that terrible morning. Back then, these valleys were overgrown by thick forests that were infested with dangerous snakes and Vietcong fighters. By the time your fa-

ther's outfit was dropped onto this mountain, large numbers
of North Vietnamese Army soldiers had already infiltrated
into the area from Cambodia. The VC and the NVA were
coordinating their forces for a joint push southward to overthrow Saigon, hoping the departing Americans would leave a
power void for them to fill. They were eager for battle by the
time your father's unit arrived. I was just an infant then, but
while growing up, we always knew this as Massacre Mountain, famously the first communist battle victory of many
more to come."

Meggan stared again at tiny faraway Bong Dung, then
looked over the neatly planted fields in the valley below this
breezy cool mountaintop. She struggled with the incongru-
ency of this peace and beauty, and the terror that Tam had
just described.

Tam started putting the folded chairs and food bag into
the jeep. "Should we return to Dalat?"

"I'd like to walk along the crest a little way, alone if you
don't mind."

"Of course. Take all the time you want."

Meggan stopped at the wooden cross, which was about
four feet high. Although weather-worn, she could see a faint
painted inscription that said "In memory of the brave fallen
from Co A, 32nd Inf Batt." She wondered how the tangled
morass beneath the crest allowed anyone to find any remains
of those men. But then she wondered if it mattered. Would
her life have been any different if her father's body had been
found and returned, and then ceremoniously buried in the
United States? It wouldn't have helped her know anything
about him or his life, or how and where he died.

When she started to return to Tam, a strong gust sent
a frightening chill through her, and an overwhelming sense

came over her that something about her father was with her right now. Was his spirit speaking to her? A part of her wanted to believe that; another part couldn't.

She looked up, and Tam's jeep seemed so distant, as if she had wandered too far from him. She squinted to see him sitting inside waiting behind the sun-glared windshield. Although she wanted to run to him so he could take her away, she also felt reluctant to leave. As she got closer, Tam stepped out of the jeep and watched her, as if feeling concerned about how she was handling the experience.

"I think I'm ready to go back," she said.

"Before we go, would you like me to take your picture?"

"Yes, that would be nice."

She gave her cellphone to Tam. He guided her to one side, to include the mountain and valley below.

"Tam, let's get one together."

She let him hold the camera at arm's length while they both smiled into the camera.

***

Their descent down the now-familiar winding mountain trail seemed quicker than the climb had been, even though Tam was carefully creeping down in low gear.

They both waved at smiling Mrs. Hoa as they drove past her blue corrugated metal home, and then made their way back up the rough trail to the highway. This leg of the trip was made in silence, with only side glances and separate thoughts trying to sort out their shared experience. Meggan checked her watch: almost three o'clock—they would probably be in Dalat a little after four. When the temperature got warmer, she took off her long-sleeved wool shirt and tossed it onto the backseat.

On the way back, Tam lifted the silence by telling Meggan how the government had arrested his father after they discovered his clandestine coffee and vegetable gardens.

Tam said he and Bien were children, but old enough to remember the military thugs who handcuffed their father and took him away while their mother wailed helplessly. That was in 1986, and his father faced many years in prison without trial for the crime of capitalist activities.

But by then, however, Vietnam's communist leaders had seen Stalinist Communism collapse in the Soviet Union, and Communist China was struggling out of its socialist dark ages by allowing private enterprises. The communist model was also starving the Vietnamese, a people not afraid to revolt when desperate. Vietnam's leaders had begun looking to Japan, Singapore, Hong Kong, and South Korea for answers, and came up with *Doi Moi*—free enterprise—but they treaded cautiously with this risky economic experiment. They started by letting farmers cultivate a few hectares of land and sell their harvest at prices fixed by the government. That increased farm production but not enough, so they tried giving the farmers title to the land, with permission to eventually give it—but not sell it—to one of their children. That urged more progress, but recovery was still sluggish. The government then allowed farmers to bargain for prices, and sell their land to anyone—with police approval, of course. This stage tapped into Vietnam's enterprising spirit. But although rice farmers rebounded to pre-war production levels, coffee farmers had lost the knowledge and skills to produce reliable yields, and concentrated on planting vegetables and mountain rice.

Tam said that shortly after his father's arrest, government officials saw the healthy plants and production levels that his father had achieved illegally in secret gardens, and they offered to forgive his serious crimes if he helped the government teach other farmers his secrets.

"My father has such green thumbs," Tam said with a grin. "When the threat of famine passed, Vietnam started looking at export opportunities, and officials asked Father about his coffee growing techniques. Since then, he has helped many farmers start coffee gardens, and it helped Vietnam become a successful coffee exporter."

"How much land did the government give your father?"

"Only ten hectares, which I think is about twenty-five acres. But he was very busy teaching other farmers, so he let another farmer work our land and then we split the harvest with him. As a teenager, this seemed like a revolutionary business idea, with both the worker and the owner benefiting. Then I learned how coffee brokers made even *more* money without *any* land. A much better idea! The brokers gave operating money to the farmers for seeds and fertilizer, and then guaranteed the harvest price. The brokers earned a profit by finding coffee buyers in other countries, and then shipping unroasted coffee to them. I encouraged my father to experiment with that kind of coffee business, but he wasn't interested. When I promised to do all the business work, he got interested. We eventually made money as small-time brokers, and then we bought more land to sharecrop. Other growers began letting us broker their coffee because they liked and trusted Father. After a few years, we stopped buying land and only brokered coffee for other landowners."

"So, you became the family's business brain."

"My father is good at business, too, but he was too busy with his first love of perfecting his growing methods, something he still loves. I wasn't much help for that. My thumbs have no green."

Tam parked in front of the Royal Tiger Hotel just after four o'clock. After a long, slightly awkward look between them, Tam said, "May I walk you to your room?"

Meggan said yes, and Tam reached back for her bag on the back seat.

She picked up her key from the front desk clerk, and when they got to her room, she said, "Thank you for the wonderful picnic, Tam, and for an experience I'll never forget. You made my trip to Vietnam an even better success than I hoped for."

"I'd like to show you a little more about Dalat, not the tourist sites, but places where the original people live. There is a nearby village of Lat people, the hilltribe that first settled in this area."

"I have a reservation for a flight to Saigon tomorrow."

"That's easy to change; just tell the hotel clerk to call the airline."

Meggan looked at him with a tilt of her head. "Did you, by chance, tell the hotel to make any flight changes for me?"

"I hoped you wouldn't mind. I just thought you could use a little help. The airline's president is my friend, and he has given you diplomatic status in their system. Any request will have top priority."

"And, per chance, did you offer to cover my hotel expenses?"

Tam shrugged his shoulders playfully. "Secretly taking care of a bill for someone special is a Vietnamese custom. But don't worry about the cost. When I instructed the hotel manager to forward me your final invoice, he insisted on simply writing off your expenses as a visiting travel writer."

"Another friend of yours?"

"He and I play tennis sometimes. He likes playing tennis with me because neither of us are good at it."

She couldn't hold back her smile any longer, and she looked into his brown eyes. He rested his hand on her upper arm and their lips slowly met. They held each other closely during a soft kiss that seemed both brief and endless to Meggan, and then Tam nuzzled into her hair and they held each other tighter.

She whispered, "I'll cancel my flight."

"I'll see you in the morning."

CHAPTER 26

Meggan canceled her flight to Saigon without reserving another one. Her feelings about Dalat had completely shifted after today and she wanted to let things play out with Tam before scheduling her return. She couldn't imagine a long-term romantic relationship with someone who lives on the other side of the planet, but she couldn't imagine just forgetting him, either—not after today.

The evening was chilly when she stepped out for a walk, so she was glad to have her father's tartan wool shirt on. It kept her warm, and now meant so much more to her.

There was lightness in Meggan's step while she strolled toward Dalat's central market, feeling braver about venturing beyond the now-familiar few blocks around her hotel. Stalls were already erected along the sidewalks leading to the central roundabout. As it got darker, bright lights glowed inside canvas roofs, where people could buy plastic bags filled with dried fruits and dried strips of indiscernible meat, clothing, mostly for cold weather, like coats and knit hats, all stacked in tidy piles. Smoky grills covered with roasting meats, snails, and strange vegetables skewered by wood sticks. Two pots of steaming soup sat on portable gas stoves next to a basket filled with baguettes. People of all ages leisurely roamed the area, mostly younger couples and groups of giggling teenage girls twittering like birds from stall to stall, with a few solo males plodding along not far behind. Many shoppers roamed around with something to eat or drink, sampling the seemingly endless snack choices.

Heeding the advice of travel websites, Meggan avoided raw foods, but the grilled treats looked safe. On one of the grills, a crispy flat bread being prepared for someone by a grandmotherly woman, with bits of various vegetable and slivers of meat, all held together by a thin layer of cheese. Meggan pointed to it and then to herself, and the woman slid one off the grill with a metal spatula onto a sheet of brown paper. Meggan took folded dongs from her pocket and followed her usual method of letting the woman choose the appropriate payment.

The vegetables tasted fresh, the meat fragrant, and the light cheese did its job of holding everything in place. She ate while strolling with the ebb and flow of the now-thickening crowd. She decided to join a few scattered people who were sitting on concrete steps that led up to an almost empty fancy clothing store. At this slight elevation, she could see most of the market area, but nothing could compete with her mountain views that afternoon. She thought about the excitement of the trip, her emotions on top of the mountain, how Tam had looked after her, his protective embrace, the gentleness of his kiss…

Her brief reverie was interrupted when she saw Tam's jeep slowly circling with other cars in the roundabout. He exited on the other side from where she was sitting, and then parked along the curb farther down the block. When he got out, she saw him open the back door and lift a girl with a pink dress from the backseat. A woman wearing an expensive-looking tan waist jacket stepped out of the passenger door and they walked together with Tam holding the child, and entered one of the shops just beyond the chaos of the central market.

Meggan's stomach tightened, realizing she might have made yet another blunder about a man, and so soon after being betrayed, cheated, and divorced. She wondered what she had been expecting with Tam, after such a short time, with just a few days left before she would be leaving Dalat. She felt as if she had been acting out some kind of foolish romance story, perhaps as an antidote for the sting of her last relationship.

She sauntered down the steps to a trash barrel and tossed away her half-eaten sandwich. Picking up her stride, she wove through a meandering crowd that began to feel oppressive to her.

On the way back to the hotel, she shifted some of the blame to Tam. How could he so convincingly deceive her, and then go home to do the same thing to his wife and child? She knew that rich men had willing mistresses in some countries, but was that acceptable in Vietnam? Or was this something less significant, simply a one-time fling with a naïve tourist, an unattached woman just passing through, never to return? Perhaps something to brag about with his tennis partner?

When she got back to the hotel, she asked the receptionist if married Vietnamese men wear wedding rings.

"Not traditionally, miss, but now some men do, especially younger men. It's a Western fashion."

Meggan started toward the stairs with her thoughts racing. Maybe the woman and child were just friends or relatives needing a lift. Or he might be a rich playboy. But that didn't seem reasonable; he seemed too sincere and kind, not self-centered or egotistical in any way. But then, she had also trusted Brent…

Meggan decided to not leave Vietnam without at least trying to learn the truth about Tam. She went back to the receptionist.

"Do you know where Tran Van Tam lives?"

"Somewhere on the west side, I think."

"How can I find his phone number?"

"I don't know, miss. Maybe you could ask him."

When Meggan got to her room she saw a sealed envelope that had been slipped under the door. She tore off one of the ends and read a note from Tam that said he'd be at the hotel at ten o'clock in the morning. Frustrated that she had been given no choice, she tore the note up and tossed it in the trash can. She thought about leaving a note for him at the front desk, saying she had other plans and would be gone all day. If she was going to see him again, she'd do so on her terms.

She opened a beer from the minibar and sat on the edge of the bed, wondering if she was judging him fairly. Had she expected him to be completely unattached, just waiting for her to enter his life? After all, she hadn't told him about her recent divorce, or revealed anything else about her past. And he did retrieve some of her ransom money, and he helped her fulfill her reason for coming to Dalat—without asking anything from her in return.

Sipping her beer and feeling lonely, she almost wished he had.

CHAPTER 27

Just before 10 AM the next morning, Meggan sipped coffee in the quiet reception area, nervously glancing at the hotel's entrance. When she saw Tam coming up the steps, she took out her phone and pretended to be looking at something interesting.

"Good morning," Tam said from just inside the door.

Her head bobbed up, as if she was surprised to see him.

"There's no hurry," he said. "Finish what you're doing."

"I'm done," Meggan said, getting up. "I was just emailing my mother to see how she was doing." She made a mental note to do that when she returned to the hotel's Wi-Fi.

"Is your mother well?"

"Oh, sure, just fine. Are we going to see the Lat people today?"

"Yes, I hope you find them interesting."

Tam opened the lobby door for her. While descending the steps, he said, "The Lat village is on the edge of the city. Because they are the hilltribe people who first settled here, the city was named for them. In their language, *Da* means a stream of water, so *Da Lat* roughly means 'the water source of the Lat people.'"

Meggan got into the jeep before he had a chance to open

the door for her. There was no child seat in the back.

He got in and closed his door. "The Lat people have kept their traditions through the years, with a few changes. For instance, in the early 1900s, during the French colonial period, missionaries came from France to open schools. Many Lat people eventually became Catholics."

Tam navigated through the morning traffic, which thinned as they got farther from the city's commercial district. After a few minutes through residential neighborhoods, he drove down what looked like an alley, and then turned onto a narrow road running between simple sturdy-looking houses, most of them built with dark unpainted wood. He parked in front of a house with a rickety wood fence that looked more like it was for keeping pets or small children in, than for keeping intruders out. Tam opened the gate for Meggan, and they walked to the back yard, which was dominated by a tidy garden. An old man wearing gray dungarees, a long-sleeved brown shirt, and a brightly colored woven vest was picking coffee berries and putting them into a small basket. Tam called out something in Vietnamese, and the man turned around. He set the basket on the ground and quickly stepped over to shake hands with Tam.

"He is the Lat chief," Tam said to Meggan.

He bowed cheerfully to Meggan and said something to Tam.

Tam responded to the chief and turned to Meggan. "Like Mrs. Hoa, he asked if we were lovers."

She wanted to ask Tam what he said in reply, but instead said, "I don't know why he'd think that."

"The Lat are not afraid to be openly curious. I told him we were friends."

The chief said something to Meggan, which Tam interpreted.

"He invited you to his meeting lodge for some entertainment."

Meggan walked alongside Tam while they followed the lively old chief, wondering what kind of entertainment he had in store for her. They followed the chief up a few steep wood steps to the door.

The inside looked more like a storage shed than something she'd expect to be a chief's official meeting place. The planked siding had many gaps, some wide enough to allow in sunlight. A few heavy-looking boards rested above on log rafters, and simple benches lined the walls. Almost knee-high brown ceramic jugs were stored under most of the benches, all of them with green fabric over their openings, tied in place with twine. A wooden box on the floor dominated the center of the room, about one foot high and four feet wide on all sides, lined inside with charred stones around burnt wood fragments and ashes. Hanging by a rope over it was what looked like barbecued snakes to Meggan.

"What are those things above the firepit," she whispered to Tam.

"Dried meat strips. Smoking it keeps insects and bacteria away, always ready for a snack."

She thought, *Oh God, don't let the chief offer me a snack*. But he was already busy gathering musical instruments from under one of the benches. He said something to her and pointed to one of the benches, where she sat and watched him.

He hung a tethered metal drum on his forearm and then separated three bamboo tubes that were attached to a gourd almost the size of volleyball. The chief blew into a wide hole in the gourd's neck, and manipulated musical notes with finger holes in the bamboo tubes. The musical contraption sounded like a crude flute and looked like a prehistoric bagpipe. The chief would spontaneously pound the drum with one hand while blowing the flute, occasionally stopping long enough to sing in a language that did not sound like Vietnamese.

Just when the performance seemed endless to Meggan, the chief briskly stowed his instruments back under the bench and placed one of the brown jugs into the hollow of a stump next to the firepit. His cheery look suggested this would be the highlight of the gathering.

Tam said, "That's barley beer. He's getting straws, but you don't have to drink it if you don't want to."

The chief untied the green cloth and inserted what looked like two reeds into the jug. He drew a sip and pointed to the other straw for Meggan. She looked up at Tam and he said something to the chief, presumably making a polite excuse for her. The chief nodded to Meggan and made a long reply.

"I told him your stomach was sensitive to beer."

"What did he say?"

"He thinks you are virtuous, like Lat women."

Meggan stood and averted his happy gaze, then realized this probably made her look all the more virtuous.

Tam took a few dong notes from his pocket, folded them and gave them to the chief, who nodded slightly and pocketed them without further acknowledgement. He held the door open while Tam and Meggan descended the steps, and the three of them walked together back to the fence gate. The chief said something to Meggan, but his beaming expression was the only interpretation she needed.

When they got back into the jeep, Tam said, "The Lat Catholic church is just down the street. It's decorated with Christian symbols blended with the Lat's ancient animist religion. Quite interesting, if you'd like to see it."

She glanced at him then stared ahead. "No, that's okay. I should be getting back to the hotel. I have some emails to get out."

"Do you feel alright?"

"Yes, I'm fine."

"Meggan, has something changed since yesterday?"

"No. Why do you ask?"

"You seem distant today."

"I just don't think we should get too involved."

"Because I'm Vietnamese?"

"No, of course not. It's just that I'll be leaving soon and… I'll be honest with you, Tam, I went through a very hurtful divorce a few months ago. I'm not ready for another relationship yet, and I don't want to be hurt again."

"You were hurt by another man, Meggan, not me." When she didn't respond, he said, "Please, continue being honest with me."

"I don't want an affair with a married man. That would only end with both of us being hurt, at least me."

"Why do you say I'm married?"

"I was at the central market last night. I saw you with a woman and child going into a shop. I'm not asking you to explain, Tam. You have a right to your privacy."

"If I say I'm not married, you'd have no reason to believe me."

She stared out the windshield without answering him.

"I'll take you back to your hotel, but first may I show you something to help you understand me better? It's not something private, and it will only take a few minutes. Would that be a fair request?"

"Okay, if it's just a few minutes."

"I promise." Tam tapped a number into his phone and

said something in Vietnamese.

"Who are you calling?"

"I promised it wouldn't be private," he said playfully, "but I didn't say it wouldn't be a surprise."

They drove back through the city again, eventually passing by a few fancy coffee houses and small boutique restaurants on the other side. They entered the wooded residential neighborhood where Tam had found her lost two nights before. The curvy road became almost a single lane as they drove to the top of the hill, past sprawling deco-styled villas, most of them painted mustard yellow with red clay tile roofs.

"These look new," Meggan said almost to herself.

"They were built by French colonists in the 1920s and 1930s, and authentically restored in the mid-1990s, with modern plumbing and electric systems."

Tam drove up the driveway to one of the largest houses, with a protruding sunroom and arched balconies. After he parked in front, Meggan wondered if this was the surprise destination.

"This is my family's home," he said. "Come in and I'll introduce you. Lunch is being prepared by Mai, the woman who made our picnic lunch."

"You don't have to do this, Tam."

"Mai is doing everything."

"You know what I mean."

"I'm sorry for being so mysterious, Meggan, but please let me show you enough to judge me fairly. It will be more convincing than a hasty story in front of the Lat chief's house."

Tam held the front door while Meggan went in, realizing he must have called Mai from the car; he could have told her to lie for him when they arrived. She hated suspecting Tam, and she began to resent the suspense. She just wanted to get this drama over with.

While they were removing their shoes, a young Asian woman clip-clopped across the tile floor in leather sandals. She wore denim jeans and a white blouse that draped from her olive shoulders. She stood just past the foyer in the living room and said hello to Tam, and then shyly glanced at Meggan.

"Mai, this is my new friend, Meggan."

"Pleased to meet you, Meggan. Lunch will be ready soon. Would you like lemonade while you wait?"

"That would be nice."

Mai went through a paneled door off the dining room.

"Tam, that wasn't the woman I saw you with."

"I know. Mai lives with us and does most of our housekeeping."

"Oh." She wondered who "us" was.

Mai returned with a tray holding two tall glasses of lemonade each decorated with a sprig of what looked like mint leaves. Meggan was offered hers first, then Tam.

"Should we relax here in the living room until lunch is ready?"

Meggan looked out the bay windows before sitting down. "That tall hedge makes your yard so private."

"It's very old, like the house."

She saw an old man wearing sunglasses and a floppy-brimmed hat cross the yard with an armful of cut brush and weeds. Meggan leaned forward to look closer, but he rounded the corner of the house.

"Your gardener has done a beautiful job," Meggan said, sitting at an end of the sofa so she could see the flowering bushes.

Tam sat on one of the chairs. "He has very green thumbs."

When she sipped the sweet lemonade, her nose told her the sprigs were, indeed, mint. She heard a car outside, and soon a little girl, maybe five years old, struggled to pull open the heavy front door, and kicked off her sparkly pink sneakers before scampering into the living room.

"Uncle Tam, we had ice cream!" When the girl saw Meggan smiling at her, she stopped and looked down shyly.

A woman came in through the opened door carrying a plastic shopping bag. "We came as soon as Anh finished her treat."

Meggan recognized her as the woman with Tam last night.

"Hello, my name is Bien."

"I'm Meggan."

"And this is my daughter, Anh. Say hello to our lady guest, little cookie."

"Hello, miss."

"I hope my brother has been a charming host," Bien said with a grin, "if that's the correct phrase. My English is sometimes very terrible."

"Charming would be correct, and I think your English is excellent."

"Our parents insisted on speaking perfect English at home because we were expanding our business to foreign markets. We still speak English with each other but sometimes mixed with Vietnamese."

"Mai is working on lunch," Tam said to Bien.

Bien excused herself to put her things upstairs and to wash Anh's hands and face, still sticky from the ice cream.

Meggan beamed at Tam. "You've been tormenting me."

"I wanted you to see the truth, not just hear it."

Mai started bringing plates, glasses, and chopsticks to the table, quietly placing them in front of all six chairs.

Anh came down the stairs carefully planting both feet on each step, one at a time, with Bien patiently following. Bien had changed into silky green pajama-style pants and a crisp tan blouse. She excused herself again and went into the kitchen. Anh followed closely, while sneaking peeks at Meggan. Mai was soon bringing pots to the table and setting them on trivets. She helped Anh into her booster chair, and said, "If you are ready to eat…"

Meggan walked with Tam to the dining room and then with his lead, they all sat down. Mai began scooping rice from a pot with a small wood paddle, almost filling each bowl and passing them around. She passed a plate with tomato, cucumber and pickled vegetables, and another plate with fresh spring rolls. Mai then removed the lid from a ceramic bowl and passed it to Tam, who used his chopsticks to put shredded meat onto his plate, and then held the bowl for Meggan. She was relieved that her chopstick practice kicked in, and she was able to remove, although slowly, some of the meat. Tam then passed the bowl across the table for Bien to help Anh, who was using training chopsticks that worked like big tweezers.

"The meat is pork that is grilled and pulled apart, and then ketchup sauce is added," Bien said. "Mai thought a cowboy lunch would be correct for an American guest."

Mai smiled to herself, obviously embarrassed.

Meggan furtively watched how everyone was eating, doing so with unrestrained relish as they placed fragments of pork and vegetables into their rice bowls with chopsticks, and then using them to rake in a mouthful from the bowl.

Tam paused and turned to Meggan "Would you like a fork?"

"No, I'm fine, thanks."

"The little saucers are for dipping, if you like. The dark one is fish sauce. The red one is chili sauce, but it's not as hot as Thai sauce."

Meggan dipped her spring roll into the fish sauce and took a bite. "This is very good."

The compliment brought a grin to Mai.

Anh followed Meggan's lead by biting into a spring roll, studying Meggan as if she was the strangest human being Anh had ever seen. Meggan noticed this and winked at Anh, who blinked both eyes a few times, trying unsuccessfully to master this exotic new trick.

While Mai and Bien cleared the table, Meggan turned to Tam.

"There's an extra place setting at the head of the table. Were you expecting someone?"

"Mai always sets a place at our father's chair. We never know when he might stop by."

On their way to the living room, Meggan said, "Where does your father live?"

"He lives here, but he spends most of his time overseeing research at our agriculture center. We have a residential compound there. He's lately been experimenting with new crops to export, like chocolate and medicinal plants."

"How far away is the agriculture center?"

"Almost three hours of driving. When any of us go there, we usually stay overnight."

Meggan noticed Anh lingering under the archway that separates the dining room and living room, with a serious look on her little face. Meggan winked again and patted the sofa. Anh blinked brightly and ran over to the sofa, and struggled onto it next to Meggan, her new friend.

"Is your family compound a house?" Meggan asked.

"More of a small fenced community," Tam said. "We have a family house there, and a large greenhouse for experimental plants. Another house is for a live-in couple who takes care of housekeeping and meals, and the residential grounds. There is also a dormitory for field workers who must travel long distances from their homes. Some of them stay with us a few days, and then return home for a few days to be with their families and to take care of their own gardens."

"Is it fenced to keep out thieves?"

"Yes, and worse threats. One of the large coffee brokers has tried to squeeze us out of business. Their tactics do not follow rules."

"Wouldn't the police protect you?"

"Officials are paid by both sides, which makes the police more or less neutral. We have to be prepared to take care of ourselves. Father has firearms secretly stored, and the men who work for us know how to use them. They are hill country tribesmen with a long tradition of fierce fighting during our country's many wars. Our enemies know that, so they are careful."

Bien came into the living room and sat on the sofa next to Anh. "I overheard you, Tam. Meggan must think our business is run by gangsters."

He suddenly looked worried. "I hope you don't think that, Meggan. We stay in business because our growers are successful, and we are always honest with them and with our buyers. That's how we win at business, with peace, not wars. We also have political friends in Hanoi who remember the contribution Father has made to Vietnam's coffee industry."

Bien said, "Unfortunately, Father's friends are getting older, and their young replacements have no regard for the past."

Meggan turned to Bien. "Does your mother live here?"

"Our mother died in 1986, when Tam and I were teenagers."

"Oh, how sad. I'm sorry."

"We had never imagined losing a parent," Tam said. "Our sorrow was mixed with fear about what might happen if Father died, too. He would sometimes sit for hours at Mother's gravesite, and his health weakened. Bien and I began to sit silently on the ground with him, for as long as he did, even through the night, until he was ready to come back to the house. Soon after that, he began to find life again, gradually replacing his grief with hard hours in the fields and we worked alongside him, scrounging out a living together."

Meggan felt bad about the somber mood her question triggered. Tam seemed to sense that from her silence.

"We like to talk about Mother," he said. "In a way, we feel she is still with us."

"How did she die?"

"From a poisonous green snake. She was picking passion fruit early one evening when we lived near Bong Dung village. Green snakes like to hide in bamboo and fruit trees and they eat frogs that climb up looking for insects and worms. You can hear the frogs shriek when green snakes bite into them. We didn't hear anything when Mother died. Father went looking for her when it got dark, and we met him at the door with Mother in his arms."

"You grew up without a father," Tam said. "That must have been hard, too."

"It was sometimes, but I can't imagine not having a mother."

Bien said, "After Mother died, Father found a housekeeper, a hilltribe woman named Chee. Her people had shunned her for having a mixed-blood baby. The father was a South

Vietnamese soldier who was killed in a VC ambush. Chee surprised us one afternoon, quietly peeking out at us from the tall grass with her baby while we were working at one of our secret vegetable gardens. She said in broken Vietnamese that she and her baby were alone and had nowhere to go, and she begged Father to let her work in return for a place to keep her baby. Father, of course, didn't hesitate to invite her into our home. Chee took care of the house, laundry and cooking, and became like another mother to us."

Meggan asked, "Did she ever return to her people?"

"No," Tam said. "She died mysteriously. We found her on the kitchen floor one morning. She had lived with us for over five years."

Bien said, "I think she died of a broken heart. Hilltribe people cannot be happy when they have been separated from their people."

"What happened to her baby?" Meggan asked.

Mai came from the kitchen, apparently finished with the meal chores.

Tam said, "Mai, come and join us. We were just telling Meggan about your mother, Chee."

Mai happily sat in one of the upholstered chairs. "I was only five years old when my mother died," Mai said, "but I have a few lovely memories of her. She takes care of me from heaven."

A moment of silence stilled the room.

"You are an excellent cook," Meggan said.

"I'm glad you think so. I've never cooked for an American before. I was worried about preparing the wrong kind of food for you."

"I like Vietnamese food, but your barbequed pork was among the best I've ever eaten."

Mai looked down with a self-conscious grin.

Meggan turned to Tam. "If you don't mind, I think I should return to the hotel."

"Of course," he said, getting up from his chair.

After thanking Mai and Bien, Meggan bent down to meet Anh's curious gaze and told her she was beautiful and sweet, a compliment that made Anh beam.

When Meggan and Tam got outside, she paused to look at the tiled rooftops of other villas downhill from them. She folded her arms because of a chilly breeze. Tam went to the jeep and came back with her Scottish tartan shirt.

"We forgot this on the back seat yesterday," he said.

Meggan slipped the warm shirt on over her blouse and started to button it, but then stopped and looked up at Tam. He stepped closer to her, and they found each other's lips, more passionately, with more abandon, than the first time, embracing each other urgently, as if for the last time.

Tam looked into her eyes. "Are you still in a hurry to go to Saigon?"

"I'm in no hurry to go anywhere."

CHAPTER 28

That evening Tam felt distracted from the newspaper he was trying to read, finishing a sentence or two before pausing to recall his time with Meggan a few hours ago, remembering her soft mouth and cheeks, her smooth brown hair, and the way she held on to him as if they belonged to each other.

His cellphone rang with a ringtone Tam had programmed to be unique from all other callers. He rested the paper on his lap and put the phone to his ear.

"Hello, Father. Where are you?"

"Down the road having a beer with Nguyen Cao on his patio. Is that woman still there?"

"No, I took her back to her hotel."

"A new girlfriend?"

"Something more than that, I hope. Where were you watching from—a treetop?"

"Very funny. I was walking back to the house, and you didn't notice me, that's all. You were, well, busy, so I didn't interrupt."

"I look forward to introducing her to you."

"I don't think that would be wise, Tam. I think you should keep your distance from her."

"Because she's an American?"

"Ah, then she *is* American—I thought so."

"And...?"

"She might have come here to find out more about us."

"Father, you are a cautious man. Maybe the war made you that way, and it's often been a strength that has protected us. But you might be overusing that strength right now. This woman—her name is Meggan, by the way—is interested in me, and our family, but not our business."

"You and our family are exactly what I don't want her knowing more about. If the United States government sent her, she would already know about our agribusiness, but not much about us, the people running the business, or about the people we are involved with. Has she learned anything about those things, even casually, from you?"

"Maybe." Tam set his newspaper on the side table and began pacing in the living room window. "But I don't understand why you are suddenly afraid of American spies. Why would her government care anything about us?"

"My Hanoi sources tell me the US has started secret trade talks with upper level leaders of the Socialist Republic of Vietnam. They think a trade agreement might be for real this time, Tam, but the US would first investigate Vietnamese companies that do business internationally."

"Why would they care?"

"Any trade agreement would hinge on making sure Vietnamese companies are not doing business with countries the US has imposed trade sanctions on. That would be a deal-breaker."

"We don't do business in any such countries."

"We know that, but US authorities wouldn't."

"If Meggan really is a spy, then it might alarm her if I suddenly stopped seeing her. That's one consideration. Another is that I'm in love with her."

"Well…I've never heard you say that about a girlfriend."

"I've never felt like this."

"You might be stepping into a deep river, son."

"I know, but I also know that our family comes first. What do you think I should do?"

"You must follow your heart. But also follow your mind."

"And if those two things conflict?"

"Then you become trapped."

"As always, Father, your advice is wise, but the specifics are wanting."

"I like to leave the hard part for you."

"I'll work on that part. Enjoy your beer and tell Cao I said hello."

Tam walked out onto the balcony and welcomed the gentle distraction of evening birds chirping and hopping, pecking at whatever the lawn was offering them, and then flying away in a panicked flock toward the late afternoon's pale sky—only to return seconds later for another hasty snack. Although he respected his father's usual call for caution, Tam wished Meggan was standing here with him to share this peaceful scene.

Bien came in from the front door and paused at the bottom of the stairs to watch her brother, who was seemingly entranced about something on the balcony. When she walked out to join him, he didn't react to the sound of someone behind him.

"Tam, is something the matter?"

He turned his head and said, "I just talked to Father. He thinks Meggan might be a spy."

"A spy? Father is afraid of so many things."

"But often for good reasons. I would take a chance on Meggan, but I must respect his warning. I was just wondering what I should do."

Bien stood next to him and watched the birds. "Did he suggest anything?"

"Oh, sure. He said to follow my heart *and* my mind, but failed to say which one carried the most weight."

"That doesn't help much if you are falling for Meggan, and I think you might be."

"I think so, too. I told him so."

"Does Meggan know anything about Father?"

"I told her about his struggles after reunification but no secrets, nothing she couldn't have learned elsewhere. And she didn't seem to be digging for information. But maybe that's the talent of a good spy—to not seem like one."

"Well, I don't think it matters now. Meggan will soon return to America and you'll still be here, and our lives will go on as usual. I'd say just enjoy your time with her, and don't tell her anything else about us."

Tam grinned at her. "I chided Father about his vague suggestions, but you've never had that problem."

CHAPTER 29

America's ambassador to Vietnam, Wendall Ness, nervously anticipated his critical early-morning meeting with Cuong Hoan, Vietnam's Minister of Foreign Affairs. The message from Washington that Ness would soon be delivering to Hoan offers an opportunity for reciprocal trade with the United States. There will be conditions, however, that might seem impossible to Hoan, at least at first, but will be necessary before top-level negotiations, and perhaps even a presidential goodwill visit, can take place.

Wendell Ness knew one thing for sure: the American president was determined to negotiate a trade agreement with Vietnam; not just for economic reasons, but to restore a collective defense with more allies in Southeast Asia, something the now-dissolved Southeast Treaty Organization had failed to accomplish. The pressure was on Ness to help Hoan find a politically-acceptable pathway to that vision.

Ness had arrived in Hanoi two days ago from a series of Department of State policy meetings in Washington, DC. Some of those regarding Asian trade were even attended by the president, which signaled their priority. The president made it clear he wants a mutually-beneficial trade agreement with Vietnam after so many years of post-war sanctions. He knew, however, that unless he satisfied the passionate demands of human rights activists, and of American veterans, many of whom belonged to well-funded veterans' organizations with powerful lobbyists. Without those two groups on board, trade talks with Vietnam would be politically impossible.

While waiting in Minister Hoan's reception room, Ambassador Ness reminded himself to remain optimistic about his proposal.

A thirtyish staff woman calmly glided into the room. "Mr. Hoan will see you now," she half-whispered, and led the way to an office with a high open doorway.

When Ness entered, Cuong Hoan got up from the formal position behind his desk, and said, "So good to see you, Wendell."

"Thank you, Hoan, for finding time for me on such short notice."

"Of course. I always have time for you. Please sit down." Hoan settled regally into the upholstered side chair across from Ness. "I understand you recently returned from Washington. I hope you have cured any jetlag by now."

"I think my brain is finally getting used to living on both sides of the globe."

Hoan acknowledged this polite humor with a well-mannered chuckle. "Please tell me how I can be of service to you."

"Thank you, Hoan, and I hope I can be of service to you, too. During recent meetings in Washington, our president made it clear that he is eager to begin serious trade talks with the Socialist Republic of Vietnam. He believes that open trade between our countries will bring new levels of prosperity and friendship to both countries, and allow us to help you protect your waters and borders from potential intruders."

"I see," Hoan said dryly, as if he was unaware that Ness was referring specifically to China.

"However, before our Department of State can begin discussing possible diplomatic meetings, some conditions must be addressed."

"Ah, yes. Conditions. Can you tell me the nature of those conditions?"

"A few minor differences will have to be discussed, but I'm sure we can easily settle them."

"Any major differences?"

"A couple, yes. Americans, as you know, believe that one-party rule can sometimes overlook human rights. But that's a complex issue that must take differing national traditions and philosophies into account. Therefore, we feel it is best suited as a mutual intention for long-term discussions."

"We are willing to consider new ideas, as long as foreign powers are not forcing them upon us. Although we had to fight for self-rule over many generations, we have made many progressive changes in the way we rule."

"Of course. And the United States will always respect your country's sovereignty."

Hoan sat back in his chair. "And your other major difference?"

"It's a more specific problem, one that must—and we feel can—be resolved between us. As you know, almost three million Americans served in the war here, which represents almost ten percent of their generation. Most came home, but some were left behind. Of those who were imprisoned, killed, or were missing in action, about twelve hundred are still unaccounted for. In the United States, black POW-MIA flags continue to fly throughout the country as a constant reminder to find them, and until we do, those flags will continue to arouse strong political opposition against forging economic and defense agreements with Vietnam."

"But we have cooperated with American officials and volunteers for decades to find the remains of those Americans. We are still missing many thousands more of our own people."

"I understand, Hoan, but Americans have fought all their wars on foreign soil, so bringing home remains of their dead and missing is considered a patriotic duty. I personally believe this sense of duty is a way of healing our grief, and perhaps a way to mollify our guilt for sending so many of our young people into wars they did not understand.

"I wish we could account for everyone who served in the war, American and Vietnamese, but if that impossibility is a locked gate between our two countries, then I fear we will never find a key.

"Hoan, I have just delivered my official message to you. Now, perhaps I can informally pick at that gate lock a little. I suggest we focus on forty-eight unaccounted-for MIAs who were reported to be captives. Finding verifiable remains would be ideal, but confirmable reports of their demise might suffice for now. In addition, there are seven MIAs who were reported to be seen alive in Vietnam after the Americans had pulled out, either staying behind to work here, or were married with Vietnamese families. Finding anything about those two groups could be an opportunity to demonstrate your country's ongoing desire to honor those who served on both sides, and would likely become an encouraging news event in the US. If public opinion shifts positively toward Vietnam, the president will have a much wider pathway toward finding common ground between us, the way we did with Japan and Germany after our war with them."

Hoan tilted his head slightly in thought, and then narrowed his gaze at Ness. "Officially, I cannot confirm those reports of living MIAs, or even comment on them."

"I understand. I also understand that some of the sighting reports might have been fabricated."

A trace of amusement softened Hoan's expression. "Let me see what I can do, unofficially, of course."

"Thank you, Hoan. And I will encourage the Secretary of State to let us continue these discussions."

After Ambassador Ness left, Cuong Hoan tapped the direct number of the Deputy Prime Minister into his phone's keypad. It was answered after only three rings.

"Sir, I believe our meeting was productive, but to move to the next step we will have to do something that will be very difficult. They want us to reveal the identities of any lost Americans we know about. To save face, we could say their remains were recently discovered, but we could never make that case for Con Rong. We have kept his identity a state secret for too many years, but that may no longer be possible. I suggest we make him and his family disappear, without any evidence that they ever existed."

***

Later that day at the Lam Dong Province offices in Dalat, Mr. Bao, the Provincial Secretary, knocked on the governor's doorframe and waited in the open doorway for Governor Minh to look up from the letter he was reading.

"Yes, Bao? Come in."

Secretary Bao stepped in and closed the door behind him. In a measured, anxious voice, he said, "I just received an urgent phone call from Hanoi. It was the Minster of Foreign Affairs."

"Come and sit down." Minh set his letter on the desk without taking his eyes off Bao. As governor, Minh was the top governmental official in the province, but Secretary Bao was directly answerable to the Communist Party of Vietnam, which gave him political clout from Hanoi's highest-ranking officials. His advice to the governor carried more weight than from any other subordinate or advisor.

"The minister himself called you?" Minh asked.

"Yes, sir. He instructed me to inform you of a serious problem erupting in Dalat, a problem that could embarrass the party, and could stop trade talks that are now secretly underway with the United States. The minister made it clear this information is highly classified."

Minh's mouth opened slightly, as if searching for the right words. "Of course. What can you tell me?"

"There are reports from our undercover agents in Dalat that an American woman has been making strange inquiries about a US soldier whose status has been 'missing in action' since the American War. One of the agents interrogated her hired driver, a local man named Duc, who said she claimed to be looking for evidence of her American father. Duc also said she bribed a policeman with several thousand dollars to obtain classified government information. Duc didn't know the policeman, and he didn't know what information she obtained. The bank confirmed that she did, indeed, draw over sixty-eight million dongs with her credit card. And she has been seen several times with Tran Van Tam, a rich coffee broker."

Minh tried to mentally make connections from that tangle of information, a thread to what seemed to be random events. "I don't see how there's enough to prove she's a spy for the American government."

"Our agents contacted the woman's airline for information about her. Her point of origin was from the American state of Minnesota. She was also listed by the airline as an American diplomat. Our agents checked her hotel's photocopy of her passport, but it was not a diplomatic passport, a possible deception that puts her purpose, if not her identity, in question."

"What, or who, would she be spying on, and why is this such a serious problem?"

"The minister fears that the 'father' she claims to be looking for is the notorious Con Rong, who is actually the father of Tran Van Tam. His real name is Peter McHillston, an American who was secretly detained by our government during reunification, and has not been allowed to leave Vietnam since then. That would classify him as a POW still in our custody. All these years his true identity has only been known by a few top government officials, and if the Americans discover this, it could make further trade talks and US military protection politically impossible. As you know, Americans are fanatic about bringing all their POWs and MIAs home, dead or alive, but finding an alive veteran that we've been concealing for over forty years could disgrace us in front of the entire world."

"Did the minister say what we should do about this?"

"Yes, he said we should do nothing. The Central Government will handle the matter, and we are to stay out of their way."

"I'll notify our local police chief."

"That has already been handled by the Military Intelligence Department in Hanoi."

***

While sitting in the backyard reading, Peter McHillston's phone rang, a rare occurrence because only family members and a handful of his closest friends knew his phone number. He stood and pulled the phone from his jeans pocket. The caller ID showed it to be from General Khai, an old friend he first knew when Khai was just a captain.

"Hello, General."

"Peter, I hope you and your family are well, my friend."

"I am, thank you, and I hope you and your family are well."

"Oh, yes, we are very lucky. Peter, I have something to tell you, but please keep this matter a deep secret, just an unofficial call from one old friend to another."

"Of course, General, and I appreciate your trust."

"Something has started troubling rumors at the Central Government's Hanoi headquarters. An American spy has apparently been discovered in Dalat. Some ministry officials think she is trying to uncover information about you, which would be disastrous for secret trade talks that have begun with the United States."

"The spy is a woman?"

"Yes, and she has been seen with your son, Tam. I hope she hasn't seduced information about you from him."

"Tam is used to being careful. Is the woman in danger?"

"If it becomes evident that she's a spy, she will likely, shall we say, have an accident."

Peter missed a breath while his mind raced.

General Khai filled the silence.

"If this sounds extreme, keep in mind that if your existence is uncovered, it would reveal an inexcusable and embarrassing cover-up by our government. And if you were turned over to the Americans, they might arrest you for desertion, collaboration, or worse, treason. Our Central Government cannot let either of those events explode into international news media headlines, which puts you and your family in great danger. All of you will have to disappear, Peter, either by your actions, or the Central Government's. The first option would be difficult, the second one disastrous."

"I've stayed awake many nights wondering when this storm would hit."

"Yes, and you've talked to me about it. I hope you still have a plan in place."

"I do, General. I am indebted to all your guidance and support through the years."

"And I honor all that you have done. It's a shame that most of our people will never know the sacrifices you and your family has made to help rebuild post-war Vietnam. But old men like us are considered obsolete, and we're being replaced by young firebrands with university degrees and little regard for history. They were not old enough, or not yet born, to suffer a terrible war like we did, followed by the bitter reunification."

"There have been blessings, too."

"And I hope you and your family can continue enjoying them during your long lives. For now, I will say goodbye, and then you should start preparing your family. The storm is almost at your doorstep."

After he hung up, Khai's warning fired Peter's thoughts about the emergency plans he had put in place many years ago, when his children were young and without a mother. But now there was a wildcard to consider. An American woman has come into Tam's life, either perchance or by calculation. And when Peter saw Tam kissing her last night—wearing the Scottish tartan shirt with the McHillston clan's colors—Peter knew she would probably be entering his life as well.

CHAPTER 30

Meggan had eaten a light supper of pho at the hotel restaurant early that evening, and sat on the bed in her underclothes to knit her orange scarf and watch a silly British sitcom. Tam hadn't called or stopped by all day. Last evening, he had been so warm and affectionate, but when he drove her back to the hotel he had been unusually quiet. Perhaps he was having misgivings about their budding relationship, and rightly so: different cultures, families and friendships, living so far from each other.

She started to wonder if she had been misreading his feelings, the way she had misread other men in her life. But she felt differently about Tam, and wanted to trust him. He didn't seem like a womanizer—more of a business nerd— and he could certainly attract any number of local women if he wanted to. Besides, he had made no attempt to go any further than a kiss.

She finally decided that he probably had to catch up on business matters, given the amount of time he has been spending with her. After all, she was on vacation, but he had a complex business to run.

Meggan turned off the TV and thought about last evening's meal with him, and with Bien, Anh, and Mai. It left her puzzled about where all this was going. Should she extend her stay in Vietnam, or had this been nothing more than a vacation romance? She didn't want to decide that alone, but she might have to.

A knock at her door startled her. She put her knitting down and padded barefoot to the door.

"Yes," she asked, putting her ear near the closed door.

"It's Tam."

"Just a minute, Tam."

Meggan excitedly slipped her feet into the terrycloth hotel slippers and pulled on a hotel robe. She shuffled back to the door and opened it.

"Come in," she said happily, forgetting all the angst a moment ago. "I'm surprised to see you this late in the day".

Tam's face showed a side of him that confused her.

"Is something wrong?"

He closed the door behind him. "There might be, Meggan. I would like for you to move into our family's house."

"Why? Is the hotel manager kicking me out?"

"No, but you will be more comfortable at our house. We have a guest suite with a private bath and a sitting room. You will be safer there."

"Safer…? Safer from what, Tam? What's going on?"

"The winds of politics are shifting against our family, Meggan."

"Okay—whatever that means—and I don't want to sound selfish, but what has this got to do with me?"

"Too much, I'm afraid. My father has just been told by a high-ranking general, a longtime friend of our family's, that you have been under investigation by the Central Government. They think you might be an American spy, Meggan. Secret trade talks are beginning with the United States, and someone reported that you have been sent by your government to find something that could upend our position in the negotiations."

Meggan sat heavily on the edge of the bed and glared at Tam. "That's ridiculous. Why would the United States government send me to upend anything?"

"Because some Americans apparently think the Vietnamese government has been hiding wartime POWs and MIAs. Some Vietnamese officials think that's what you came here to find out."

"I never thought my father was being hidden by the government, if that's what you mean. I just wanted to see where he died."

Tam sat on the desk chair and scooted it closer to her, looking into her eyes. "I know. But what we know doesn't matter."

"You're scaring me, Tam. My God, will problems with the police ever stop?"

"This is beyond the local police."

"Okay, I'll be on that flight to Saigon tomorrow, and then I'll get out of Vietnam as soon as I can. Maybe we can meet again in another country."

"I'm afraid it's too late for that, Meggan. You'll almost certainly be arrested at the airport, and you would become as missing as your father. We need to get you out of the country another way, and we are able to do that. My father and I will arrange everything, but for now, you need a safe place to stay."

"Are sure your house is safe?"

"Yes, for now. And Bien, Anh, and Mai said I can't come home without you."

"Okay, I'll go with the majority vote. But what will your

father say? He doesn't even know me."

"No, but he wants to."

"Even though I might be a spy?"

"He knows you're not."

Tam moved to the end of the bed next her and stroked her hair once with the back of his fingers. "You'll be honoring all of us by being our guest, Meggan, and it would give us some more time together before you leave."

"Okay." She stood thinking about how to quickly put her things together. "I need to get dressed."

"Should I wait in the lobby or stay here with my eyes closed."

She felt relieved by his playfulness. "Just close your eyes at the appropriate time. I'd better get used to trusting you."

As soon as Meggan dressed and had her travel bag packed, Tam was at the door ready to open it. When they walked through the lobby, the receptionist asked Meggan if she was checking out, and Tam said no, she would be back in the morning.

The town had quieted for the evening, with most people having supper or resting from the busy day. Twilight gave a last glimmer to the mountain tops, and interior lights were illuminating most shops and houses. Corner street lights popped on intermittently as they drove through the city to the west side of town.

As soon as Tam parked and shut off the engine, Meggan jumped out of the car, opening the back door for her bag, and wheeled it toward the front door ahead of him.

When they got into the house, Anh ran to them with a big grin and yelled, "Auntie Meggan!"

Tam said, "Close friends of Vietnamese families are often called aunts and uncles by the children. It's a traditional endearment."

Bien soon appeared, dressed in blue jeans and a red tee shirt, barefooted in her leather sandals. "Meggan, I'm so glad you came. I hope Tam didn't force you too much."

"He didn't have to, after telling me the alarming news."

"Yes," Bien said, "but we are always prepared for bad news. Mai is fixing pizzas for supper. Americans like pizza, don't they?"

"It's just about my favorite food."

Tam took Meggan's suitcase and led the way upstairs to her room. Even though it was a big house, the wood-floored bedroom was larger than she would have imagined. A queen-size canopy bed with a white bedspread and white throw pillows was draped on all sides with mosquito netting that almost reached the floor. Tam showed her how to use the shower controls, which were mounted above a claw-foot tub, next to a large window overlooking neighborhood rooftops. A shower curtain could be drawn around the entire tub for privacy. On the other side of the bedroom was a sitting area, with a loveseat, lemonade-yellow upholstered chair, and a corner writing desk with windows to the corner.

"This is so cozy," she said, going to the window where she saw a faraway valley beyond the sprawling city. She hadn't noticed before, but this house was on the highest location in the neighborhood.

Tam put her suitcase on a folding stand and then showed her how to use the electric heater if it got too chilly at night. "We have private Wi-Fi, if you want to use it. The link name is *dragon*, and the sign-in code is *happy339*. I'll leave you to refresh, if you like, while I make a couple of quick calls. Just come down whenever you want to and feel at home, alright?"

"Okay, thanks."

Meggan sat on the sitting room's loveseat and signed into the Wi-Fi. A text from an internet app popped up on her screen. It was from her mother's phone.

I am Alice Horton, your mother's nurse, and she asked me to send this message to you from her phone app to make sure you would receive it. Your mother had a heart attack this morning and was brought by ambulance to the hospital in Bigfork, Minnesota. A neighbor had found her unconscious near her mailbox. She will remain in our intensive care unit until her condition stabilizes, but at least overnight. As you might know, she has been using nitroglycerin tablets for angina episodes that have been more frequent lately. Her cardiologist plans to insert a stint into two mostly-blocked arteries as soon as her strength increases. I will check this phone during my regular morning shift tomorrow, and let you know if her condition changes. Rest assured, she is in good hands.

Meggan jumped up and yelped, "Oh my God." With shaky hands she tapped a thank-you reply to the nurse.

There was a light knock on door, and Bien asked if she was alright. Meggan hurried to open the door.

"Bien, I shouted because I just got a text from a nurse that said my mother had a heart attack."

Bien put her hand to her mouth to hide a gasp. "Did the nurse say if your mother will be alright?"

"No, she didn't say. My mom's in a good hospital, though. The nurse said they are going to insert stints to widen two of her arteries." Meggan pressed her lips together to steady her composure. "Bien, I wish I could be home right now, with my mother. I should not have come to Vietnam."

Bien squeezed her shoulder. "You can't judge your decision so soon. Your mother's trouble doesn't mean you are not following your destiny. Remember that you finally set foot on the ground that holds your father's spirit, and I won't ask you how you feel about Tam but I've never seen him this taken by a woman. I have no right to tell you that, but I don't think Tam means to keep it a secret. Sometimes women need to help each other understand things a man does not express."

"Thank you, Bien. I feel taken by him, too. I just wish I knew what was going to happen to my mother."

"It's very early in the morning in the US, but can you call her later?"

"Yes, with Wi-Fi I can call her on my internet app. I'm also scared about what will happen to me, and to your family."

"Father taught us to always have plans for safety. Tam, Mai, and I have grown up ready for unexpected danger."

"And now Anh is growing up that way."

"Yes, and like you, without a father."

"What happened to him, if you don't mind telling me?"

"My ex-husband thought he had married into a rich family where he would not have to work for his money. He was selfish and lazy, and he became a brute. Anh was afraid of him because he sometimes struck me in front of her. The last time that happened, Father offered him a lot of money to sign divorce papers and leave the hill country forever. He agreed without arguing, maybe because Father had a pistol in his pocket."

"He did, really?"

"Yes. Father can be a wild cowboy if he needs to."

"I hope he doesn't need to tonight."

With a hint of mischief, Bien said, "If he does, he'll have a family of cowboys with him."

That helped Meggan relax. "Tam said he has a way for me

to sneak out of the country soon, thank God, so I can get to my mother. If it's not safe for me to come to Vietnam again, maybe I can meet up with him in another country."

"Of course you can. Tam sometimes goes to other countries on business. Our government never questions his travels. Please let me know when you learn more about your mother."

"I will."

"Supper's ready if you are."

Meggan followed Bien into the dining room. The table was already set, with water glasses full and three pizzas on round metal platters, each sitting on a protective woven trivet. Tam took a chair out for Meggan and sat beside her. Bien and Anh sat next to each other, and on the other side of the table, with Mai at the end. The father's place at the head of the table was set, as usual. Everyone helped themselves to ham, shrimp, or mushroom pizza slices, and Meggan followed suit while Bien helped Anh.

The front door opened and slammed shut. Everyone stopped and set their pizza slices on their plates. Meggan turned to see who it was, but the foyer was behind the staircase. She heard heavy-sounding shoes being dropped onto the tiled floor, and after an instant of absolute silence in the house, she saw the gardener walk into the living room and stop to look at everyone. Without his hat, she could see thinning gray hair. She noticed his eyes were bright blue. Meggan quickly looked around at the others, all of them watching her with slight grins.

The man walked to the dining area and stood at the head of the table with both hands on the back of the chair. He looked directly at her.

"Hello, Meggan." His English was a perfect Midwestern

dialect, spoken as casually as if it was his routine mealtime greeting. He sat down and Bien handed him one of the pizza platters. After sliding a slice onto his plate, he turned again to Meggan. "I've been looking forward to meeting you."

"Oh? What's your name?"

"Strangers call me The Dragon, a strange name, but helpful in keeping my life private. To my family and closest friends, I'm Peter McHillston."

Meggan felt like the air had been sucked out of her lungs. She could barely utter, "That can't be…" She shot a look at Tam, wondering if this was being staged for some unimaginable, or even malicious, reason, and then at Bien and Mai for help, but they could only watch her with puzzled looks.

Tam said, "Father, what is this about?"

Peter trained his eyes on Meggan. "Is your mother Nancy Mondae?"

"Yes."

"How did you get that tartan shirt I saw you wearing last night?"

"My mother gave it to me. She said it was from her fiancé, Peter McHillston, the man who was my father." Tears pooled in her eyes and she could barely speak. "She didn't know she was pregnant with me when you left for Vietnam. When she wrote to tell you, her letters were returned because you were classified as MIA."

"You thought your father was dead, Meggan, and I didn't know I left a daughter behind. I apologize for doubting you and then shocking you like this, but I've lived in the shadow of danger for so many years, I'm sometimes too careful. But now I know for certain I've been blessed with two daughters, Bien and you."

Peter rose from his chair. He took a step toward her and

she got up. They embraced and the room fell silent while Meggan rested her head against her father's shoulder and cried. When she let go, she sniffed and dabbed a cheek with the back of her hand while Peter held her shoulders.

"I wanted more than anything to return to your mother, Meggan, and that helped me stay alive. But after the Americans left Vietnam for good, I had to face never being able to set foot on American soil again. So, I dedicated myself to making the best life I could for my family here in Vietnam— even though that meant never again seeing my parents or Nancy, and abandoning my honor as an American soldier. But I've had no regrets about the new life I found here. Our lives have often been filled with hardship and sorrow, but our love for each other has helped us survive. And then last night when I saw you with Tam, wearing that familiar tartan shirt, I couldn't believe what my eyes were telling me. Now I know that I better get used to miracles."

Meggan said "Me, too." Then something more serious struck her. She shot a look at Tam, but he was already wrapped in his thoughts.

"I didn't know you were my half-sister."

Meggan couldn't find words for him. The love she had begun to feel for Tam was now painfully tangled.

Peter stood and interrupted the silence between them. "In a moment, you'll learn something you both need to know. But first I must tell all of you that tomorrow we might be facing events that will challenge our family like never before. We'll leave together for our compound just before first light in the morning, and then I'll continue traveling with Meggan through Cambodia to Phnom Penh. Megan, I'll get you on a flight to the United States from there, but I can't go with you to America. My life will be in danger both here and in the US, but my Cambodian passport will allow me to stay for a while in Canada. Tam, you'll be in charge of our business while I'm away. I've already made you and Bien sole legal owners of the coffee brokerage. Over the years, I've stashed money, lots of money, in banks in Singapore, Japan, and Canada. Tam and Bien, you already have the bank numbers and codes. No matter what happens to our business, you'll all be safe financially. That includes you, Meggan.

"Tonight, you discovered Meggan is my daughter, our new family member. But she deserves to know more about what kept me from her and her mother, and Tam, you should know what little I do about your courageous birth-mother. Please join me in the living room for a story that will make it clear to all of you."

CHAPTER 31

When I arrived in Vietnam in 1972, I was assigned to an infantry company, which was frequently the fate of draftees. But just a few months after my arrival, the United States started pulling military units out of Vietnam, and after that our outfit went on very few operations, and none especially hazardous. We were surprised, then, to be sent on a reconnaissance mission into the heart of the Central Highlands, not far from here, where the surrounding hills and valleys were infested with Vietcong fighters. According to intel reports, they were being joined by masses of North Vietnam Army soldiers flooding in from Cambodia. Our job was to confirm these reports, and estimate the enemy's strength near the village now known as Bong Dung. Choppers dropped us onto the highest hilltop in the area, a place later to be known as Massacre Mountain.

During that battle a new guy named Roger took a shot in his chest, and I carried him over my shoulder back toward the landing zone, hoping to find help. The last thing I remember is tumbling helplessly down the steep mountainside.

I awoke lying on my back, staring up at a twilight sky. Random gunshots popped from the faraway mountain's crest above, not like those of a firefight, but more like executions. I didn't know if I could move, and I didn't dare try. Sleep soon overtook the aches of my bruised body, and the next time I awoke, it was dawn.

I listened for several minutes, maybe an hour, before trying to move. Then I risked making a sound by moving my legs and arms—they were sore but working—and I rolled onto my side. I waited for a response to the slight noise I just made, but heard nothing. When I got to my knees to look around, I noticed dried blood on the right shoulder of my field jacket. After slipping my hand under my tee shirt to check, I realized the blood was from Roger. I struggled to a crouched position and slowly stood to look around, and then I looked up at the mountain. The steepness and distance from the top made me wonder how I had survived falling so far without having my clothes torn from me and my skin peeled off. Even if I had the strength, it would take hours to claw back up there, and I'd be exposed to the enemy all the way, facing certain death before I got there.

I crawled away as quietly as I could, using the thickest brush for cover, watching for snakes and stopping often to listen and watch for enemy movement. When the sun was almost directly above, I came to a narrow, shallow stream hidden by tall grass. I low-crawled on my belly to it and pulled cold, refreshing water into my mouth with both hands. My brain started to clear, and I spotted a nearby pile of boulders around a cavity that looked large enough for me to hide in. Using a long deadfall branch, I reached in and probed around for snakes or other animals. Satisfied that I wouldn't have to share the shelter, I gathered leafy sticks and grasses to camouflage the entrance. It was a little cooler inside, and I decided to stay there a couple of days to regain my strength and give the enemy time to move out.

At first light the next morning, I pulled aside enough thatch to see that the sun was coming up on my left, which meant the stream was heading generally south. I crawled out to stand up and look around, only to see a motionless tiger staring at me a few yards away on the edge of a thicket. I instinctively grabbed a handful of cave door sticks and waved them over my head, shrieking and yelling like a madman ready to explode. The tiger bolted off in the opposite direction, and I scrambled in panic back into my cave, desperately pulling together as much of the makeshift debris as I could over the entrance. The only thing even close to being a weapon was a folding hunting knife I always carried. I kept the blade locked open and ready all night while I held onto it, occasionally daring to peek out of my fragile door.

In the morning, I carefully ventured outside for a look. No tiger, thank God, but I did see an apple sitting on a leaf about the size of a plate, just a few feet away. I looked around but didn't see any apple trees. Someone or something obviously put it there, but hunger pushed aside my curiosity and I frantically devoured the apple. I spent most of that day hiding in the cave, wondering how the fruit got there, and worrying about the tiger and the Vietcong.

The next morning, another apple waited for me on the leaf, with two shiny, very sweet fruits that looked like huge orange berries. I would later learn they were persimmons.

Early the third morning, I peeked out of the cave for my breakfast, and was shocked to see a very pregnant girl in black work pajamas, sitting in the grass with two persimmons in her small hands. I saw fear and exhaustion in her face, which lifted when I smiled and invited her into the cave using the Vietnamese gesture of drawing my downward palm toward me. She dared a grin, and with downcast eyes, shuffled quietly to the cave in her rubber flip-flops. She ducked her head to come in, and scooted to the back of the little cave. After setting the fruits on the ground, she pointed to the US Army Vietnam patch on my shoulder, and then pointed to her belly, presumably meaning the father was a US soldier. Then she pointed toward the stream and made pushing gestures with both hands, and then pointed to herself, saying "Mama-san, papa-san, number ten." I took this to mean her parents had shunned her because they were shamed by an unwed daughter who carried a mixed-blood baby, a fate that, as I have already said, would disgrace her extended family, and would condemn her and her child forever in the eyes of many Vietnamese.

Three days later she woke me with labor pains. I let her lean against me while I rubbed her tummy, not knowing what else to do. The thought of helping her give birth scared me more than the tiger and the VC combined. My only experience had been watching my father helping cows give birth on our family's farm, which reminded me that the mother will be doing the work unless the baby wouldn't come on its own. I tried to breathe calmly to transmit some calmness to the girl in my arms, but her moans soon gave way to uncontrollable cries in Vietnamese. To protect the secrecy of our hiding spot, I had to muffle her sobs with my hand. I gave her a stick and pointed to my mouth. She understood, locking it in her teeth, vainly trying to compose herself. After another hour or so, she pulled away from me and lay on her back. I helped her undress from the waist down, and from long bouts of her desperate straining, the head of a baby slowly emerged while the girl bit her stick and cried from the back of her throat. When the baby boy was finally free from its mother and started to cry, I put it into the exhausted mother's arms. Remembering the calf-birthing role of my father, I cut a bit of extra shoelace from my boot with my knife, tied off the umbilical cord, and then cut it free from the baby. The mother's sobs were quieter now, and she happily kissed and stroked the skin of her child. It wasn't long before she was breastfeeding him. My main concern now was the amount of blood and after-birth on the cave floor. The tiger would no doubt smell it. My worry grew by the hour because the bleeding wasn't stopping. I could patch gunshot wounds, but this was new to me. The girl held my hand and smiled, as if to comfort me. When I awoke the next day, she was dead. The sleeping baby stared up at me from her limp arms, and I realized it was now up to me to save his life.

To offer some dignity, and as some deterrent against the tiger, I covered the girl's body inside the cave with stones and stream mud. After praying for her soul and her baby's life, I wrapped the child in the girl's black cotton shirt, and start-ed walking along the streambank in a crouch, trying to stay out of sight against the tall brush that bordered the narrow stream. When the baby cried, I soaked the bandana from my pocket to wet-nurse the child with one hand, while carrying it with the other. I slogged on like this all day and all night, as-suming that the value of every stream and river would even-tually lead to a human settlement.

When the sun was high in the sky the next day, I came to a small wood house with vegetable gardens planted all around it. I never knew an American farm family that wouldn't help a stranger in need, so I gambled on that sentiment and went to the house. When the baby started to cry, the door opened, revealing a woman in dark brown peasant clothes. She stared at the improbable vision of an American GI bringing a new-born baby to her isolated home, and her mouth drooped.

She put her arms out, and I gave her the child. Behind me, her husband walked toward us with a hoe over his shoulder. I wondered if he meant the tool as a weapon, but when he saw the baby, he dropped it to the ground and hurried to his wife's side.

He turned to me and pointed to the mountains that confined both sides of this small valley. "Beaucoup VC, number ten," and then he pointed to me with a grin. "GI number one."

I followed the man and his wife into the house, and she set the sleeping child into a hammock. She then spooned cooked mountain rice into a bowl for me. I raked it greedily into my mouth with chopsticks, washing it down with the stream water in my canteen.

I pointed to their small window, and said, "American GI?"

The man shook his head vigorously and flicked his hand away. "GI di di." Pointing to the window, he said, "Beaucoup VC," and then pointing all around, "VC, VC, VC—number ten!"

My choices couldn't be clearer. I couldn't go back because my outfit was gone, and I couldn't go forward without being killed by Vietcong fighters. Until circumstances changed, I would have to hide out there if the farm couple would let me, and they did.

That same day, the farmer led me on a walking tour of his vegetable gardens, which were planted in various areas a short distance from his house. I asked him what kind of large berries were on the stubby trees he grew, and he said *café*.

When we turned to go back to the house, I was startled to see a beautiful girl staring at us near the door. She wore black working pajamas and her straw hat was tied under her chin. She held a reed basket of ripe red coffee berries. The farmer introduced her as Trinh, and then said *baby-son*—his daughter. I would later learn Trinh was seventeen years old, two years younger me, and she was their only living child.

Within a few days I understood my daily chores: planting, hoeing, harvesting, and watering. Lots of watering, with heavy clay pots of water from the stream. I was able to use the farming skills I grew up with on my family's farm, and the coffee and pepper plants began to thrive from a system of irrigation ditches I dug and pounded into the hard clay. I used decomposed coffee berries—discarded after removing the seeds—for fertilizer. Trinh and I always tried to work within talking distance of each other. This way, she caught on to some English, and I learned a smattering of Vietnamese. Eventually, we found ways to hide our kisses from her father. Even if I had the chance, though, I could never let it go further than that. After my experience with saving that baby, I would never leave Trinh with a child, and I held onto the hope that I would eventually return to Nancy.

Two years later, in 1975, the Americans pulled completely out of Vietnam with a hasty rooftop helicopter escape from the American embassy in Saigon. Reunification soldiers soon poured in from the north and began prowling the cities and countryside for former South Vietnam soldiers or police officers, and for citizens who had worked for the American military. Many of them were sent to starve in prisons or re-education camps. Luckily, the home where I was staying was too far from any road or navigable river to be easily detected.

I finally had to accept that I would likely spend the rest of my life in that secluded valley, and if so, I wanted to spend it with Trinh. We were married by a Buddhist monk, who was locally respected as a holy hermit, living in a cave at the base of a foothill. Bien, you were born to us not long after that.

We also adopted the baby I had saved, and we gave him the Vietnamese name *Tam*, after my brother Tom. So, Tam, you are my legal son. As you now know, your biological father was an American soldier who I did not know, and your biological mother, who I barely knew, died in my arms shortly after your birth.

It eventually became safer for us when the Vietcong guerrilla units were eventually replaced by uniformed military installations from the north. Knowing their whereabouts made it easier for me to explore the wider area downstream without trouble. Trinh's father knew a route to Dalat that was a two-day journey on foot, but I hesitated to go that far because if captured, I would likely be imprisoned or executed by the communists. Eventually I found enough courage to make the trip, dared to travel only at night. At the abandoned Dalat airbase, I managed to pilfer some equipment left behind by the Americans.

Not long after reunification, the new government followed the standard communist formula set down by Joseph Stalin, and took ownership of all businesses and farmland. It forced some farmers to clear uninhabited land for New Economic Zones, and assigned others to labor in government-owned farm collectives. It was during this time I was arrested and jailed for being an American spy. I wondered if they planned to return me to the US, where I might again be arrested, but for desertion or collaboration.

Neither happened, thanks to a new provincial agricultural officer, a young man named Captain Khai, who was touring the collective farms near Dalat at that time. Khai had been sent from Hanoi to learn why collectivism was failing in our area, an urgent problem throughout Vietnam that was threatening widespread famine.

Captain Khai made a field trip to the area where I had been arrested, and found that the plants we were secretly cultivating were healthy, compared to the failing crops of apathetic collective workers and corrupt managers. He saw that even our temperamental arabica coffee trees, a more desirable and expensive coffee than robusta, were thriving. Our black pepper plants were healthy, too. Captain Khai also saw the makeshift greenhouse tents I had built, using sheets of abandoned clear plastic left behind by the Americans, and fed water from drip tubes I made by puncturing hoses I had stripped from abandoned American army fuel trucks. While most of the collective farms' crops in that region were going to seed, ours were growing like state fair prize winners.

When Captain Khai returned to Dalat, he visited me in jail. He said his agriculture studies helped him understand my greenhouse design, with its placement and venting, but he wondered how I made my coffee plants outgrow anything he had seen in the province. I explained my techniques, such as pruning, spraying against insects with water infused with chili peppers, and fertilizing with composted coffee berries that had been discarded after removing the seeds. I told him that I buried plastic hose and bamboo pipes out of sight, to direct water from a mountain rivulet into packed clay ditches that distributed the water evenly among the plants.

Khai asked me if I would teach other farmers how to do this in exchange for permanent parole. I agreed, but on the condition that I could return to the farm I had been living at, and that my farm family could be returned from the collective farm they had been assigned to. That way, I said, we could continue experimenting and controlling crop quality, and teach other farm managers our methods. He agreed with a careful nod, but then he demanded his own condition. He said I must never attempt to reveal my whereabouts to anyone outside the Socialist Republic of Vietnam, and if I did, he would not be able to stop his superiors from executing my wife and child. He also insisted that I conceal my true identity to anyone outside my farm family. He granted me power, but erased my identity. That's when I took the alias of Con Rong—*The Dragon*. Powerful but unknown.

The Vietnamese government eventually gave up on pure communism as a utopian model. Its leaders watched the fall of the Soviet Union fail because of its communist economy and political ideology. During the 1970s, China was only able to feed its growing population by scrapping Stalinism, and allowing privatized agriculture and privately-owned businesses. Following these examples, Vietnam cautiously started returning control and ownership of agricultural land to its previous owners, and healthy production levels began to return.

Eventually, I borrowed a two-wheeled tractor from a nearby Hmong farmer to make the long trips to Dalat's military airport, where I was able to scrounge more supplies and parts abandoned by the US Army. Using wind power helped expand our irrigation systems, and life was good. Tam and Bien, you were growing fast and happily, and then, as you remember all too painfully, our loving Trinh was taken from us by the bite of a green snake.

After reunification, Amerasian children were terribly discriminated against, Tam, and I could only protect you from persecution as long as the government didn't know about you. I never told you this when you were growing up because I was afraid that you might accidently tell a friend, who might tell his parents, and the parents would likely report it to their district communist party leader. You might have been taken from me, and that would have been terrible for you. Like all mixed-blood children after reunification, you would have been officially shunned, quarantined, and then left to survive on the streets. Amerasians were called *children of dust*, and were rejected by all Vietnamese. They were never allowed in schools, and as adults could not be hired except as starvation-wage servants or cyclo drivers, or worse, drug dealers and prostitutes. I always thought of you as my son in every way, and when it became safe to tell you about your biological parents, I didn't have the heart to do it.

***

Peter felt his phone vibrating in his pocket. He stood and answered with "Yes?" and listened intently. He thanked the caller, and slipped the phone back into his pocket.

"That was my friend, General Khai. Soldiers will be raiding our house just after midnight. Pack what you need for a few days, quickly please. We'll leave immediately. Tam, you and I will lead in your car. Bien, you can take Anh, Meggan, and Mai in your car. I'll have an automatic rifle in case someone tries to stop Tam and me, so follow at a safe distance."

CHAPTER 32

Meggan already had her suitcase packed and waited anxiously for the others at the front door. It would be morning in Minnesota, so she took advantage of still being within range of the Wi-Fi and called her mother with the long-distance internet app, praying she'd answer. When the call went to voicemail, Meggan pleaded with her mother, or whoever might be checking calls for her, to call immediately through the internet app because she did not have cellphone service in Vietnam.

Peter soon joined her, carrying a black zippered tote bag and a military-style rifle. "Meggan, I'm sorry you have to go through this, especially on the first night with your newly discovered family. Once we drive across the Cambodian border, you'll be safe all the way back to Minnesota. We can get to know more about each other on our road trip to the international airport in Phnom Penh."

"You said you were going to Canada."

"Yes, but I can't get a Vietnam passport, so I travel with a Cambodian passport, a credential I paid dearly for. It gets me into most countries, although I do get odd looks from customs agents."

"My mother, Nancy, lives close to the Canadian border.

Where will you be staying?"

"Ottawa, where the US embassy is located. I want to sort out my legal status in the United States and try to confirm my US citizenship. Vietnam is entering a new era, Meggan, and I don't have a role here anymore. As of tonight, as of this very moment, I'm shedding my dragon skin. I'm just a father and grandfather. Thanks to your long journey here, I'm discovering that's what is most important to me."

That gave Meggan too much to process right away, and she was relieved when Tam joined them at the front door. He greeted her with a quick kiss and a single stroke of her hair, as if they'd known each other for ages.

"Don't be frightened about Father's gun. He's bringing it just in case. It won't be the first time we've faced trouble."

"How long is the trip to your compound?"

"In the dark, a little over two hours," Tam said.

"I'm scared, Tam."

"We'll be fine."

Peter said, "Driving to Phnom Penh will take another eight hours, but it's a safe trip. I'll have our facility manager at the compound drive us. The route near Saigon is too risky for us, so we always cross into Cambodia on backroads. There's a backcountry border crossing just north of Binh Long, which is my usual route. I know the border guards, and they appreciate my generous tips. You won't have any trouble getting your passport stamped with a Cambodian visa."

Bien joined them, carrying two large overnight bags. Mai had a small shoulder bag, and carried Anh in her arms.

Meggan took one of Bien's heavy bags. "You and I are half-sisters, Bien, so Anh is my half-niece. I suddenly have so many new family members." She then turned to Tam. "And I have a new friend—who is *not* my brother."

This triggered a round of laughter.

Bien told Mai to leave the front door unlocked so the soldiers wouldn't have to break it down. When Tam and Peter went to the jeep, Mai secured Anh into her car seat, and Meggan helped Bien load baggage into her car's trunk.

"Did you hear from your mother?" Bien asked.

"I tried to call her a couple of minutes ago, but she didn't answer. I hate to leave without knowing how she's doing. I don't suppose you have Wi-Fi at your compound."

"I'm afraid not." Bien gave Meggan a one-arm hug. "You might be able to call your mother from Phnom Penh, and then you'll soon be home to take care of her."

Mai got in the back with Anh, and Meggan sat in the front passenger seat. As soon as Tam started his engine, Bien started hers. Tam led the way through the dark neighborhood streets, while Peter was on the phone with Sawm, the Hmong facility manager who lived with his family in the compound. Sawm said he'd have the SUV full of gas and ready for the trip to Phnom Penh.

Before hanging up, Peter said, "Sawm, would you ask a few of our Hmong neighbors if they'd form a roadblock across our driveway with their tractors. This is just in case soldiers show up."

"Yes, sir. They will enjoy a chance to disturb soldiers."

"And have an extra rifle loaded."

"Yes, sir."

After just over an hour of driving, Tam's headlights caught the figure of a policeman stepping out onto the side of the road and waving him over with a white-and-black striped baton. Two other policemen stood by their squad car.

Peter pulled the AK-47 automatic rifle from the floor onto his lap, one of many weapons long-ago cached by Vietcong fighters, and later confiscated by Peter. He clicked off the safety.

"This won't do."

Tam slowed the car. "Should I keep going?"

"No, they'll call ahead. Pull up next to the squad car."

As soon as Tam came to a stop, Peter jumped out with his rifle aimed at the two policemen by the car. He yelled in Vietnamese for them to stand next to the policeman with the baton, a few feet away. They obeyed swiftly with hands high in the air. Peter ordered them to toss their pistols and cellphones onto the road, and then told Tam to pick them up and wait in the car. After opening the policemen's car door, Peter fired a burst of rounds into the dashboard radio. Aiming the rifle again at the policemen, he barked at them to run for their lives before he started spraying bullets at them. As soon as they disappeared like phantoms into the dark thick roadside brush, Peter fired a shot into each front tire before scrambling back into the jeep.

He stared into the brush for any movement, but there were no signs of them.

"Let's go, Tam, but keep a normal speed." He removed the pistols' magazines and ejected the remaining round inside each pistol's breach. He threw the pistols out the window into the grassy ditch, and after several yards he tossed out the magazines. Another several yards later, he threw away the cellphones.

Meggan fixed her wide eyes on Bien. "They'll call for more police, won't they?"

"Not with a broken radio, and father took their cellphones."

Bien was all business now, serious and deliberate, accelerating slowly to keep pace with the jeep and setting into a steady cruising speed.

Meggan said, "Has anything like this happened before?"

"No, this is something new for us."

Meggan remembered her father's recollections about the battle on Massacre Mountain. She worried that it might not have been his last fight.

Bien carefully weaved her car around the mountain's blind curves and sudden switchbacks. After what seemed to Meggan like a just few minutes, Tam's jeep stopped at the top of a rise. When its headlights went dark, Bien stopped and turned off her lights. Meggan saw Tam and Peter get out and look at something—or for something—down the road.

She got out and waited by her open door. "There must be trouble."

Bien whispered, "I wonder if the road is blocked."

Tam ran back to Meggan and looked in at Bien and Mai. "We're trying to see if there are any government vehicles at the compound. So far, it looks clear. Everyone alright?"

They all said yes, except Anh, who was still asleep in her child seat.

Meggan asked, "Will there be trouble about what Peter did to those policemen?"

"We'll probably have to pay someone a lot of money before Father can come back to Vietnam—if he can ever come back. I'm afraid that might be the case for you, too."

"What about you?"

"They're after Father, not me, and they can't prove I was the driver back there. Besides, the government needs at least one of us to run our complex coffee brokerage. We pay a lot of taxes and too many local farmers depend on us. Some key government officials will protect us, too, for either personal or political reasons."

"Is driving through Cambodia dangerous?"

"Not with Father and Sawm. They often make the trip to Phnom Penh."

"Will I see you again?"

"I hope so."

Tam stepped closer to Meggan and held her waist while she embraced his shoulders. Their kiss lingered, a kiss more from the tenderness of love than the eagerness of passion, a kiss they both knew could be their last.

"We must go now, my dear."

Meggan reluctantly let go. "I know."

They made their way down the other side of the mountain, with everyone's eyes trained to the sides of the road for intruders or possible spies, either on foot or in cars. When a pair of headlights came toward them, Meggan could see the silhouette of Peter's rifle barrel rise. As soon as the sedan passed them, the rifle went down. She turned to Bien when she saw two more sets of headlights on the far side of the valley.

"I wonder if those are policemen way over there."

"There is always some traffic on this road, even at night. It's the main route from Dalat to Buon Ma Thuot."

Soon after arriving at the floor of the valley, they turned into a long gravel driveway leading toward a small cluster of one-story white cement dwellings that were next to a large two-story house. Lights glowed in every room of the large house, and its exterior looked smooth and white in the bright moonlight, with a roof of rounded clay tiles. A high chain-link fence topped by coiled razor wire enveloped the entire compound.

As Bien followed Tam down the driveway, she smiled at Meggan. "Welcome to our quaint little country home."

"It looks more like a fortress."

"I hope you can return here when the trouble is over. This area is peaceful, and the people are so friendly. We have many friends here, and many of them have produced coffee for us since Tam and I were—"

Two sets of headlights flashed in Bien's mirror. Meggan looked back and saw that two army trucks had turned into the driveway and were gaining on them.

Bien punched her horn twice. "This is trouble."

Tam stopped in front of the compound entrance while a motorized gate slowly opened. Bien sped ahead to catch up with him.

Meggan heard a thundering rumble of motors behind them, and looked back to see dozens of two-wheeled tractors; most with trailers filled with men. The tractors spread apart and raced toward the military trucks. Some were able to rush onto the driveway in front of the trucks, while others encircled them. Soldiers with rifles jumped off and faced the large circle of farmers who far outnumbered them, standing their ground with axes and clubs.

A shot broke the silent night air, with a pop through the Audi's back window. Bien's hands dropped from the steering wheel and the car rolled to an abrupt stop in the shallow ditch. Her body was slumped against the side window, with her head dangling forward.

Meggan jumped out of the car screaming for Tam and Peter. Anh started crying herself breathless while Mai, sounding just as panicked, tried to console her.

Tam and Peter sprinted toward them, with Peter clutching his rifle with both hands. Meggan ran around to the driver's door and yanked it open, then tried to gently straighten Bien enough to unbuckle her seatbelt. Peter handed his rifle to

Tam and took Meggan's arm, saying "I've got her." He released Bien's limp body from the seatbelt and picked her up, striding off toward the compound with her body draped in his arms. Tam kept pace alongside him with the rifle in hand, occasionally glancing back at the on-looking crowd of farmers and soldiers.

While running along the other side, Meggan tried to hold Bien's blood-soaked head in place. "Bien, can you hear me? Oh, God, please be alive!"

Mai ran as fast as she could to keep up, moaning prayers while carrying Anh, who was screaming constantly for her mother.

Sawm held the house's front door open with a rifle in his other hand. His wife stood behind him, wailing helplessly. Tam gave his rifle to Sawm and followed Peter inside to help him gently lay Bien on the sofa.

Peter knelt and searched her neck artery in vain for a pulse. He started sobbing, while slowly stroking her black hair. Then he stilled and fell silent. After a few seconds of quiet, split only by Anh's hysterical begging for her mother, he got to his feet with a faraway look and walked to the still-open front door. He noticed his blood-soaked shirt for the first time and looked back at Tam, who returned his glance after resting Bien's limp arm onto her body.

Peter took one of the rifles from Sawm and bolted out the front door.

After Meggan swallowed back her grief and fear, she grabbed the other rifle from Sawm's hands, and ran after Peter.

"Stop!"

He glanced back at her while in full stride. "Take that gun back to Sawm."

The army trucks were still hopelessly sealed off by scores of tractors and hundreds of angry farmers who seemed ready to pounce at the slightest provocation. Most of the hapless-looking soldiers were already slinging their rifles over their shoulders, and some were climbing back into the trucks.

She caught up with Peter and stood in his way.

"What are you going to do?"

He walked around her. "Put an end to this."

"Shooting at those soldiers won't end anything, except you."

Peter stopped but kept his eyes trained on the army trucks, his finger was still on the rifle's trigger.

"Go back, Meggan. I mean it."

"No! I'm going with you. I've had to live without a father all my life, but now that I've found you, I won't let you die alone. If you want to fight until we're both destroyed, then let's go."

Peter gave her a stupefied look. "That's a ridiculous idea."

"I know."

He put his rifle over his shoulder and lightly touched her tearful cheek. "You're right, Meggan. You and I have to leave for Cambodia very soon. Let's spend the time we have here with our family."

CHAPTER 33

Nine Months Later

Nancy put her apple pie into the oven late in the afternoon so it would fill the house with delicious smells and be ready for supper. Meggan had just called and said she and Tam would be there soon, but their adopted daughter, Anh, insisted on staying longer at a logging camp museum in Grand Rapids. It was a forty-minute drive from there to Nancy's lake home in Marcell, so Nancy had plenty of time to blow up the balloons for Anh's fifth birthday party.

The wedding three months ago had been at the border city of Fort Francis, Ontario, only two hours north of Nancy's home. The ceremony was punctuated afterward by tears for Bien's absence. For Anh's sake on this otherwise happy day, the loving tears for her mother were dabbed without comment.

Peter had already been cleared by the US Department of Defense of any legal wrongdoing after they considered his forced detention in Vietnam—a fact confirmed by a top-secret letter from General Khai to the US ambassador in Hanoi. Peter's confinement in Vietnam, and arguable abandonment by the US Army, made his status something of a POW/MIA blend, a potentially controversial status that could embarrass both countries and disrupt their current trade talks. It was eventually solved by classifying the incident as a state secret, something Peter happily acceded to in writing. But he had not yet received his American passport, so having the wedding in Canada allowed him to proudly escort his daughter down the church aisle and give away the bride to the man he had long ago helped bring into the world.

Nancy and Peter had spent hours together the evening after the wedding ceremony, sipping wine and talking late into the night like two old night owls catching up on the last forty-five years. She joked about being lucky for having two new stints inserted into her arteries, otherwise the excitement of seeing Peter alive and smiling after all this time might have given her another heart attack. Peter shared some of the hardships he went through while raising his children in Vietnam. He struggled with tears when he got to losing Bien. Although most of their lives had been worlds apart, they quickly found the chemistry that had attracted them to each other so long ago.

Peter told Nancy he was looking forward to retiring, and turning management of the coffee brokerage over to Tam and Meggan. Meggan was already organizing plans to open untapped markets in the United States for Vietnamese coffee. They planned to spend summers in Minnesota and winters in Dalat, where Mai would still be taking care of the family villa, the place she had called home since childhood.

Nancy's doorbell rang, startling her while she took the pie out of the oven: how could they be here so soon? She quickly set the pie on a cooling rack and hurried to the door. When she got there, she saw a familiar sun-browned wrist pressing an opened American passport up against the door's small single windowpane. She couldn't read it without her glasses, but she didn't need them to recognize Peter's photo.

The End

Sign up for pre-publish announcements and discounts for forthcoming books by James Luger by visiting

www.JamesLuger.com